For my wife Nicola

'Religion is what keeps the poor from murdering the rich.'

Napoleon Bonaparte

CHAPTER ONE

Ewan Striker pushed his palm into the print reader that controlled the door mechanism of Lancashire Constabulary's Anti Terrorist branch offices. It was the most secret and clandestine part of police headquarters.

The building was silent. The majority of the highly skilled souls employed on these floors worked daylight hours; after midnight, well, they were, indisposed.

For the most part, contrary to the big budget detective movies, once darkness fell, the corridors of power rattled empty. '

When the shit really hit the fan and the press was knocking on the door, then of course a full complement of highly polished operatives was nailed on, twenty-four-seven.

Trouble was, so far, the shit and the fan hadn't quite ticked that highly polished box.

The LED on the machine turned from red to green; an almost inaudible click gave the detective entry into the darkened rooms.

As he stepped silently inside, no mean feat for such a big man, he still felt the unique rush of being in a genuinely hallowed place.

The gentle hum of the desktop computers may have been the only audible sound, but his blood pounded in his ears.

This job was a live one, a big one, he just knew it.

Striker walked to the vending machine and selected a black coffee; it clicked and popped before delivering the drink. He gently removed the plastic cup between a thick thumb and forefinger, sipped, grimaced and set the cup four inches to the left of his report.

He was thirty-two, but as he looked out from the one-way glass onto the silhouette of the city he felt much older. His shoulders and back ached; his neck was stiff. He rotated his head and felt the tendons crack. The sound reverberated in his skull and masked the thud of his heartbeat for a second.

From the cool air-conditioned room, four floors above ground, he could clearly see the fires that were devastating the city of Preston, an ancient town that the Romans considered as important as London.

Striker knew that one blaze was a mosque. Rioting had erupted between the Asian and white communities, and despite the best efforts of the police to regain control the city was in chaos.

He checked his Omega.

11.37 pm.

He'd been roused from his bed and ordered to report to the 'office'. He was on call most weekends. Striker volunteered for most out of hours duties. No wife, no family, no problem.

The detective was an anomaly. His father had been an American Navy SEAL who had been on attachment to the British SBS in Northern Ireland in the late 1970's.

A whirlwind romance with a pretty but stubborn Irish Catholic girl, Margaret Mary O'Dowd, had resulted in an unplanned pregnancy. It may have been the era of free love for the rest of the western world, but in Ireland the shame on the O'Dowds was sufficient to force the couple to live Stateside to avoid the gossiping locals. Striker was born and raised in Chicago, Illinois, until his seventeenth birthday.

When Striker's father was taken by cancer, his mother, who had always had little time for the American way, decided her heart was still in the Emerald Isle. They moved back to Belfast. Two years on, he was completely alone, Margaret Mary the victim of a hit and run driver.

He lifted his cup and considered another sip of evil coffee, thought better of the process and set it even further away from his report. Several hundred yards from the burning mosque was a murder scene and the victim was 'flagged' by MI5.

According to the intelligence brief, Abdullah Mohammed Hussain had visited Pakistan three times in twelve months. He was loosely associated with individuals of interest to the Firm, and had been arrested at a recent anti-government protest.

More significant to Striker was his alleged association with the Black Flag movement; a radical Islamist group, who were intent on bringing Shariah law to the UK.

Hussain had been secretly filmed by the EDL, harassing couples walking the streets of West London. Their crime had been drinking alcohol, or holding hands.

Striker considered that the boy's profile was interesting enough.

But there was another, more pressing matter, which made the detective's presence a priority.

Abdullah Hussain had been kidnapped, tortured and killed.

He lifted his desk phone from its cradle and dialed.

"I'm going to need a car and a space-suit."

His accent was immediately recognised by the stores officer. A strange mix of Irish-American, that made him sound like a caricature from a fifties US cop show.

Few people had the courage to mention it to the detective, though. He had inherited his father's tremendous strength and toughness, together with his mother's red hair and temper.

It took Striker twenty minutes to get within half a mile of the scene; then another twenty of detours and doubling back.

The delay aggravated him, but despite his irritation and the occasional vocal outburst toward the odd rioter, Striker was calm...ish.

In spite of his horrible temper and frightening appearance, Striker had what his mother had insisted calling, 'a gift'.

His father had been more pragmatic and called it intuition.

Striker could visualize things in his head that others couldn't.

And when something wasn't quite right, well, he just knew it.

Roadblocks were set at every junction; some official, some no more than residents with makeshift barricades trying to protect their homes.

He eventually eased the Audi forward through the riot cops that were a thin line of defence for the fire crews, trying valiantly to douse the burning mosque thirty yards further down Deepdale Mill Street. His roof light flashed blue neon into the night sky. It reflected off the clear plastic shields that protected the cops from missiles, and back to Striker's windscreen.

Young Asian men, their faces hidden by scarves, thumped on the roof and bonnet of the car, shouting abuse at the detective sergeant as he edged ever closer to his destination.

Older men, in national Pakistani dress, sat on their haunches at the curbside, dazed and subdued. It seemed they were oblivious to the violence in the air, and simply watched and waited.

The rioting had started almost thirty miles away in Nelson, but had spread like a malignant virus across the county. Despite three neighbouring forces assisting the Lancashire officers, resources were stretched to their limit.

Striker studied the stunned faces of the older men and wondered if they even knew why it had all started.

He took a left and was immediately faced with a further line of cops. This set, protecting an altogether different scene.

He dropped the window, flashed his ID and was waved through.

Mill Autos was a small industrial unit, the last in a line of five. The garage, turned car repair shop, was protected by metal gates and a G4S sign. How often the area was patrolled by the private security firm, Striker had no way of knowing. He did consider that it was extremely unlikely that any guy on less than seven pounds an hour would have risked a visit to Deepdale in the anarchy that surrounded the site this night.

The not so protective gates had been pushed open but the opening was sealed by yellow crime scene tape. A young detective with birdlike features and an unfortunate chin, dressed in an overcoat far too big for his slight frame, stood at the gates. He held a clipboard and did his best to look important.

Striker parked behind the long line of murder scene vehicles, walked around to the boot of his car and removed a set of paper coveralls from a sealed plastic bag. He added shoe covers and what resembled a surgeon's face mask, before tramping over to the thin-shouldered detective.

He nodded at the fresh-faced man. He pulled down the mask and held out his ID long enough for him to record his presence at the scene, and strode to the half-closed roller shutter doors that formed the garage entrance.

The sergeant dipped his muscular frame just enough to enter and was forced to shield his eyes from the glare of halogen lamps.

The Crime Scene boys had set up enough lighting to drain the National Grid.

Striker did not need to see the victim so clearly. No human being with a single ounce of heart muscle would.

The garage was small and surprisingly neat, with a single hydraulic ramp sitting over an inspection pit in the centre.

Suspended over the pit, was a very dead teenage boy.

The SOCOs had rigged ladders and even more lighting to gain access to the corpse and were busy doing what they did best. Striker couldn't take his eyes from the body.

The spell was broken by Phil Grover He was what the Americans call a medical examiner. "Mess, isn't it?" said the police surgeon in his thick Liverpool accent.

Striker knew the man of old from his days on CID; he nodded, "Always one for the fuckin' understatement, you, Phil."

The doctor beckoned the detective closer to the body.

"He's had a beating before this happened, a pretty sustained one at that. I've had a quick look in his mouth and he has a few missing teeth; you can see the facial damage for yourself. They tied him with plasti-cuffs, the proper police or army issue ones, inserted that meat-hook behind his collarbone and dangled him over the pit by it."

Striker grimaced at the sight of the hook that impaled the boy's body. It protruded grotesquely out of the chest cavity. It was connected to a metal chain, which the offenders had fastened to the car ramp. The boy's face was a mask of sheer terror, his eyes wide open, his mouth fixed in a silent scream. If Striker needed any further evidence that his involvement was imperative, the boy had a printed sign dangled from a cord around his neck. It had one word laser-printed on it.

'Terrorist'.

Striker's eyes moved downward from the torso to the shoeless, blackened feet of the victim.

"Jesus, Mary and Joseph!"

Grover pointed into the pit. "Apparently the fire was still smoldering when he was found."

"What killed him, Doc?"

"Can't say for sure at the moment, shock, maybe? The chest wound wouldn't be enough in itself, but the pain from the burns, the hook and the beating combined, well..."

"Who found him?"

The doc pointed a thumb over his shoulder in the general direction of the street. "Garage owner; he came down to look after his investment after he saw the mosque fire on the TV. He's with the local boys outside. That's his puke in the corner over there."

Striker held up his hand to halt the conversation. He had seen a SOCO remove an object from the victim's jeans pocket and drop it into a plastic bag.

"What will you be havin' there, son?"

The SOCO looked at the detective and then to the ME for support. Grover nodded his consent to the man; he held up the object.

"Mobile phone, a Blackberry, sir."

"I'm not a sir, I'm a sergeant, sunshine, now be handin' that over to me."

Grover shook his head. "Now come on, Striker, even you know you can't remove anything from the scene. The OIC isn't even here yet."

"Yes he is." The booming voice of Detective Superintendent Errol Graham emanated from behind the men. They turned to see the source, "and I agree with the good doc here, nothing will be removed from *my* crime scene unless I say. Now, who are you, Detective?"

Striker ignored the superintendent, stepped toward the SOCO, snatched the plastic bag containing the phone from his hand and stuffed it in his pocket.

Graham was on him in a flash. "What did I just say to you, Detective? We haven't even identified this kid yet."

Striker's piercing blue eyes flashed in anger. The tufts of his flame red hair protruding from his hood almost matched them for ferocity. He removed his warrant card from his wallet and held it out at arm's length.

"My name is Striker, Detective Sergeant Ewan Striker, Anti-Terrorist Branch and, yes we have an ID for this kid. These boys have found his driving licence, and the second it was checked by PNC it triggered at our end because he's 'flagged'."

Graham wasn't about to back down, he had the rank and the experience to go with it.

"That doesn't mean that you can ride..."

"Yes I can, Superintendent. You can make the call right now." Striker pulled his own mobile from his pocket and pushed it under the nose of the burly man.

"Call the Chief Con, tell him that Abdullah Mohammed Hussain is hanging from a fuckin' meat hook in a back street garage and he's been tortured. Tell him, he's just off the plane from Pakistan for the third time in a year and tell him that the chatter tells us, he's active."

Striker moved to turn away from the senior detective, but changed his mind.

"Oh, and tell him he's got that sign around his neck, for good measure."

The two men were locked in a stare, neither wanting to be the first to blink. Dr. Phil Grover intervened.

"Come on, gents, this isn't getting us anywhere."

Graham poked a finger into the chest of Striker. "Sign for that phone, Sergeant, and make sure you're at my briefing, nine a.m. sharp."

CHAPTER TWO

Barry Williams stepped out into the street, lit the man's cigarette and then his own. He made a show of clicking the lid of his Zippo closed. The change in temperature, from the warmth of the bar to the chill of Plungington Road made Barry shiver as he inhaled. The man standing opposite him, sharing his love of nicotine, was a new face to the regular meetings of the Preston branch of the English Defence League.

The regular clientele of the Miners Welfare Club stayed away on the second Wednesday of the month. They were replaced with around twenty-five men, who drank their way through a couple of barrels of beer and plotted the next white revolution.

Somewhere over to the east of the city, sirens wailed.

"Somethin' is going off over Deepdale, pal," said Barry, blowing out a plume of smoke.

The man nodded.

He was a big guy compared to Barry. Then again, most were. The males in the Williams family were notoriously small and wiry. Standing just over five feet five, Barry fitted the model perfectly. He had also inherited the family penchant for violence. Despite his lack of physical bulk, Barry had the reputation of a hard man, who would take on men much bigger and stronger than himself; hence his nickname 'Mad' Barry Williams.

"Probably something to do with that fuckin' mess in Nelson this afternoon," said the big man, stubbing out his cigarette with a booted foot.

Barry mirrored his action. "Saw it on the news before I came out. Fuckin' black twats need a lesson. We're all going on a march to protest about it."

The man let out a short laugh. "Oh a march; well that will leave the Pakis quaking in their boots, eh? A bunch of piss-heads sitting in a back street boozer, moaning about how the twats are fucking the country; well that is gonna make a whole lot of difference."

Barry squared himself; he didn't like the guy's tone. The lads at the EDL meetings were good sorts. They all felt the same way. They could see what was really happening in their town; how the blacks were taking over; taking jobs, playing the race card to get houses and benefits. The EDL were the ones to sort out the mess the government had made. Barry was sure of it.

"We'll be going up Deepdale if it's a kick off, pal." He threw a thumb in the direction of the door of the bar. "None of them lads in there are scared of a few Pakis." He jutted out his chin. The big man had to restrain himself from punching it.

"I'll bet," he said calmly.

Barry's short fuse was burning. "So if you don't like it, why don't you fuck off?"

The man held up his hands.

"Whoa, mate, steady on. I'm on your side."

Barry balled his fists. The drink had given him just enough Dutch courage. The guy looked a real handful, but you couldn't let that stop you. Not when you were 'Mad' Barry Williams.

"Don't seem like it to me," snarled Barry.

The man was not intimidated. He knew what would happen, should the stupid drunk try it on. It wouldn't be pretty. But he wasn't there to break heads; he was there to recruit.

The man unzipped his jacket and found his wallet.

"Listen, are you working at the minute, mate?"

Barry took on the look of a puzzled bulldog. He hadn't seen the change of tack coming.

"Might be, why?"

"I'll take that as a 'no' then," said the man, who flipped open the wallet and found what he wanted. He could quite happily put 'Mad' Barry in the hospital, just for his bad attitude. That said, the sap was just the type his boss was looking for, so he smiled and played the game.

"Look, pal, I can see you've got some bottle; not many would square up to me outside a pub." He removed a business card from the expensive-looking leather wallet and held it out.

"Give this guy a call. He provides security for Alistair Sinclair, the politician. It's good money, cash in hand."

Barry took the card, all thoughts of violence temporarily suspended, as his brain slowly processed the information on it.

Danny Slade, Security Consultant

"Err…thanks, pal…I'll give him a call."

"You do that," said the man, walking away.

Barry shouted after him, "Cheers, pal…err…sorry about before…err…I didn't get your name."

"I didn't give it," said the man, and disappeared around the corner.

CHAPTER THREE

Westland found the whole thing ridiculous. The human body was just not meant to be up and awake at eight-thirty a.m. Not unless accompanied by loud, new school punk and naked women. His often abused bones had never quite got used to the shock of finding that not one, but two, eight o'clocks existed in the course of a solitary day.

Westland was convinced that his head was about to split into tiny pieces; he rummaged through his uniform pockets for aspirin. Bile prickled his throat and he felt his own sweat drip cold onto the base of his spine. Total confirmation; Westland felt like shit.

The sun had forced itself from a no doubt prettier view, to shine over the less than delicate skyline of Avenham. Tonight the whole town had seemed to be on fire. Rival factions had fought running battles in the streets and from the sound of the radio traffic, the rest of the county was in a similar state. Westland had mercifully been spared the duties of quelling the disturbances and had, instead, been kept back to deal with the usual matters of city policing that went on at night, riot or no riot.

One high-rise tower still pierced the sun's perfect circle. A twenty-storey, four families a floor job, eight different races, six religions, one lift and one dustbin. Westland wasn't too sure which held more monetary value, the contents of the flats, or the contents of their solitary skip.

He'd once suffered the misfortune of being too close to this particular building when a disgruntled Croatian on the twentieth floor 'accidentally' dropped a bin bag of heavily soiled nappies from his balcony.

Even young constables should know better, and he had found the shame of being forced to walk the one and a quarter miles to the station covered in a positive smorgasbord of excrement, a particular piss off.

Now, surveying the interior of his patrol car, he decided it smelled little better than the contents of that very bin bag; a vague mix of fags, stale farts and whatever take-away the previous driver had managed to spill on the seats.

Six months he'd been a street copper. He'd been shit on, spat at, punched, gouged and been forced to stay up all night for no apparent reason.

To add insult to injury, his boss, Mr. Jeremy feckin' Thomson, Inspector and all round bastard, together with every other copper at the station, thought he was an alien. If he didn't play feckin' rugger, he was obviously a prime candidate for the gay police officers department on the third floor. Add his grave distaste of 'rugger' to the fact that, whilst very pissed on his first invitation to the divisional ball, he announced that 'all bloody Masons were bigots,' well, let's just say it wasn't going too well for Tag Westland.

During the previous seven hours of his life, Westland had reported nine crimes that would never be investigated never mind solved, fought his way out of an Indian take-away using CS spray and attempted to rescue a woman who had locked her keys in her Lexus, very close to the rioting hordes that were going to make headline news.

It was as Tag Westland struggled with the very capable locking system of this particular luxury model, that serious doubts were cast into his mind regarding his suitability to the job of police officer.

"Hurry up, will you?" pouted the twenty-something obvious avid Friends watcher who insisted in speaking in that student-like drawl where every sentence rises with the final inflection.

Westland had given the woman his very best 'I know I'm wearing a uniform, therefore I am a public servant but shut the fuck up' look, but it hadn't registered.

In fact, with one manicured hand on hip, she continued, "Nick Cage would have had it open by now. YOU'LL never make it in the movies, will you?" and let out an inane giggle.

Tag had countered with the reasonable explanation, that indeed Nick Cage was a god, and that his performance in Leaving Las Vegas had reduced him to tears. Despite this, Gone in Sixty Seconds was hardly gong material and a tad unrealistic. Tag's obvious grasp of movie trivia would have gone down quite well had he not muttered words to the effect of, "Now, stop getting on my bloody nerves, whilst I get this door open."

A strong complaint had been registered to Mr. Feckin' Thomson by the woman's husband within an hour of the incident. As most of Deepdale was burning and the Muslim League of Great Britain, the English Defence League and The British National Party were massing all around Lancashire, the complaint had fallen on temporarily deaf ears, but Tag would undoubtedly suffer eventually.

So, at stupid o'clock in the morning, feeling like shit, stuck in a stinking, knackered patrol car, Westland made the biggest decision since his last biggest decision.
He was going to resign from the police.

CHAPTER FOUR

Ismi curled into a ball so tight she had to fight for each tiny breath. When Ismi was scared, really scared, the ball always helped. It was almost a hug.

Her bedroom was okay. It was warm and dry in there and they had electricity all the time. Her father was a hard man but never struck her. Indeed life would be pretty cool now if it weren't for the noises.

There were bangs from the spare bedroom and definitely a woman's voice.

Ismi heard her crying. The woman sobbed, pleaded and begged. It sounded as if she was choking on something. Her dad was making funny grunting sounds and swearing.

And there were other noises. Ismi tried her best to curl tighter when she heard those.

Ismi suddenly wished that they lived on the ground, rather than three floors up. If they could live on the ground, then whenever Ismi got scared, really scared, she could climb from her bedroom window and run into the garden and hide; just like she'd done back home. She would wait in the bushes until the danger had gone and her mother would find her and make it better. But the last time Ismi hid in her garden back home, her mother never came.

Even at such a tender age, Ismi had been fully aware of what the soldiers of the American Army had done to her mother; and what they would have done to her should they have found her.

The man that came to save her that day was her father. A man only previously seen in a dusty picture, her mother kept in her purse back home in Iraq. He was a war hero and he escaped the Americans to rescue his only daughter.

Yes, Ismi knew the noises, and they still haunted her. They had followed her all the way to England and again, this night, the noises meant her father had found another of the evil infidel women whilst at work in his taxi.

Westland checked his watch.

0842 hours, or quarter to nine in the morning to most human beings, time to start his reluctant patrol car and head for the nick. Even if the fire brigade were damping down and pockets of rioters still skirmished the streets nearby, he was due to go home. Fourteen hours was enough for any man.

Tag was warming to his pending resignation with each passing moment. He could see himself in a suit, with a company car, finishing work at five o'clock on a Friday and out with the lads all weekend, like normal people.

Joining the job had been rash. He had liked the idea of the uniform and racing around in a big car with the sirens wailing. He hadn't quite realised though, just how long it took to get into the sirens wailing department. Everyone was forced into staying up all night and fighting his or her way out of Indian restaurants for a minimum of two years.

In reality Westland could readily expect to be stuck in his stinking patrol car until he reached the five years of service mark.

This concept was now completely out of the question. Another four years and six months of nights like tonight would see Tag Westland scratching a premature beer belly whilst falling asleep in front of Sex and the City re-runs.

He'd seen them, the 'five years in a patrol car' men. They had the same look as 'five years in casualty' nurses; pale, broken creatures. Five years of eating a junk lunch at three in the morning. Five years of frontline work with bottom-line pay.

The massive workload took its toll, but it was complete excess in everything, when blessed with time off, that finally broke the donkey's five-year-old back. Most would see both marriage and divorce inside that time. Those who remained single would spend the other half of their lives in the cattle markets of northern nightlife.

No, the price was just too high. Tag was twenty-four and still warmed to the idea of making thirty.

Until tonight he had never really considered that walking into an Indian Restaurant in police uniform could be his last social outing. The situation in the Bombay Duck had been bad. It wasn't the violence, no, savagery was everywhere, but it was the way the general public reacted towards Tag that had disturbed him.

Their sheer hatred of a total stranger in a blue uniform, who after all was present as a result of their telephone call, puzzled him.

There he was, jammed into a corner, fighting two oafs from Moor Nook Estate for the retention of both his testicles, and not one good soul came to his aid. Indeed some found the whole scene so entertaining that they felt the need to encourage the two dangerously pissed toe-rags.

One diner shouted so much support that Tag considered he would give Angelo Dundee a run for his money.

The bigger of the two Moor Nook boys had picked up a wine bottle from the table and Tag decided enough was enough. He knew this kind. These boys hadn't had a good night without thirteen pints, a curry, a fight, and sex (not necessarily in that order). He drew a CS canister from his belt and gave both parties a blast.

In his haste to save himself from certain GBH he also took out a full row of diners with the spray.

Over the screaming patrons, one lone voice was raised in his defence.

"Leave him alone, ya bastards!"

Tag looked over briefly before giving Moor Nooker number one a swift kick in the bollocks for good measure.

The voice came from a somewhat dishevelled bloke who had obviously seen better days. He looked like he'd suffered from the Moor Nook boys himself and was bandaged in various areas. He was probably forty-five but looked a good ten years older. Tag noticed he had a 'Help for Heroes' badge on his coat and a bottle of cider in his pocket.

Ex squaddie?

Ismi was really scared now. The woman in the spare room was screaming and glass was broken. This was not normal. The noises should be gone now. Her father should be back on his way to work; making sure decent people got home safe.

There were angry cries from her father. They sent shivers down Ismi's back. The woman screamed again. Bad words, some Ismi didn't even know.

Then the flat door slammed and all that remained were her father's quiet sobs.

Sandra smashed her fist into the lift controls. She had little care for the choice of floor, just as long as it wasn't this one. The lift doors refused to close so she pushed her head out into the empty corridor and screamed.

"Bastard!"

Her eyes were wild, her voice had all but failed her, and her sobs were transformed, into strange hacking sounds.

She slid down the cold metal wall of the lift, uncontrolled, shoulders heaving.

"Fuckin' bastard!"

As the lift doors shuddered to a close, Sandra whispered a childhood prayer.

She felt the chilled remains of her attacker seep from her. For a brief moment she sensed her anger subside, and the first insolent pangs of guilt.

Strangely, her attention was drawn to her feet.

Her new shoes were missing.

The lift doors opened onto a foul-smelling entrance hall. First glimpses of sunlight only pinpointed the squalor of a front door used by over a hundred inhabitants.

Sandra stepped onto the cold tiles, oblivious to the Saturday night human deposits.

It took her a few moments to work out how to open the electronic exit. She pushed the heavy reinforced door ajar and almost fell onto the concrete outside.

Then she ran.

Not far, just the thirty yards or so to Tag Westland's patrol car.

Abu Al Zachari felt at the wound on his head and found a towel to stem the blood that flowed freely from it.

The whore had caught him out. No man had ever got the better of him before, let alone an infidel female.

This could mean trouble and he knew it. The months of planning, the grooming of the soldiers, the glory of victory, could all be compromised.

He reached for his mobile, plugged it into the encryption device and dialled.

"Salam Alaikum."

The voice five hours ahead in the mountains of Pakistan was wide awake and didn't question why the great warrior needed a clean-up team in northern England.

"It will be done," he said, in perfect Queen's English.

CHAPTER FIVE

Wilson sat in the Eagle and Child. It was one of those wonderful new pubs that opened at breakfast, and closed when the last drunk left. He'd been on a real bender. Exactly where was unclear. He had memories of a curry and throwing up.
Hair of the dog and all that.
He twisted his pint glass with his fingers, eyeing its rim with some suspicion. Once confident he had detected half the shades of Max Factor's most recent range ingrained around it, he stood and edged to the bar. He held the glass outward with his good arm, keeping the offending lip-gloss and the offensive pourer in his slightly blurred sights.
If this was to work for a second time he would need all his wits about him. Before Wilson could consider formulating the wording of his very justified complaint, the steroid-enhanced barman cut off his approach.
"Don't come that fuckin' shit, pal, that's twice now! I washed that fucker myself and, anyway you've drunk it!"
Wilson considered the glass and its remaining quarter of a pint of Stella Artois. In his peripheral vision he could see Sky News flickering behind the beetroot-red face of the barman of the year. He hadn't seen the news for a while. In fact he didn't know what day this was.
He screwed his eyes up in an attempt to focus.
It appeared a group of Muslim women had thrown paint on some poor bastards returning from Afghanistan during their homecoming parade in Nelson. Small electric pulses fought to connect memories in Wilson's head as he watched the story unfold.
As a result of the action by the unnamed Islamist group, the reporter gushed, there had been rioting in Padiham, Burnley and Nelson; all of which boasted BNP councilors and, according to the newsreader, were strongholds of the renegade right-wing party.
The English Defence League was planning a march in protest and police had cancelled all leave as a result.
To his surprise, Preston too was already in chaos. A mosque had been burned to the ground. Someone was dead in a garage.
He hadn't noticed.

By the time Wilson looked away from what appeared to have been a terrible day in Lancashire's recent history, Mr. Happy the barman had him by the throat and he was being moved toward the exit, none too slowly.

Wilson's ribs were already broken, as was his left cheekbone. The muscle-bound arsehole that was propelling him outside might have noticed this due to Wilson's bandages and various other dressings that were looking grubbier by the day. The population of the Eagle could see too, but were too scared to say anything against the skinhead. The word was, he was connected to some Nazi extremist group spreading its own vile wings in the town.

Wilson was pushed through the door and felt the cold blast of air on his face seconds before his back hit the pavement, sending rivers of pain through his previously healing body. Two kids in school uniform stepped over him and made a comment about piss-heads behind cupped hands. The street noise hammered at his skull until it vibrated his teeth.

He rolled onto his side and sat up. A movement that caused him further agony. Wilson raised his face to the perfectly blue sky. An aircraft was low overhead; so low he could read the orange letters on the fuselage; the Airbus on its final approach into Blackpool airport; bringing passengers home from a warm and beautiful place. He cursed it.

He brushed himself down and reattached his 'Help for Heroes' badge to a filthy lapel; then felt in his coat pocket and found his meds. It wasn't time but what the fuck.

They kicked in twenty minutes later and he found himself sitting with his back against a large steel dustbin, examining his ribcage. He'd collapsed in an Avenham back street, somewhere between Tokyo Joe's and the Jalgos Club. The alley smelled of piss and junk, but he hadn't many options until Fox Street Mission opened its doors at four p.m.

Wilson heard voices and knew from the particular street drawl they were Asian. To his left four boys loped toward him with looks ranging from disgust to pure hatred.

"It's a fuckin' tramp, innit, Shaz." The smallest of the four stood in front of the others with his arms crossed, displaying an array of golden fingers.

"Fuckin' sponger, that's what it is," said a taller more muscular youth in a Nike baseball cap.

Then the small one saw Wilson's badge depicting two soldiers carrying a wounded comrade in silhouette and the mantra, 'Help for Heroes'.

He only felt the first kick.

Three miles away, Asquith's was a barristers' chambers specialising in Criminal Law, Financial and Regulatory Crime, Public Law and Immigration and Nationality issues. Under the watchful eye of Tariq Hussain QC, the chambers had developed into a thriving business with no less than seventeen expert barristers.

Tariq ensured his clerking team was the most energetic and resourceful in the county. Clients could use the services of any of his advocates without the use of a solicitor, though most of the lower profile cases came via what had become known in legal circles as the 'taxi rank' system.

Tariq himself had made a name for himself defending high profile terrorism and fraud cases, together with any individual who considered themselves to be unfairly treated by the powers that be. His cases had involved murder, manslaughter, drugs and firearms offences. His defence of people charged under Section 57 of the Terrorism Act, where defendants were alleged to be in the preparatory stages of being 'about to commit' an act of terrorism, had gained him many plaudits, both from the judiciary and colleagues alike. It was these cases where the defendants seemed impossible to prove innocent, which made Tariq Hussain a shining star.

He defended the 'un-defendable.'

That said, Hussain was a moderate; a conservative; he had no affiliation with any political party or radical groups. Indeed, he could never agree with acts of terror.

Nonetheless he could not stand by and watch if an act of injustice had been committed; where legal process had not been followed to the letter.

It was not his job to judge; it was to ensure that fair practice was followed by the prosecution, and that it applied to all, no matter what the allegation.

Tariq sat in his plush office, flicked the remote and killed the sound of the television. The fire brigade was still hosing down after a night of violence in the northern mill towns of Lancashire. The hostility was building, spreading like a disease. A mosque had been set ablaze not a mile from his chambers in Preston.

He paced his office for a few seconds and then called his secretary. "Call the offices in Burnley and Nelson and see if everyone got to work okay today, okay, Gina?"

"Yes, Mr. Hussain."

Tariq was convinced Gina was looking at him differently this morning. She'd worked as his personal secretary for eight years, a Preston girl born and bred, straight talking, honest as the day was long. But she was definitely different today.

He scanned the TV again. What the hell did these people think they were doing when they made the plan to disrupt the parade? Did they not realise that Pakistani businessmen like him had to live and work here?

He was well on his way to being the first man of Pakistani origin to become a circuit judge, outside of the capital, and these fanatics were about to plunge him into a legal wasteland by alienating every good Muslim in Lancashire.

It was one thing to defend notorious criminals; but to lose the trust of his peers due to social unrest in his community, would be another matter.

His intercom buzzed. It was the ever-reliable Gina with bad news. "Your cousin Abdullah didn't make it in to the Nelson office yet. You want his mobile?"

Tariq felt his stomach turn.

Abdullah was a firebrand; a vocal, political, nineteen year old on the edge of activism. He wasn't the kind to stay at home if his people were being attacked by the BNP fringe. He would have been part of any retaliation. He lived yards from the fire-bombed Preston mosque.

"I've got it, Gina, thank you."

Tariq pushed the number for the third time that morning and got the Orange answer phone.

He dropped the phone on his desk and brooded. If Abdullah had got himself arrested Tariq would be duty bound by his family to defend him.

The conflict of interest wouldn't bode well.

He called his secretary into the office.

She stood in front of him holding a pad and pen. At just over five feet tall and around a hundred and forty, Gina Williams was a stout woman with a jolly nature and sarcastic wit. She wore sensible shoes and sensible everything else.

Childless, but married for eleven years to Barry, she oozed reliability and northern normality.

"You seem different today, Gina, everything all right?"

Gina inspected her sensible footwear for a moment, took an obvious deep breath and spluttered out the sentence.

"You don't agree with them that threw that paint on our boys, do you, Mr. Hussain?"

"I knew you were different today. Is that what's bothering you?"

"Well yes. I suppose it is."

Gina put down her pad and stepped closer to Tariq.

"I didn't bother when you defended them boys for terrorist stuff in Blackburn like, even though you go to the same mosque and everythin'. But this is different, Mr. Hussain; them lads on that parade yesterday had been off risking their lives for their country, our country, your country, Mr. Hussain; and I think, well, I think, if you agree with them that did that terrible thing, well, me and my Barry don't think I should work here another day."

Tariq's mobile vibrated on the desk. He checked the display. It was Abdullah.

He held his hand up to Gina in apology and put the phone to his ear. But it wasn't his cousin's clipped tones.

It was a strange accent. Belfast? Dublin? American? Tariq couldn't tell.

The voice was hard, each word sounded like it had been carved from stone and it clattered against his ear.

"Hello?"

"Yes?"

"Are you acquainted with or a friend of, Abdulla Mohammed Hussain, the registered user of this telephone, sir?"

Tariq's mouth was dry, even Gina looked scared.

"Who is this?"

The voice softened slightly as the speaker introduced himself.

"Striker, sir; Detective Sergeant Ewan Striker."

Tariq thought for a moment and considered insisting that he see the cop face to face before divulging any information about Abdullah. His fear for the safety of his cousin stopped him.

"Yes. He's my cousin. Is something wrong?"

"I would say that's a possibility. What's your location at this time, sir?"

The man sounded tired, but there was a distinct edge to his tone, not just his accent. It was a voice that you would not want to hear behind you in a dark alley.

Nonetheless, Tariq was not easily intimidated and felt his own temper rise.

"I'm at work in my office, my own legal practice. My name is Tariq Hussain QC."

Tariq heard the scrape of a chair, some footsteps and the tapping of computer keys at a fantastic pace. Whoever this Striker was, he knew his way around a computer.

As if reading the lawyer's previous thoughts, the detective said, "I think it's best you come over to the station, Mr. Hussain. I see your chambers are close by. Shall we say thirty minutes?"

"Do you have Abdullah there?"

Tariq heard more ferocious typing.

"I think it best we have a wee chat here at the nick, sir. It's eight fifty-five now so I'll expect you at nine twenty-five."

Tariq was furious at the man's attitude.

"I assure you, officer, that I am well aware of legal process and if you want me to go anywhere, you are going to have to give me more information than that. Do you get my drift?"

The detective sighed. He almost sounded in pain, the conversation alone causing him injury.

"This wee phone here, the one registered to your cousin there, has two hundred and thirty-four contacts on it. Out of those, there are eighty-two mobile numbers, with no direct evidence of a relationship with the owner, for example Ahamed, Ismail, Iftikar etc, twenty business listings within Lancashire, seventeen others in Greater Manchester and a hundred and six international numbers, mostly Pakistani and Middle Eastern in origin. "

Tariq's hand shook as he held the phone.

"That leaves your number, Mr. Hussain."

"I don't understand."

"You, sir, are listed as 'Jihad' and you have attempted to contact this number three times this morning."

Tariq felt his throat tighten. Whatever his cousin was mixed up in, it had nothing to do with him. Despite Hussain's reputation for defending the un-defendable, he didn't need any connection to a crime on his CV.

"Where do I come to?"

He wrote down the address, even though he knew exactly where Lawson Street was. A new mosque had opened just across from the station.

When the call ended he looked up. His long-standing employee was standing stock still in front of him. His legs felt like jelly.

"I have to go, Gina. I think there may be trouble and my cousin may be hurt."

Gina's bottom lip started to tremble. She had always liked Tariq Hussain. He had been a kind and respectful employer. He'd been wonderful when she'd miscarried for the second time and needed sick leave. He was a good man, but her Barry had been right. She couldn't work for a man who supported those women yesterday.

"I'm very sorry, Mr. Hussain, but I still need your answer."

Tariq looked at Gina and his anger rose further. She earned good money by him. Four weeks' paid holiday and a good bonus at Christmas. He could have hired a bright young thing from the family for half the price. A respectful girl, who knew her place, never took a day off.

"This is not the time to start talking politics and religion, Gina. You know my views all too well. I have a family emergency."

Gina produced an envelope from under her arm. Tears rolled onto her round red cheeks. She dropped it on the desk and her voice finally cracked.

"That's what my Barry thought you'd say."

Tariq stood as she turned.

"Gina! Wait!"

She didn't turn to him, but waved her hand behind her for him to be silent, praying to God he didn't continue to challenge or cajole her.

Barry had been insistent. Ever since he'd started going to those meetings at the club on Plungington, he'd become a man who hated, rather than tolerated.

Barry had always been trouble; he'd been to jail a couple of times, but Gina had loved him for as long as she could remember. She knew he was a racist, but she knew many more people just as bad. In recent months it had got worse. Barry wouldn't even pick Gina up from work anymore.

When he saw the news and the paint on the soldiers, he had made her promise to leave the office.

They'd fought more than they had ever done in all their years of marriage.

Finally Gina agreed to ask the question.

And now she knew the answer.

"Oh no!"

Tag actually verbalised the words and immediately made a note that he was talking to himself.

He watched the forty-something woman burst from the door of Penrith House. She had mascara all over her face, no shoes and was obviously pissed off about something. She staggered at first, then picked up pace.

Now, worse still, she was running, well, wobbling toward his car; one very white knee protruding from her very black unfashionable tights.

"Shit, shit, shit," hissed Tag under his breath.

After all, it was now close to nine a.m. and the last thing he wanted was to have to deal with some domestic between this drunken old tart and her latest pick up.

Sandra reached the car door before Tag could hit the catch to open it. She grabbed violently at the handle, nearly wrenching it from its mounting.

She screamed at him, "Let me in!"

Tag tried to lift the interior door catch but it was never going to shift whilst this lunatic pulled on the outside handle.

"Let go of the handle!"

"Let me IN!"

Tag realised it was useless to try to communicate through the glass of the car door so he stepped out himself. He felt the cold morning instantly. He was about to ask the first and obvious question of the hysterical woman when she collapsed on the tarmac.

"This is fuckin' marvellous," he muttered as he knelt beside her. He reached for his radio. "Delta Bravo Five to control, over."

No response.

"Typical."

He lifted the woman's head gently and manoeuvred her into the recovery position. Her eyes flickered and for the first time Tag noticed her injuries. Some hard arse bastard had given her a right going over.

He tried the radio again and on the third call he got a reply.

"Go ahead, PC Westland."

The voice of the operator was unknown to him, probably drafted in due to the nightmare unfolding around the town. The tired sounding soul had probably worked through the night, just as he had.

"I have a collapsed female on Avenham Lane, near to the flats, " he said. "Looks like an assault, request an ambulance and a relief, over."

"Stand by."

The radio fell silent and Tag suddenly realised that other than he and this poor sod, not another living soul was on the street. They were probably watching Sky and thinking 'fuck that'.

He stroked her hair and spoke gently.

"You'll be okay, now, love the ambulance is on its way. You'll be fine."

The woman repaid his kindness by coughing briefly and then throwing up all over his left leg.

The inside of the ambulance smelled as it should. All disinfectant masked death, blood and snot. The two paramedics worked on the woman but they, unlike Tag, had not already made their hypothesis about her situation. The woman's pulse and breathing was steady and to Tag's relief she had stopped throwing her last meal everywhere. That said, the medics were concerned that she simply refused to rouse from her faint.

They tried the usual trick of pain, the one where the medic digs his nail into the patient's finger just at the cuticle, but the woman didn't flinch.

"Well, she's not just pissed up," commented the medic as he released her digit. The rather overweight man was clad in bright green coveralls. They gave him the appearance of a large apple. He placed a small clear mask on the woman and delivered some oxygen to it. As he lifted her head to secure the mask with the elastic tape, he let out a low whistle.

"I think you better have a look at this, pal."

Tag leaned forward cautiously, aware that he had been caught by projectile vomit on the trousers, but a direct hit to his face would be a totally different matter.

"What is it?"

The medic turned the woman's head away from them to reveal her neck. A very nasty purple and red coloured lesion was evident around three-quarters of her throat.

"She's been strangled with somethin'," said the medic in a flat, matter of fact tone.

Tag stared at the injury for a moment, his mind temporarily blank, and then turned to the medic.

"I think... err... this might be a... err, CID job, eh?"

He instantly realised he sounded like a southern ponce with too much university education to be of any use, but it was too late. The Golden Delicious guy gave Tag a knowing look.

"Well, I reckon it might need someone with a bit of experience, son."

Tag grabbed his radio, looked sideways at the medic and muttered a sarcastic, "Thanks, mate."

No one wanted to talk to him on the air. He presumed that the radio operators were in it up to their eyes. He could hear sirens in all directions. The shit had truly hit the fan somewhere close.

Tag reluctantly directed his comments to the fat medic. "Looks like I'll be the one following you to Casualty."

"Whoopee doo," said the man.

CHAPTER SIX

The parade story ran like old newsreel in Wilson's head. He knew every millisecond of it and he now knew why it mattered to him. Burka-clad women screamed at the soldiers as they marched by; eyes front. The men and women were used to the abuse on the streets of Jalalabad but not Nelson.

As the paint struck, he heard the physical gasp of the crowd, the sheer shock of what was actually happening on a British street. Women covered their mouths or wiped tears as the reality struck. Then placards appeared as if from nowhere.

'British Murderers', they said.

One paint-covered soldier broke discipline and flailed at the crowd, damaged and ashamed, before being floored by his own kind to preserve his dignity. The police finally made it, and arrested several angry bodies, none from the Islamist group.

That was my Charlie's parade.

Wilson opened the drawer 1989.

Back then he worked for a living. Charlie had just arrived and Molly still loved her husband.

He had a good yard; seventeen wagons and twenty drivers worked for him.

Another year, said the accountants, and he'd be a millionaire.

He still liked to drink and fight of course.

The English love to fight, everyone knew that.

He was the county's middleweight champion three years running and was as feared out of the ring as in.

Molly had bathed his broken hands and face more times than he could remember. He'd drive a wagon to Cork; make a grand on the sale and then bet it on himself at a travelers' fair.

All comers.

He'd fight the gypsies for hours; bare knuckle too. Man after man, hoping to take the ever increasing purse.

Wilson never lost.

Well. Not in those days.

He'd stagger into his cottage back in rural Howick, battered and bruised but three thousand pounds better off.

Molly adored him.

Men admired him.

"Wilson!"

"Come on now, Wilson, you can hear me, let's have you, old mate, open those eyes. Talk to me."

The paramedic worked on him. Wilson could feel himself being moved around. Something was pushed into his throat and he wanted to gag but could not.

Then there were straps and he could breathe easily again.

He opened his eyes to see the medic shaking his head as the ambulance made its way through traffic.

"This is the last fuckin' time, Wilson," he warned.

"You're forty-five years old, you stupid bastard, your body won't take this shit anymore.

You've been fighting again, haven't you? You're all busted up and you've overdosed on the meds."

The medic sniffed at him.

"And you've been on the piss. What did the docs say to you about the meds and alcohol? They can fuckin' kill you, mate. Kill you! Understand?"

Wilson couldn't have answered the medic, who he recognised from several recent casualty visits, even if he'd wanted to.

What was he to say, anyway?

He'd been fucked over again?

He should've run away?

The guys who'd broken his ribs again within the first minute of the beating had been easily twenty years younger. They'd done him good style.

Back in the day, well, that would have been a different story.

He closed his eyes and thought about Charlie's parade; his Charlie.

That wasn't right.

Something should be done about it.

The Royal Preston Hospital, like most NHS trust units, was overworked and under-funded. The hopelessness of the whole situation seemed to rest on Tag's already knackered shoulders. After all his fine decision-making it seemed he was destined to continue as an 'un-resigned' police officer, at least until Mr. Feckin' Thomson returned to duty that night.

Meanwhile, he slouched in a rickety chair at the foot of the mystery woman's bed in the vain hope that someone would relieve him. But from the radio transmissions he was eavesdropping on, there was a major incident ongoing, and that did not seem likely. Sandra had been admitted to Ward 20, an observation unit. A place where they take you if they haven't a bloody clue what is wrong, or indeed, if there is anything wrong, with your body. She was sandwiched between a suspected epileptic fit and a suspected paracetamol overdose.

In fine company.

A ray of sunshine appeared on the horizon in the form of the tea trolley and Tag sat up and smiled briefly in the hope that he may be entitled to a cup himself.

A young woman that Tag considered to be of about perfect proportions controlled the trolley. Things were definitely looking up, he thought.

"Morning, gorgeous," he attempted.

The look of total horror on the face of the tea person, told Tag that his rather feeble line had gone down about as well as Gary Neville did with England managers.

She rummaged around on her trolley, busying herself, head down, her lovely shiny strawberry hair falling around her pale near perfect complexion.

"Would you like tea or coffee, officer?"

Her voice was soft, yet clear; northern, local and lovely. Tag perceived a slight tremor in it. She glanced up and caught him staring intently at her.

Tag felt himself visibly blush. "Err, I'm sorry, sweet. I mean, miss...err... tea, yes, that would be nice, thanks."

The girl wore a lapel badge and Westland noted her name; Scarlet with one't'.

She poured dark, over-brewed tea into a pale blue hospital cup and handed it to Tag. Her hand visibly shook and she withdrew it with great speed once he had taken control of the saucer.

"Sorry," she cleared her throat, "I'm a little nervous around the police."

Scarlet one't' managed a weak smile before retreating behind her trolley.

"I must get on."

Tag found her gentle mix of beauty and nervousness absolutely engaging; he couldn't let her escape.

He did his best to regain his lost charisma.

"Scarlet?"

She stopped her task and gazed at Tag. She had taken on the appearance of a rabbit caught in headlights.

"Yes."

"Can I ask a personal question?"

"Can I refuse?"

Tag smiled kindly, "Of course."

"Then no, I don't mean to be rude, but," she moved the trolley forward, "I don't answer personal questions. And I don't date, I mean, if that was the question, I mean, sorry…"

And she was gone. With a swish of starched cotton the vision of beauty that could have held Tag enthralled for, well, months disappeared.

A very overweight staff nurse had witnessed the exchange and nodded in Scarlet's direction.

"Funny one, that. Doesn't say much and doesn't like men if you ask me."

Nonetheless, for some reason, known only to him, Tag felt happy. Happiness is generally short-lived in hospitals and Tag's was no exception. His warm self-satisfied glow was transposed by hysterical screams from his mystery woman. He attempted to calm her by making shushing noises and holding her hand. Two nurses, including the fat one with the Scarlet 'one t' information, pushed him roughly aside. They both gave him a look that reminded him how useless he was. He stood back and watched the experts deal with his charge. Without warning the woman stopped screaming and stared directly at Tag. Her chest heaved as she took great gulps of air. She raised a finger and pointed directly at him. It seemed like an age. Tag felt guilty. He had no idea why.

Her arm sagged; her voice faltered and she began to cry. Great hacking uncontrolled sobs that tore at Tag's hardened heart.

The two nurses pulled the curtains around the bed of Sandra Mackintosh. The fat one gave Tag a 'get lost' look and he took the hint.

Ms Sandra Mackintosh had survived where eleven of her rapist's other victims had not. She also had the dubious honour of being the hundredth hospital admission that morning.

Two floors below Sandra Mackintosh was the reception area. Molly had told the hospital over and over not to ring her, but Wilson's only ID was his driving license, probably his last possession, and she was still his named next of kin.
Her very ex-husband was in hospital again, had more broken ribs and the doctors were concerned he had a perforated stomach ulcer brought on by his overdose of medication and heavy drinking.
Molly had long since moved on. She had a new man in her life, a gentle, kind man who didn't fight, in or out of a ring, a man who came home at night sober and in good temper; a man who had been more of a father to Charlie than Wilson ever had.
He had grieved at the lad's loss as if he had been his own blood.
When the Taliban had taken Charlie, her Henry never left her side until a week after the burial.
Wilson had been on a five-day bender and couldn't be found.
Charlie had been dead eleven days before his so-called father knew of the roadside bomb that had torn him limb from limb.
They never saw his body.
It was best, they said.
Wilson went straight back on the booze and missed the fucking funeral for good measure.
"I don't give a damn if he lives or dies," she spat down the line at a young but tired casualty receptionist.
Nineteen year old Ayesha returned the phone to its cradle and adjusted her hijab.
"It's a good job somebody does, love," she muttered to herself with a thick Lancashire lilt.
She punched in the numbers for Wilson's ward and admired her new henna on the back of her hand. There was a click and the ward sister answered.
"Mrs. Wilson won't be attending, sister," said Ayesha. "They are divorced and she doesn't care about him."
"Really?"
"Really."

There was a pause until the sister added, "Okay, leave it with me, thank you."

Ayesha held up her hand to the light and inspected the intricate design her aunt had created. If she needed proof that the love of alcohol and divorce were epidemic, or that British society and its sense of community was self-destructing, she had witnessed it first hand. She witnessed it every shift. She saw that the British had no morals or values.

Their women paraded around half naked and inebriated, dreaming of being Jordan or Chantelle. They staggered into the hospital, abusing her and the staff, swearing and fighting like, well, like nothing she could imagine.

Ayesha studied hard at UCLAN. She would be a pharmacist within five years. Two shifts a week as a casualty receptionist was her contribution to the family. It was a small price to pay.

Her most secret friend Abdullah Mohammed had told her that it was good for her to witness such things. It showed the British for what they were.

Ayesha sighed. Abdulla Mohammed made her stomach do back-flips each time she saw him.

He was strong and handsome and came from a good family. They had met three times now. Always in secret for fear of bringing shame upon them; each time swearing it would be the last; each time knowing it could not be so.

Both were promised to others. Abdullah was less than a year from his arranged marriage. Ayesha was yet to meet her proposed husband.

Not a living soul could know of their love.

She leaned, opened her bag and carefully withdrew the small package Abdullah had given her to deliver. She wondered about its undisclosed contents.

She shook it against her ear but there was only silence and it felt light as a feather in her touch.

When she finished her shift and had seen her family, she would take it to the flat in Avenham.

Abdullah Mohammed had trusted her with this important task. She was proud to deliver this treasure he held so dear. Ayesha would do anything for him; anything at all.

Tag turned the key in his own front door. He was too exhausted to even pick up his mail, and simply trod on it in the hall.

He climbed thirteen polished wooden stairs to his bedroom, dropped his clothes to the floor and slipped between welcoming sheets.

To his horror he was not alone.

A sleepy blonde head popped into view, followed by two stretching arms and a pair of naked breasts.

"You are very late, Tag, babe," pouted the blonde.

Westland jumped from the bed. His anger at the intrusion to his most hallowed place would have boiled over into rage had he been clothed, but the realisation that he stood clad in Winnie the Pooh boxer shorts and one black sock tempered his tone slightly.

"Amy! What the hell are you doing here?"

"Surprised?"

"Well," spluttered Tag. "Quite frankly, yes, I mean we are finished."

"Are we?"

"Aren't we? I mean yes, we bloody well are!"

"But, Tag, babe…."

"No! Never mind the Tag babe bit, you shagged Quinton."

"It was Quentin, babe, and all that is in the past now."

Amy pulled the covers further back to reveal a little more stunning figure, and patted the mattress.

"Come back to bed, babe, you're spoiling my surprise.

Tag felt himself losing the battle. The trouble was, or had been, that Tag always lost the battle with Amy, and that was the reason they had split for the last time three months prior to this particular bed invasion. The fact was, Amy was about as trustworthy as a pit-bull.

Despite all this prior knowledge, the sight of her wonderful form already warm in his bed was causing some hesitancy in throwing her bare face out onto the street.

It was then that God or some other superior being that occasionally watches over the truly 'not that bad' people came to Tag's assistance.

Amy leaned over to her left and lit a cigarette.

The fact that the two-timing tart had the audacity to break into his house, purely on the presumption that he would perform degrading sex acts at the snap of her fingers, just because she was beautiful, and naked, (well, he couldn't really be annoyed at that, as he had done it before,) was bad enough. But she knew that Tag hated smokers with a passion, and to add insult to injury Amy was using his treasured Liverpool FC Treble winning plate as an ashtray.

All thought of temporary reunions and great sex went straight out of the window. Tag ripped at the duvet and threw it to the floor.

"Get the fuck out of my house."

"But….."

"No buts, get out, oh, and give me my key, and don't stub that out on my plate."

Amy looked hurt. The look was very brief and quickly turned to a… 'I suppose I'll have to go back to Quentin' type look. Tag stomped downstairs, sat on his sofa, and listened to Amy collect her things.

She didn't say goodbye.

CHAPTER SEVEN

Detective Superintendent Errol Graham bit at a rogue piece of skin on his left thumb. He read the press release again and it didn't get any better.

Half the town had been on fire overnight. He had every spook that MI5 and 6 could muster setting up camp in his police station, and now he had a teenage boy hanging from a hook in a back street garage.

Errol spat the offending skin onto the carpet and pushed his tired frame from his desk.

Standing, he walked to the full length mirror his wife had insisted he have fitted to his office when he made Detective Superintendent.

Errol straightened his tie. He stood well over six feet tall. His once muscular frame was going to seed, and he patted his ever increasing gut and vowed to restrain his wife from making such large portions of home cooked food. Perhaps he could take up a sport, badminton maybe?

He opened his office door and stepped straight into the mêlée that was the incident room. It was buzzing with excitement. The Chief Constable himself was to facilitate the first briefing.

Half the elected membership of Lancashire was downstairs, including the BNP and the Muslin Council of Great Britain.

The whole thing was a political nightmare.

He took his seat next to the chief, moved the mic toward his mouth and waited for silence.

He commanded it without a word and received it in seconds.

"Ladies and gentleman, for those of you who don't know me, I'm Detective Superintendent Errol Graham.

I've been a police officer for twenty-two years. I was the first black senior detective to work on Operation Trident in the Metropolitan Police area. I've seen more hate crime than most men alive, I've seen every race colour or religion you care to mention dead on the pavement and heard all the reasons why it shouldn't happen. That qualifies me to run this investigation, and I intend to do just that starting now."

Graham eyed the front row of detectives.

DS Ewan Striker sat toying with *that* mobile phone in its plastic evidence bag, oblivious to the briefing. Graham instantly disliked him. He'd had the audacity to countermand his direct order within seconds of meeting him. He was a loose cannon. Striker had the social skills of a slug. Despite his credentials as an excellent intelligence and counter terrorism expert, Graham thought Striker brash, tactless and what his wife would call 'common'.

He continued to annoy the chief by first messing with the mobile and then tapping furiously into an iPad.

Graham did his best to ignore him.

Abu Al Zachari gently placed Ismi in the back of the cab as it idled noisily on Avenham Lane. Within two hours, every trace of his being would be erased from his flat. The team would have done their job without question.

He considered, not for the first time, that his failing may be overtaking him. The infidel whores were his duty to defile, degrade and kill. This was the will of Allah. But the last one had escaped, and the great plan could be undone by his weakness.

The Council would never understand his flaws, and so it must remain a secret that he and Ismi would take to the grave.

Ismi was now of an age where she understood life's urges and temptations. He could no longer depend on her naivety or her silence.

In the boot of the cab were two suitcases that contained almost all he would need in this life. All that remained was the final tiny piece in the jigsaw.

This worried Zachari somewhat as delivery of the item had been arranged for this very night at his flat. He walked the ten meters to the public phone and grimaced at the smell inside. He would need to contact Abdullah to arrange an alternative site for the delivery.

He closed his eyes and mentally put the last hours behind him.

He dialled the number from memory and inserted the coins in the box.

"Yes?" the voice answered.

Not an English voice. Not the voice of his brother in arms.

Scottish? Irish? Zachari had difficulty in discerning the difference between the two.

He dropped the phone into the cradle and walked briskly to the cab.

This was not good. Not good at all.

The sound of the mobile ringing in the briefing room was as welcome as a fart in a spacesuit.

Striker struggled with the small buttons through the plastic bag, but eventually on the fourth ring managed to accept the call.

His analytical brain moved into overdrive. The screen pronounced the caller ID as 'unknown.'

"Yes."

Silence on the line. Well, not quite silence. Striker heard breathing and the unmistakable ambient noise of a phone box.

The line went dead.

The detective closed his eyes. What else had he heard? A car idling nearby? A diesel car?

A taxi?

Striker opened his eyes to see the furious face of the Chief Constable glaring at him.

A shrug was all he could muster, he didn't apologise, because he wasn't sorry; he wasn't sorry at all.

Westland was freezing. This was hardly surprising as he had fallen sound asleep on his sofa after Amy's departure and lay prostrate without covers. His newly acquired house had yet to have the benefit of central heating.

It hadn't been the cold that had caused him to wake, but the constant simultaneous ringing of both his house and mobile phones. In his delirium he attempted to answer both.

On the house phone was a pushy little nerd trying to sell him a new kitchen. Unfortunately in telling the call-centre complication to go forth and multiply, he insulted his mother on his mobile.

"Sorry, Mum, I was talking to someone else, I...."

"I should hope so, Trevor."

Westland winced at the use of his name. He had been christened Trevor Arthur Gordon by his delightfully middle-class parents, and instantly hated all three options. Their various abbreviations were no better; he couldn't bear the thought of Trev or Gordy or, for God's sake Arty, and therefore always used his initials.

Tag scratched his nether regions and shivered.

"What do you want, Mum, I'm on nights."

"What have you said to poor Amy, dear?"

"Poor Amy?"

"You know who I mean, Trevor, she's been on the phone in a terrible state, the child could hardly speak she was so upset."

"Really?"

"Yes really! There is no need for that kind of attitude, my boy; you know full well that your father and I hoped that the two of you would..."

"Stop!"

Tag took a deep breath and forced himself not to raise his voice to his mum. "Stop right there, Mother. Have you forgotten the little matter of Quentin the chartered accountant?"

His mother sighed.

"She was taken in by his money, darling, that's all. That and you going off to do this dreadful police job, I mean, any girl would have her head turned. If you had taken the job in the city that Daddy had organised for you, none of this would have happened."

"I don't want to talk about this now, Mother."

"Well you should, I was married and pregnant with you by the time I was your age."

"I'm on the pill, Mum."

Tag's mother knew she was on a loser with this one. She secretly didn't care for the girl anyway but she did play bridge with Amy's mother Wednesdays and Sundays and quite liked her. It was just a shame that, Amy, as with most of the upper classes these days, couldn't keep her legs together.

"So it's really finished?"

"Really."

His mother did not give up on her matchmaking that easily.

"Shame, still the Allcocks's daughter is just home from Cambridge University for half term, she's lovely and we are having supper with them on Saturday."

"No, Mother."

"But!"

"No. Anyway I have a date," he lied.

"Tell me more, darling."

"Nothing to tell, Mother."

"Well at least tell me her name."

Tag thought for a moment.

"Scarlet, Mum, she's called Scarlet, one 't'."

Tag put down the phone, all thoughts of sleep pushed to the back of his mind.

He rummaged in the kitchen for instant coffee and clicked on the kettle.

He opened the fridge and peered suspiciously at the milk carton. One sniff told him the good news.

"Shit."

He pulled on his tracksuit and strode back out into the chill of the day.

Ten minutes later he queued patiently for the Spar checkout. A large guy who needed a shower more than the contents of his basket obscured most of his view, but he did see a flash of a blue uniform further down the line. To his delight and amazement he realised that he was only two human beings away from the delicious Scarlet. Coincidence?

Some things, he mused, *must be fate; she must live nearby.* No one in their right mind would shop at the Spar unless desperate, (most likely), lazy, (Tag's excuse) or local.

His mind was a frenzy of activity. How could he make an approach? He'd heard that the trendiest place to pick up a woman was the supermarket, but how, dressed in muddy trackies, clutching a bottle of semi-skimmed and a copy of Loaded, was he going to impress the stunning redhead?

He needn't have expended the energy on the thought process. It was like something from Fawlty Towers.

Tag leaned just a little too far right to get a better glimpse of Scarlet and his two-litre plastic bottle of semi slipped from under his arm, struck the Spar floor with the velocity of a guided missile, and exploded.

The back-splash from the milk bomb coated the school blazers of the two children directly in front of smelly man-mountain; but far worse, the meteor-like rise of white liquid stuck Scarlet a bulls-eye. Tag considered he couldn't have intentionally covered a human being with so much milk had he been given a fire hose and a tanker full of the stuff.

Worse?

Oh yes, much worse.

In obvious distress, Scarlet leaned forward to allow the excesses of dairy product to drip from her nose. In perfect concert, Tag had decided that the obvious thing to do was to dab Scarlet with his copy of Loaded magazine. He too bent toward the distraught woman.

The clash of heads was spectacular. Not since Norman 'bites your legs' Hunter retired from professional defending had there been such an astounding meeting of skulls.

Both sat clutching their heads whilst their lower garments soaked up the remainder of the milk bomb.

"Sorry," managed Tag, "are you okay?"

"No thanks to you," replied an obviously angry Scarlet.

"It was an accident," whined Tag.

"I'm glad about that," Scarlet pulled herself to her feet, "as the thought of suicide milk bombers in your local Spar beggars belief."

Tag felt instantly better, well a little, at least she was able to joke about the disaster.

"I usually strap them to my body with tape and throw myself to the floor."

Scarlet looked puzzled.

"The milk cartons," clarified Tag, "on my milk bombing runs."

The beautiful girl actually smiled; he was winning after all. He continued with the triumphant chat up line.

"You've probably seen me on America's Most Wanted. I think I was number seven last week."

Scarlet looked into Tag's face; it was dawning on her. "I have seen you before, haven't I?"

Tag didn't quite know what to say so he stayed quiet.

The look of realisation on the girl's face did little to inspire Tag Westland.

"You're that, that copper, aren't you?" she spat, "you're the one at the hospital, the one with that poor woman."

"That's me, Scarlet."

"How do you know my name? Have you been spying on me?"

Tag realised that the suicide bomber routine had definitely failed and that there was a need for emergency modification of his initial plan.

"I know your name because of the nameplate on your uniform at the hospital, I wasn't arresting that woman, I was trying to help her and I just thought…."

"Thought what? Thought that you could just smile and twinkle those brown eyes of yours and I would come running? I told you I don't…'

"Don't date; I know I heard you the first time. I just want to take you for a drink, just friendly sort of stuff, you know, a pub, bowling, whatever."

Tag purposely twinkled. "No tongues."

Another smile, "I don't like policemen."

"Join the club, I'm resigning tonight."

"Really?"

"Really."

"But what about that poor woman?"

And so it was; oblivious to the carnage he had left behind, Tag walked Scarlet from the shop.

Her anger had subsided and her nervousness, previously displayed in the hospital, had returned. Tag had no idea why this was so, but he tried his best to ease her disquiet by being funny.

The trouble was, being funny is far easier when you don't smell like a small primary school has thrown up on you.

"I'm not doing too well, am I?" he conceded.

"You're doing okay."

"I am?"

"Look...err..." Scarlet fumbled for his name.

"Tag," he prompted.

"Yes, Tag... I... err...just...well... I'm not too good at this right now and..."

"You don't need to be good at it; I'll be good for the pair of us. Please?"

She captured him with another smile.

He pleaded, "Look, just once. If you hate me, I will never bother you again."

"I...err...I... don't know," she wavered.

"I won't bring milk."

That was it, those four words, did the trick. She laughed, and said..."maybe."

Striker sat opposite Tariq Hussain. The QC looked every inch the successful lawyer he was; expensive suit, expensive shoes, Rolex. He was a slender, handsome man and as articulate as you might expect from someone in his position.

He'd checked Hussain on Google. The barrister had a reputation for defending terror suspects, drug dealers, paedophiles; the lowest of the low.

He made Striker's teeth itch.

The detective considered that not unlike himself, the lawyer might be someone unlikely to show his emotions; but Hussain cried genuine tears.

Striker waited for the lawyer to compose himself.

"Would you like some water, Mr. Hussain?"

"No, thank you. I would like to know how Abdullah died."

The detective looked into the face of the brief. His sharp blue eyes telling everything the powerful and eloquent man needed to know.

"He was murdered?"

"Yes."

"My God!" Hussain held his head in his hands. "Oh my God."

Striker's tolerance was draining away, impatience being one of his ever problematic flaws. He had always found sentiment difficult to express; there was no time for any sentiment in this case, no time for any emotion. He'd considered keeping the details of the murder from the QC, but with modern communication, Twitter, Facebook and the blogging community, what was the point? The garage owner would have told his wife what he'd seen, she would have told her friends, and they would have told theirs. Before the day was out it would be all over the internet.

The jugular was Striker's favorite place to start.

"He was tortured before he died, Mr. Hussain. Why would that be?"

Tariq's head shot up from his cradling hands, eyes wide in shock. "Tortured? What do you mean, tortured?"

"I mean, he would have told whoever did this, exactly what he knew."

Striker tapped at his iPad, and changed tack; a classic interview technique.

"Your cousin had visited Pakistan three times this year. Why was that?"

Hussain shook his head and raised a finger, tears still present but drying as he regained his professionalism.

"Now don't even begin to suggest that Abdullah had connections with terrorists, Detective."

Striker snorted.

"What? He was arranging his marriage? Visiting family?"

"Yes, of course. He is..." Hussain corrected himself. "I mean...was... about to arrange his marriage. He parents live in Islamabad. Why should he not visit the homeland?"

"His home is here, Mr. Hussain."

"Don't play politics with me!" Tariq banged the table with a clenched fist.

Striker grabbed the man's hand and held it to the desk. There was little contest.

"Don't? Don't what? Don't tell you that we already know where he's been and who he's been associating with? Don't say the 'T' word? Be politically correct?"

Hussain struggled to free his hand. Striker gave him the option.

"Exactly what are you implying here, Detective?"

Striker sat back in his chair, opened a brown envelope and removed a single black and white proof of the murder scene. It showed Abdullah Hussain, hooked like a carcass for butchery; that sign around his neck; the look of sheer terror etched on his face. He held it toward himself; briefly considered the implication of showing it to the lawyer and then dropped it on the table in front of him without another thought.

Hussain gasped.

Striker almost punched a hole through the photograph with his finger.

"I know what is happening here," he said, his voice no more than a whisper. "And I don't like it one bit."

He pushed the image closer to the QC.

Tariq shook. "These people, the ones who did this terrible thing, they are vigilantes?"

"Call them that if you like. How long did the Islamists think this shit would go on before some good old flag-waving Anglo Saxons started to fight back? They swallowed the 7/7 bombings, I was surprised it didn't kick off then. I suppose the English had seen it all before; the IRA, bombs in litter bins, that kind of thing. Even soldiers being brought home in body bags and paraded through Wootton Basset didn't light the fire. Muslim hate preachers walking the streets, and employing fancy lawyers just like you, to ensure they stay in the country;

What the hell did you think would happen when Lee Rigby was run over and half decapitated in broad daylight? It was the straw that broke the donkey's back."

Striker picked up the photograph and held it inches from Hussain's face.

"The Irish, the PIRA, were hard to spot, hard to target, but it still happened. Innocent Irishmen were murdered on English soil in the name of so called justice.

The Islamists, well they are not so difficult to see; the dress, the beard; you know what I'm saying?

This murder has not been carried out by some right wing thugs. This is a professional job."

He pushed the image back into the envelope. His eyes bore into the QC. They flashed with anger. If Tariq had been facing the man in the courtroom, he would want him behind bulletproof glass.

"If it was the hope of the Taliban to wake a sleeping giant," Striker hissed, "They finally have their wish. The chatter on the internet will bring the Muslim community out in their thousands tonight. The EDL and BNP will do the same; together with every racist thug the town can muster. If it continues, there will be troops on the streets within a week."

"You're alleging that my cousin is Taliban?"

"I'm saying that your cousin was connected to an active terrorist cell, and that he has been radicalised enough to take part in some kind of atrocity."

Hussain glared at the detective.

"Abdullah was a nineteen year old boy, who wore Superdry fashions and shaved every day. He went to Preston North End; a season ticket holder. He may have been angry at government policy, but that hardly makes him a terrorist."

Striker held up the Blackberry phone.

"The same boy who has you listed as 'Jihad' in his phone?"

"Don't be ridiculous, Striker. Knowing Abdullah, it was probably his idea of a joke. He viewed me as a moderate, part of the system. He often teased me about my 'Englishness'."

Striker moved the goalposts again; changed his tone and used the brief's first name.

"Look, Tariq; I know all about disaffected youth. My mother was Irish Catholic and lived in a time when your beliefs either got you employed at the local factory and a nice council house, or firmly in the slums and trapped in the benefit system.

My uncles fought running battles on the streets of Belfast with the RUC and British army. To them Ireland was, and still is, an occupied country.

You want to see segregation? Want to see hatred? Go visit the States where I grew up. We all read history at school, Tariq; trouble is, no one ever learns from it."

Hussain was an expert cross examiner. He knew exactly what the detective was trying to do. To lull him, cajole him, show empathy; he was having none of it.

"You haven't produced any hard evidence to even suggest my cousin was involved in any kind of radical behaviour. If you had that information, he would have been in custody and not dead in the morgue."

Hussain was warming to his task. "So my question is, what are you and your fellow officers doing to catch his murderers? All you have done so far is implied that three innocent visits to my family in Pakistan have turned an astute, well-balanced boy into an Islamic terrorist."

Striker shrugged his massive shoulders.

"Believe what you wish, Hussain. I'm not here to catch your cousin's killers; not in the sense you think anyway. There are dozens of detectives upstairs right now, doing just that. I'm here to find out why he was killed. Because if I'm right, and your cousin was about to commit some kind of terrorist act, something spectacular, then we are in trouble, big trouble. This time, the security services seem to be a step behind. Up to now we haven't considered that an opposing vigilante force would appear, especially not one as professional as these guys. Whoever did this to Abdullah is very serious. Serious enough to torture and kill to get information. Now what did Abdullah tell them? That's the million dollar question."

Hussain stood.

"You give a good speech, Striker. Maybe you should be in politics, rather than a policeman; but as I said; unless you can show me that my cousin is involved in anything more than giving me a funny name on his phone list, any more than your gut feelings or childhood experiences, then this conversation is over."

Striker waited for a second, but the brief was right, he had nothing more to add.

He walked Hussain from the interview suite, to the door of the station and watched him walk down the steps to his Mercedes car. Black, top of the range, private plate.

"Money talks," he said under his breath.

Tag Westland had returned to duty at six o'clock to find Mr. Feckin' Thompson had been seconded to 'Bronze Command,' meaning he was sitting in a mobile control room somewhere in the division, attempting to co-ordinate officers on the ground, who in turn were getting the shit kicked out of them by both the Asian and white rioters.

The station was full of unfamiliar faces, all dressed like Robocop; they looked as tired and pissed off as Tag himself felt.

Resignation would have to wait.

He pulled a thin file from his 'in' tray and studied the note attached to it by a paperclip. The spidery handwriting was the work of the early shift detective, responsible for Avenham. It explained that he was too busy to look into the Mackintosh assault, and the task would fall into Tag's not so capable hands.

"Bugger!" he said under his breath.

He yawned theatrically, selected the set of keys for his patrol car and shuffled down to the garage.

Much to his dismay, he saw his Astra had a smashed windscreen and severely dented bonnet, courtesy of some mystery miscreants. No doubt the early driver had suffered the misfortune of driving too close to the rioting hordes.

He let out a second, "Bugger," turned on his heels and went about the task of finding alternative wheels.

By seven-thirty, he was back in the Royal Preston Hospital, sitting at the bedside of Sandra Mackintosh. The injuries to her throat had blossomed from the original angry red welts to a spectacular blue-purple bruise that circled her throat like a bizarre collar. She was also very much awake and lucid.

Tag introduced himself to the woman, and explained it had been he who had been outside the flat the night before. She appeared as unimpressed with Tag as his senior officers did.

"Where's the CID, then?"

"Erm...they are a bit tied up at the moment, Ms. Mackintosh, erm... sorry..."

Sandra gave a very hoarse-sounding *humph* and sipped her tea. "So they sent you then, Sherlock?"

Tag gave a weak smile.

"I'm more of a Watson type myself."

Sandra sat up painfully. She was a big woman, with a once pretty face that had been eroded by a life of excess, a lifetime on Avenham estate, and three kids by three different, useless men.

"Fucking marvelous! Some Paki tries to kill me, and they send me a bloody comedian to sort it."

"I didn't mean..." started Tag, "and Paki is not the preferred term, Mrs..."

Sandra cut him off.

"Look, son. I was pissed last night. I was on the vodka from tea time, had a right good night too. I'd been in the curry house and this Paki taxi driver was in there. He had his cab outside and offered me a free lift. I knew exactly what he was after. He weren't bad-lookin' either, so I thought fuck it, why not; a shag is a shag, right?"

Tag winced at Sandra's coarseness. She was not going to enamour any jury with her testimony, that was for certain.

He scribbled a few notes in his pocket book.

"So erm... you went up to his flat for erm...?"

"Sex. Yeah. Listen, son, how old are you? Twenty? Twenty two?"

Before Tag could answer, Sandra was off again.

"Look...I'm forty-seven. I've lived in my shithole flat since I got up the stick at sixteen. I've now got three lads who haven't worked a day in their miserable lives and spend more time in Preston nick than you do. I work three jobs cleaning and get to go out once a month. So if I want some cock, then I reckon I'm entitled, right?"

Tag felt himself blush. Sandra noticed immediately.

"Oh, Jesus; you are a proper posh boy, aren't ya? Look, son, I should tell you this before we go any further. I'm not going to make a complaint on this one."

Tag made to speak but the woman held up a meaty hand, cleared her throat agonisingly and continued.

"If I make a statement against a rag-head, my life will be a misery on Avenham, lad. I'll get untold grief from the lot of them. Then my lads will get the hump and before you know it, they'll be in the nick again for bottling one of 'em. It's not worth the hassle."

Tag was tempted to get a short retraction statement in his pocket book, ask Sandra to sign it and get on with the rest of his life. Then again, that would not endear the lovely Scarlet one 't' who, on exchange of mobile numbers outside the Spar shop, had been insistent that Tag look into the matter. She would be very upset by a lack of progress in the case. Alternatively, she would be seriously impressed with his detection skills, should he solve the crime within the day.

Tag considered his position; he knew the seriousness of the assault meant he wouldn't need a complainant statement to make an arrest. Therefore he did what he always did in these circumstances; he bullshitted.

"How about I just go round to this gentleman's flat and give him a warning, then?"

Sandra eyed the young cop suspiciously.

"Yeah right, the guy is fuckin' massive, must be near on seven feet tall, son."

"No, really," said Tag, attempting bravely to keep any sound of pleading out of his voice. "I'll just give him the gypsies."

Sandra thought about it for a few moments.

"One condition."

"Okay," said Tag.

"You get my fuckin' shoes back. They cost me twenty-five quid, them; only wore 'em once."

Striker had slept for two hours when his mobile shocked him awake. It was the office. The call to Abdullah Hussain's mobile had been made from a phone box at the junction of Avenham Lane and Oxford Road.

His rubbed his eyes and powered up his iPad. A quick check of Google Earth showed the area; he zoomed in and looked at the phone booth in question.

He called the incident room and was patched through to a very weary-sounding Errol Graham.

Striker did his best to be polite.

"Hello, sir."

"Where the hell have you been, Striker?"

"I grabbed a couple of hours."

Graham was not a happy bunny.

"Well, before you went to the land of nod, did you think to mention that you had interviewed a family member of the deceased? I had him in the morgue this afternoon for the formal ID and he tells me you more or less accused his whole family of being terrorists! Not only that, the guy is a fucking QC, he'll be a judge in a year. What are you thinking, Sergeant?"

Striker rubbed the top of his head and let out his trademark sigh. The one that told any party within hearing that he was bored with the conversation.

"It's in my report, sir."

"What fucking report?" The chief's voice was rising with each sentence.

"I emailed it to you at ten-twelve this morning."

There was a brief silence and a tapping of computer keys.

"This tells me nothing, Striker."

Striker would have loved to explain that the lack of content was deliberate, due to the fact that his investigation was on a need-to-know basis and that Graham didn't need to know. A full and detailed document had winged its way to the security services with all his findings.

Instead he replied,

"Little to report, sir; the man was distraught. He must have misunderstood my line of questioning."

Graham was unimpressed.

"What do you want anyway?"

"The call I took in the briefing this morning; you remember?"

"How can I forget, the Chief Con was fuming."

Striker smiled to himself and pressed on.

"Well, that call was made to the victim's mobile from the phone booth outside Penrith House, Avenham. It was a silent call; when they heard my voice they terminated. I need full forensics on the booth a.s.a.p."

Graham's voice hit another octave.

"Let me get this straight here, Striker. You want me to pull the only SOCO team that is awake off the murder scene to examine a phone box that has been pissed in more times than my toilet?"

"That's the strength of it, sir. I have a feeling about this one."

Grahams booming voice rattled Striker's ear.

"A fucking feeling!"

"Just trust me on this one, boss, okay? Get me the team down there and I'll be in your office within the hour. I'll brief you; give you all I've got."

Another silence; then, "Be here in twenty minutes."

Striker knew he wouldn't be in Graham's office any time soon. It wasn't that he was being awkward, although that was a formidable character trait of his; it was the inherent way of the anti terrorist squad, as was Special Branch before it. Keep as much information out of the public domain until it can work in your favour.

He knew it would only be a matter of time before his own boss would come under pressure and MI5 would come sniffing around and try and take the case from him.

That was not going to happen.

Striker's house was situated on Buckshaw Village; a new housing development created by the private sector. After the royal ordinance factory had been demolished it left sixteen square miles of prime building site slap bang in the middle of the M6/M61 corridor. The village had a pub, a school and a supermarket, but was still soulless.

On his rare social outings, Striker preferred to visit Preston's old quarter, around Friargate. There you could find pubs with character and more importantly, for a man who was teetotal, great jazz.

He'd paid two hundred and twenty-five thousand pounds cash for the three bedroom, two reception, three-storey. Something that had raised eyebrows during his vetting procedures for the anti terrorist unit; that was, until it was seen that the cash had been raised from the sale of his mother's house, in what had become a very trendy area of Belfast.

Striker pulled on a pair of US Navy issue boots. He had spent thousands of hours pounding the sidewalks of Chicago with his father and latterly the pavements of Belfast and Preston alone. He'd considered buying some new training shoes, maybe some Nike or Asics, but his father had used boots all his life, therefore they were good enough for Ewan.

When faced with problems, some cops turn to the bottle; Striker turned to the sidewalk.

He lifted a heavy backpack that contained eight rubber bricks, each weighing five kilos, onto his shoulders and adjusted the straps. His final touch was to push the earphones from his iPod into his ears, select a Charlie Parker album and hit 'shuffle.' He stepped out into the chill of the evening and ran.

Striker headed onto Dawson Lane and toward Leyland, the Lancashire town once famous for manufacturing buses and tyres. He dug in hard as he climbed the railway bridge that would take him toward the town centre; by the time he hit the ancient stone cross on Towngate, he was feeling the burn and his head started to clear. He turned right past Tesco supermarket, and headed for the main shopping street.

Darkness had fallen and the air was the perfect temperature for his run. The only outlets open were the small independent takeaways and the pubs.

As he approached The Ship Inn, he saw a smartly dressed man standing just outside the doorway handing out leaflets. Striker dismissed it as a promo guy, drumming up business for the latest local band. He'd seen two or three decent blues bands there since moving to Buckshaw. One, 'The Vendettas,' reminded him of the days his father would take him to backstreet Chicago bars to see the real deal. He ran past the pub; the smell of beer and the lingering odour of cigarettes from the smokers' shelter filled his nostrils.

Ten meters or so further on, Striker felt the usual tingle of suspicion. He never understood why it happened; it just did. He turned and jogged toward the suited figure; as he closed he saw the man was in his thirties, heavy set, crew-cut.

"What you got there, man?"

The figure didn't answer; just thrust the A5, single colour document into Striker's hand.

He scanned the page and immediately understood why his senses had kicked in.

"You part of this crew?" he asked the suit.

The man answered in a south London accent. "Me and thousands, mate. Be thousands more by the end of this week, 'bout time eh? This guy is gonna change things, mate; put the Pakis back in their place."

Striker folded the leaflet and pushed it into his combats.

"And what place is that, friend?"

The guy smiled. "You're a soldier, mate, eh? That or ex squaddie? You know what I'm saying? They're takin' over, mate. Gotta be stopped; and this guy is the man to do it; forget the BNP or the EDL pal. This is the real thing."

Striker nodded.

"The Real Thing? Seventies band, weren't they? Black guys?"

The suit puffed out his chest.

"You being funny, pal? You a Paki lover?

There was a momentary staring contest, which Striker won hands down. He stepped forward until his nose touched his would-be opponent's.

"No, pal. I'm not a lover, I'm a fighter."

CHAPTER EIGHT

Ayesha parked her Fiat 500 in the multi-storey car park, just off Avenham Lane. She locked the doors, adjusted her clothing to ensure she was appropriately dressed, and for the third time, checked that Abdulla's package was still in her handbag.

Ayesha was unfamiliar with Avenham, her own home being in the far more affluent area of Fulwood to the north of the city.

She wasn't scared, but it would be obvious to anyone that Oxford Road was not an area to be wandering around alone at night. She walked from the car park, the only sound being her shoes on the damp concrete that shone black in the streetlights.

She crossed Avenham Lane and broke into a jog toward the electronic doors of Penrith House.

She had memorised the entry code but needn't have bothered, as a solitary beer can wedged the door open.

As she stepped inside to the starkly lit entrance hall, she was forced to hold her nose against the smell of stale urine.

Why would Abdulla have to deliver this package to such a disgusting place?

She pressed the lift request button, and heard the clank of machinery as the car started its descent.

The doors creaked as they opened and she stepped reluctantly inside the elevator, the first creeping feeling of genuine unease turning her stomach. She came close to a dry wretch as she saw a used condom dropped on the floor of the lift.

Ayesha steeled herself and pressed the button to take her to the third floor, and her ultimate destination. Then she would call Abdulla to inform him that she had completed the task he had entrusted her with, and hopefully organise another secret meeting, which would make all this worthwhile.

As the lift rose, she heard the sound of a crying child and a mother bellowing at it. She said a silent prayer.

At floor three the doors scraped open and Ayesha was forced to peer into near darkness; every ceiling light on the corridor had been broken, shards of glass crunched under her feet. She held her bag containing the package to her breast, took a deep breath and stepped further toward her destination. She could feel her heart beat in her chest. She was sweating and beads formed at her temples.

Nothing to be scared of, Abdulla wouldn't send me into danger.
The doors closed behind her with a final scrape and she was plunged into total blackness; the distant screaming of the child temporarily replaced by an arguing couple somewhere above her. Ayesha rummaged for her mobile to light her way. Where was it? As she looked downward she noticed the red dot on the floor. One of those laser pens her youngest brother liked to play with?
It moved steadily toward her, up her body and to her forehead. She never heard the shot.

Tag Westland drove steadily from the Royal Preston. Sandra had remained adamant that she would not furnish him with any written testimony. She had also refused the services of the rape crisis unit. All he had was the name of the offender's taxi company, his address and the agreement to recover Sandra's black patent heels. After hearing Sandra's description of the offender, he'd considered asking for another officer to support him, but the radio traffic suggested that he would have little chance of back-up.
Tag may have been inept in many areas of his life, but his physical abilities, especially in a fight, were considerable; he was fairly confident he could deal with the man, even though Sandra's descriptive powers seemed to be limited to how big the guy was in every department.
He also considered that any man who was prepared to attack a woman, deserved some summary justice. This was always best dished out without witnesses.
As he pulled up his patrol car outside the flats, he noticed a SOCO unit was setting up at the junction, their attention seemingly on the telephone box. He gave a cursory wave, but the paper-suited men and women ignored him.

Please yourselves.
He tutted to himself as he kicked away the beer can wedged in the electronic door ensuring at least some modicum of security for the residents of Penrith House, and made to the lift.
Despite his best efforts, the car wouldn't move from wherever it was parked above him. He could hear the doors attempting to close, but that was the sum of it.

Bloody marvelous!

He found the stairwell, which smelled even worse that the entrance hall, unclipped a mini Maglite from his belt and negotiated what was laughingly called the fire-escape stairs. He climbed over two mattresses and a discarded pushchair in near total darkness, before he reached floor three. Tag had spent some considerable time in the flats and knew the layout well. 307 would be at the opposite end of the corridor.

He opened the heavy fire door that led to the landing. It was pitch black. He felt his way into the narrow passageway and immediately slipped on something wet. His right leg gave way and he landed with a splat on his back. His torch flew from his grasp and skidded across the floor, spinning as it went.

He cried out in surprise at his lack of footing. "Fuck!"

He tried to lift himself but his hands slipped away again, failing to find the grip they needed to lift his bodyweight.

On the second attempt, he managed to haul himself to a sitting position. His Maglite was some fifteen feet away and shone a narrow beam of light toward him. His eyes adjusted and he saw the cause of his downfall, the corridor floor was covered in thick oxygenated blood.

Tag grimaced and wiped his hands down his shirt.

As he found his feet, he was aware of a scraping sound, further down the passage. Every ten seconds or so, it repeated its laboured clatter.

What is that?

Whatever it was, this job had gone from a straightforward, summary justice stroke shoe collection, to something much more serious. He drew his baton and inched toward the noise.

What he found would live with him forever.

Striker checked his watch. It was almost twenty four hours to the minute since Abdullah Hussain had been discovered; now they had a second body. The operation to complete a forensic search on the telephone booth had been temporarily suspended. All available SOCO members were now changing into fresh kit to avoid any cross-contamination and were being briefed about the latest murder scene less than one hundred meters from where they had been working.

Striker walked over to the very pale-looking beat officer who had found Ayesha Chowdry. He was sitting on the curb edge, directly outside Penrith House.

"What's your name, son?"

The cop looked up. He was a handsome lad with a floppy haircut; he reminded Striker of a young Hugh Grant. When he answered, he sounded like the ponce too.

"Westland, sir."

"I'm not a sir, I'm a sergeant." He held out a hand. "Striker."

Westland took it and shook weakly, but didn't speak.

"How long you been in the job, son?"

Tag swallowed hard, seemed to find some strength from somewhere and used Striker's grip to pull him to a stand.

"One fucking day too long, sergeant," he said.

Striker looked up at the block of flats and considered the scene he had just inspected.

A young girl, no more than eighteen or nineteen, lying on her back, her body wedged between elevator doors; dragged there, her hijab soaked in her own blood, a single perfect shot to the forehead, an execution, professional, very professional, a small package in her hand and that sign again, the same A4 laser-printed sign.

'Terrorist'.

Westland was covered in the girl's blood. Striker thought back to the first murder scene he'd witnessed as a young cop. It didn't measure up to this one and he felt a twinge of sympathy for the lad. Sympathy was one thing, but now he had two dead bodies. This one held a suspicious-looking package with Chinese and Arabic script printed on it.

The doc had given him little useful information, cause of death was obvious, but he did offer that her corpse had been posed postmortem, this had been done for maximum effect; he needed answers and quick.

"So run it by me, pal, the reason for your visit to the flats; don't leave anything out, son."

Striker removed an iPad from its cover and started typing. Tag may have sounded like a southern ponce, but when Tag met the detective's eyes there was something in there that told Striker the kid was tough. Tag cleared his throat.

"I was dealing with an assault, happened yesterday morning a woman, Sandra Mackintosh, came running out of the flats about nine a.m. She'd been sexually assaulted and strangled, very nasty, won't make a complaint, says she would suffer at the hands of the locals if she did, I persuaded her to give me the flat number, was going to give him the Gypsies', she wanted her shoes back."

Striker took on the look of a puzzled ginger rhino.

"Shoes?"

"You would have to know the woman, sir...I mean...sergeant. She's, well, she's a bit of a tough nut, says that during the struggle the guy pulled off her shoes. They were new, she wanted them back."

"You got a name for the guy?"

Tag shook his head. "A strong possible; I know he lives at 307, he's a taxi driver, probably Arabic, works for J and G on Manchester Road. The victim says she was convinced there was a child in the flat during the assault."

Striker scratched his red locks.

"A kid?"

"So she said. She went there willing enough, she was drunk, went up to his flat for sex. Seems he got very rough, tried to strangle her with a belt, she said he was shouting or chanting throughout the attack. She hit him with one of the afore-mentioned shoes and managed to escape. Looking at her injuries, I'd say she is lucky to be alive. The guy needs sorting, sergeant."

"And you were the one to do it, son?"

Tag shrugged.

"I was going to wind him up a bit. See if he cut up with me, hopefully lift him for public order, take it from there."

Striker considered the story. "What makes you think he's an Arab, rather than Pakistani?"

"I went to J and G first, the taxi firm. They weren't too helpful. They did tell me one driver hadn't turned in for his shift tonight; dropped them in the shit. I asked to see his badge, personnel file, passport copy whatever, but they clammed up, said I'd need a warrant. He's probably an illegal. I did chat to another driver outside, nice guy, very devout Muslim, had no time for our missing driver, said our man was a Syrian who had an eye for white women. He told me he'd picked up the guy and a young kid on

Avenham Lane just before the end of his shift; took them to Burnley."

Striker felt his tell-tale tingle.

"What time was that?"

Tag shrugged. "I didn't ask, sorry, but he works nights. I'd put a few quid on just after he attacked Sandra Mackintosh. Lots of the night guys stay on for the school run; so about half-nine, I'd say."

There was a squeal of tyres as a large black BMW pulled up.

Striker saw Errol Graham step from the rear. The detective turned to Tag.

"If you are up to it, get back to the nick, get cleaned up and meet me at J and G in thirty minutes."

Westland gave Striker that look again.

"You think this fucker killed that girl up there?"

"Possible."

"See you in thirty, then."

CHAPTER NINE

Even at two in the morning Alistair Sinclair looked immaculate. He shaved three times a day through necessity, cut his jet black hair weekly and wore the best suits money could buy.

Of Scottish Protestant descent, he had been schooled in England and studied politics and history at Oxford. He was married to Catherine, had two daughters and had no sexual skeletons in his cupboard.

Other than his wedding band, he didn't wear jewelry of any kind. His watch was an Omega, which had been his father's. Major Robert Sinclair (retired) of the Queen's Own Lancashire Regiment. He had the perfect family, the perfect background and more guts than any other politician in Westminster.

He had taken the seat as MP for Nelson under an independent candidate banner eight months before. Now it was time to head his own party and govern the country.

He did not take calls from Grant Bliss; either via mobile or landline. Sinclair knew that if his plan for political greatness was to work, their arrangement had to be the most secret since any hatched in the Second World War; and this was a war, make no mistake.

It was acceptable for Bliss and his right hand man, Slade, to provide security at Sinclair's speeches and rallies; after all, security was his business, and few were better, but all conversations concerning the great plan were face to face.

The room that was Sinclair's campaign office was situated over a hardware shop in Nelson, Lancashire. It was small and inexpensive. Sinclair had added a computerised switchboard and BACS facilities to enable donations to the Party to be taken directly by phone or the web. The switchboard took up to seventy messages simultaneously, and recorded them. Even now, at this late hour, the lights that indicated the machine was busy flickered satisfyingly.

The only other hardware was desktop computers, and a laser-printing machine that churned out flyers and posters, advertising forthcoming events and meetings. As a major televised rally was less than twenty-four hours away, the machine and Sinclair's faithful had been flat out.

There were three desks, staffed each day between eight a.m. and midnight by volunteers, who took calls and cash from the public; the money and members were rolling in at a rate the BNP could only dream of.

As Bliss stood patiently in front of him, waiting for the brute of the man that was Danny Slade to finish sweeping the room for bugs, Sinclair checked the traffic on the Party's website, Twitter and Facebook accounts.

Twenty four hours ago, the Party had posed the question on the website; *'Are you a white Christian? Have you suffered discrimination by the Islamist community? Tell us about your troubles. Ring 0845 000 888 or Tweet @Justice4GB or go to our Facebook page, Facebook.com/Justice4GB'*

Sinclair smiled a Hollywood smile.

Twitter now boasted 191,600 followers and was trending faster than One Direction.

The Facebook page had 237,000 'likes' and was struggling to keep pace with friend requests.

Finally he checked the graph showing web traffic to his own site The Justice for Great Britain Party. Membership was increasing by over nine percent per day. Sinclair was going to need a bigger server.

The party philosophy was simple enough. It had worked for so many great leaders over history, but in order to succeed in the here and now, Sinclair needed the moderate white community on his side. It was all very well having the shaven-headed extreme right on board, but they were also counterproductive and frightened the middle classes away.

Firstly, just as Hitler discovered, people who were living through a depression were vulnerable and scared. If you gave them something to focus upon, someone to blame for their woes, it solidified the community. They could easily identify the culpable, and protest against the perceived threat to their livelihood. The people could blame this section of society for their lack of jobs, even lack of food, and it was a modern day fact that families were unable to provide even the basics on the minimum wage, let alone benefits.

Food banks were a modern day fact of life.

They had opened in every major town in Lancashire. In recent times mothers had seen their kids go without a hot meal, whilst others drove around in new German cars.

Not having a job was one thing; not being able to eat was quite another.

All those issues were more than enough to engage the working classes in his plan, but the better off were still better off, and didn't have to live in the areas where the biggest changes in British society had taken place.

Sinclair considered Enoch Powell a visionary. His foresight had left him damned by his peers, but many now rued the day they stood against him. He foretold what Sinclair now considered a national disgrace.

It had always been a far thornier issue to engage the middle classes and prise them away from the main parties; especially if the race card could be so easily played against them.

Fortunately the community he was so eager to disperse, or better still remove from British society, had given him two of the most powerful weapons he could ever ask for; their fiscal success and the terrorists that flourished from their ranks.

The backdrop of social unrest was essential and it would be Bliss and his men who ensured that it festered and worsened, spread like a plague. The sight of the police surrendering the streets to the army would be enough to destabilise the already fractured coalition of the Con-Lib alliance. Labour were a spent force, with a weak leader and too much union involvement; that left UKIP and the BNP.

To Sinclair, it was already a no-contest.

Danny Slade, a frightening figure of a man, finished sweeping the room and nodded to Bliss that all was well.

Bliss in turn jutted his own chin in the direction of the door. The man duly obliged and left silently. Sinclair waited until he heard his footsteps fade to the street below before he spoke.

"Let me see," he said

Bliss opened a laptop, hit the power button and selected an icon on the desktop. He turned it to face Sinclair, who scrolled through the content.

"When does this go live?"

Bliss checked his own Rolex.

"Six hours and thirty seven minutes."

Sinclair nodded slowly and checked the content one last time.

"Security?"

"The site server is in Amsterdam. Everything on the page will be downloadable by anyone visiting it, for as long as it's up. The site will automatically Tweet its own web address to a hundred random Twitter accounts and then close itself fifteen minutes later, gone forever."

Sinclair gave the trademark smile again.

"Good work, Bliss, very good work."

Striker had endured the hairdryer treatment from Errol Graham, dismissed it as an occupational hazard and walked the short hop from the flats on Oxford Road, to the J and G taxi office.

Westland was parked outside; a young girl with the shortest of mini-skirts was leaning into his patrol car. The young cop appeared to be enjoying the attention.

Striker stood watching the show for a moment before he spoke.

"When you've finished, son."

Westland turned at the sound of the detective's voice. The girl, however, was unimpressed at being disturbed in her attempt to chat up the good-looking officer.

Striker would never be described as handsome. His nose had been broken once too often and his square jaw and lack of any noticeable neck, gave the impression that his head had been set on sideboard-like shoulders without the necessary attachment. His wayward red hair curled wherever it felt the need. His best asset were his eyes; sparkling blue; trouble was, most of the time, they gave the impression that he was about to rip off your head.

"What do you want, Ginger?" slurred the girl.

Striker considered a witty retort. Instead he pulled his ID.

"Fuck off," he said.

The girl teetered down Manchester Road in impossibly high heels, giving Striker the finger as she went.

The detective leaned into the police vehicle. "You okay now, Westland?"

Tag felt better, as he was now blood-free. It had been the first time he had ever seen a dead body, let alone a murdered one. Despite the trauma, the recently departed girl, who had insisted on protruding her naked breasts through his car window, had cheered his mood even more. He'd even forgotten Scarlet 'one t' briefly. Tag wasn't shallow; he was positively superficial.

"Yes, not bad, sir...I mean sergeant."

"Call me Striker, son. It's fuckin' easier for you to remember."

Tag smiled meekly. He had to admit, he was a little scared of the weird-sounding detective. The man was a cross between a marauding bull and a rabid dog. He alighted from the car.

"Are you...erm...are you an American...sergeant...I mean...Striker?"

"Northern Irish mother, American father; I have dual nationality, son. That means I can piss people off in four different countries."

"Nice," was all Tag could think of.

The two stepped into the cramped taxi office. The operator had changed shift from Tag's last visit but, as before, was protected from the general public by the same counter and a metal grill.

She was a very overweight woman who was intent on adding to her problems by stuffing a kebab and fries down her neck. She spoke without turning around to see her potential clients, spitting fragments of lamb and chili sauce onto her console.

"No taxis 'til three-thirty."

Striker took a fist to the grill. Tag thought he would punch it clean through. The woman jumped, "What the...!"

"Police," Striker stated, holding his ID against the metal squares. The woman dropped her pitta, and wiped grease down the front of her already stained top.

"I don't give a fuck who you are, pal. I told you..."

"We don't want a taxi," interrupted Striker. "I want to see the boss."

Despite the obvious threat to her well-being, the woman had the advantage of her metal cage for protection. She had regularly seen aggressive behaviour at this time in the morning and was unfazed by two cops.

"Yeah right; he's always around at this time of the day, pal. Come back at seven."

Tag sidled up to the mesh and gave his best twinkle.

"Sorry about my friend here, love, he's a little tetchy, he hasn't eaten."

Striker gave Tag a look that could kill at a hundred yards, but he ignored it and continued his charm offensive.

"It's very important that we talk with him tonight. Could you give him a call, please?"

The woman shifted in her seat and pushed out her considerable cleavage, before licking her fingers to remove the last remnants of grease and sauce. Striker was impressed. The kid had a gift with women, no doubt.

The woman brushed a bleached blonde lock behind her ear and admired the uniformed officer.

"I can't, honey, he'd give me the sack."

Tag was in there like swimwear. "Oh, I don't think so. He wouldn't want to lose such an attractive receptionist."

The woman actually giggled. Striker was redundant, he knew when to let go. This was the time.

Tag pulled out his Lancashire Constabulary business card. "I'll do you a deal, sweetheart. You give me his mobile; I'll give you mine."

Minutes later the two cops were back on Manchester Road. Striker eyed the rookie with a look that rested between suspicion and admiration.

"What?" said Tag.

Within the hour, the J and G owner had been roused from his bed and Striker had obtained the personnel file of the missing driver. The man had been reluctant to hand over the documents to the detective, just as he had hours earlier with Westland; but where Tag had the charm with the ladies, Striker had the tools in his locker to persuade the man it was in his best interest to co-operate. This involved holding the man in the air by his neck with a single hand, whilst threatening him with the might of every agency known to man.

The man said he would make an official complaint. Striker didn't give a shit.

The detective studied the photocopied documents using the interior light in Westland's car. A copy passport which was actually Iraqi, a visa and work permit, a British driving licence, a CRB check and a single sheet of paper that formed the agreement between the taxi owner and the driver.

The name on the documents was Khalid Mustapha; address, 307 Penrith House, Avenham, Preston. According to the documents, he had been resident in the UK for three years.

Striker pulled his iPhone from his pocket and photographed each sheet in turn, attached the files to an email and forwarded them to the office. He didn't hold out much hope that they were genuine, but it was worth a try. He then took a close-up of the passport photograph and enlarged the image using the phone's software. He stared at the picture that filled the screen.

"Now what?" said Westland.

"Take me to the Royal Preston, let's wake up Ms. Mackintosh," said Striker.

Gina Williams hadn't slept.

It was three a.m. and her Barry had not made it home. Even when the EDL held an event, Barry would be home by one, half one at the latest. He might have had a lock in at the Princess Alice, but even so it was very late. The bloody cop sirens had never stopped all night. Gina had to turn up the television so she could watch Emmerdale on catch-up. By the time Corrie had finished, she'd necked a Valium and done a bottle of red. Before News at Ten started she went to bed, but sleep still wouldn't come. She wanted Barry home. Gina knew her husband only too well. A late arrival and a police siren always meant trouble for her Barry.

Barry Williams had been Gina's first love. It had started at school, when she was just fourteen. Barry was the cock of the school.

The 'cock' meaning he could fight any boy there, and win.

Barry wasn't big; he was just good at fighting. He'd always been a scrapper.

When Gina was young, it was Barry's reputation, his confidence, and his swagger, which had drawn her to him. He wasn't particularly good-looking. He didn't even treat her that well, spending much of his time with his mates, drinking and getting into mischief.

Despite it all, she loved him beyond anything else.

They married at eighteen, and as most young couples found in their early years together, money was always a problem. They struggled to pay regular bills; especially as Barry liked to drink and gamble. To make matters worse, Barry would fall out with his boss and get the sack on a regular basis.

Gina had progressed from a schoolgirl who found being the girlfriend of an exciting dangerous boy, fun and exhilarating; to a young woman who had continued her education, got a decent job, hated violence and desperately wanted a baby.

In his twenties, Barry became part of a football hooligan crew attached to Preston North End.

His behaviour started to put a massive strain on their relationship. His short temper and naturally aggressive nature saw him jailed for three months after a number of minor fracas and assaults; but it was the unprovoked attack on a police officer that saw him incarcerated for two years.

Gina was just twenty-one when Barry was sent down for the assault on the policeman. On her meagre salary, the bills just kept on adding up; the electricity, the gas the council tax, the rent. Two weeks before Christmas her landlord turned her out of their flat and she was forced to swallow her pride and live with her mother. After listening to her parents tell her 'I told you so' for eleven months, Barry was released.

The thing Gina had wanted and prayed for most was not to be. Gina had been desperate for a child since her sixteenth birthday. It was how life should be, the procreation of God's children.

Gina touched her stomach absently and checked her watch for the thirtieth time.

No not to be.

She had fallen pregnant and lost her child twice. The doctors said she would never carry full term.

All she had left was her Barry, and the job that she loved.

Now, Barry had ensured her resignation, half her life was over. Regret filled her heart. After all, Mr. Hussain hadn't said he supported those women who disrupted the parade, he'd been so worried about his poor cousin, he wasn't thinking straight.

She got up, made a pot of tea, and set down two cups, just in case. The central heating had clicked off at eleven and the house was cool. Gina pulled her toweling dressing gown around her to ward off the chill and poured herself a cup.

She looked around her new kitchen. Barry had finished the ceramic tiles just yesterday. How would they pay the loan for all this, now she wasn't working? Barry hadn't worked since being laid off at Leyland DAF two years back.

Barry blamed cheap labour from Eastern Europe for his lack of luck in the job market. The Poles had been added to Barry's hate list, alongside the Pakistani community, who he blamed for just about everything from the closure of the local pub, to their house price falling.

Then Gina heard the key in the lock. Her heart skipped; grateful that he was home safe, yet she steeled herself for the row. Barry would be upset she was awake and waiting for him, he would be drunk.

To Gina's surprise, Barry was as sober as a judge and walked into the kitchen with a spring in his step. Anyone would have thought it was three in the afternoon rather than three in the morning.

"Ah, you've got a brew on, love," he chirped. He sat and poured, adding a minuscule amount of milk, the way he liked it.

"How come you're up? All this racket from the riots I suppose, eh?" He sipped his tea. "Hmmm, good cuppa, that, love."

Gina hadn't seen Barry so happy in months, maybe even years. She couldn't help but smile. Since losing his job, Barry's change of character had been a major concern to her; she was terrified it could even end their marriage.

"Yes, love, all the sirens kept me awake, and I was a bit worried you wouldn't be able to get through."

Barry sipped more tea, and nodded.

"Was a bit awkward; you wouldn't believe it out there. Deepdale is completely sealed; a no-go area. You can't get in or out, the cordon is as far north as Blackpool Road; west to Garstang Road all the way down, past Meadow Street, right over to New Hall Lane on the east side."

Barry gave a chuckle.

"The Pakis always wanted it to themselves, eh? Well they've got it now."

Gina winced at Barry's language but ignored it as usual.

"Well so long as you're alright, love."

"I'm better than alright, Gina. I've got a job!"

Gina jumped from her chair and hugged her husband; and for the first time in months he hugged her back. "Oh, Barry, that's fantastic!"

Barry even cupped her considerable breasts and gave them a squeeze. Gina couldn't remember the last time he'd paid her any sexual attention.

She felt tears begin to fall.

"Hey, don't be cryin', love," he said. "This is the change of luck we needed."

Gina wiped her eyes. "Sorry, Barry, I'm just so happy. I thought you'd been on the march, is all; didn't think you'd been out lookin' for a job. Tell me about it, come on; I'll put some toast under the grill and do you some beans with it, eh? You must be starving."

Barry sat and puffed out his chest. He was a slight man, but with a naturally athletic build; he'd never carried any excess weight and still boasted he could fit into his wedding suit. His hair was thinner than in those days, his widow's peak retreating ever further along his scalp, and he had lines around his eyes and mouth that were exaggerated by his thirty a day habit.

"Well," he began. "You know I've been going to them meetings?"

Gina's heart sank. "Yes, love."

"Well I met a bloke there the other night, he gave me a card and I followed it up, didn't I? You must have seen that MP Alistair Sinclair, he's all over the news at the moment."

Gina nodded.

"Well I'm workin' for him; not exactly for him personally, but for his security team."

Gina opened a tin of baked beans and emptied them into a small saucepan.

"I thought you said you'd never do security work, love."

Barry shot Gina a look. She desperately didn't want to spoil his mood, she knew he'd turned down two security guard jobs in recent months, so why change now for this man?

"This is different. This job has prospects; this Sinclair guy is going places; right to the top, Gina; he'll be running the country before you know it."

Gina stirred the contents of the pan with a wooden spoon and then touched it to her lips to check the temperature of her husband's snack, poured the beans onto hot toast and put it in front of him. "So is it full time, love?"

Barry cut a corner of toast and shoveled beans onto it, before pushing the concoction into his mouth.

He swallowed quickly.

"Not exactly; not just yet anyhow; but soon will be. Good money too, eight pound an hour in your hand."

He pointed his fork at his wife.

"I've been in Leyland all day, and I've to be back in a couple of hours, setting up a stage and barriers for Sinclair's big rally, helping with the sound system and lights, bit of everything really. Then we'll do crowd control, not that they'll be any bother, people love him."

Gina looked at her husband and felt a twinge of sadness.

You mean, white people love him.

Westland was concerned that Striker's idea of gaining access to Sandra Mackintosh's ward would involve him strangling the life out of a staff nurse or two.

As it turned out, he needn't have worried.

As the two cops strolled toward the hospital entrance at just after four a.m. Sandra was in plain sight, sitting on a bench and smoking. Another patient, who Tag vaguely recognised, was with her, he too indulging in the habit that Westland found so offensive.

"That's her," he said.

"Classy," muttered Striker.

As Westland approached, Sandra stood. "I thought I told you, I'm not making a statement."

Her fellow nicotine junkie mirrored her movements and added, "Yeah, she's not saying anything to you lot."

Striker walked over to the man. "Who the fuck are you?"

Wilson did his best to square up to the detective, but his injuries were against him, as were the last ten years of alcohol abuse.

Westland had seen his type before, he had all the signs of a street brawler gone to seed.

Sandra came to the man's aid. "It's okay, Wilson; I'll see you inside in a minute, love."

There was a brief staring match, before Wilson reluctantly shuffled toward the entrance, stubbing out his cigarette between thumb and finger as he went.

Striker turned his attention to Sandra. "Friend of yours?"

Sandra inhaled deeply before answering. "Sort of; we had a thing a few years back; not seen him in a while. He fell off the perch with the drink. I heard he got worse after his lad was killed in Afghanistan."

"Tough one, was he?" asked the detective.

Sandra gave a wry smile as if remembering better times. "Hard as fucking nails Wilson was, still is on a good day. He'd have given you a run for your money back in the day, pal."

Striker ignored the comment as irrelevant, pulled out his iPhone and displayed the picture of the man he knew as Khalid Mustapha. He gestured toward the blue-black bruising around Sandra's neck and held the screen toward her.

"This the animal who did that to you?"

Sandra took a glance at the screen.

"Could've been, but like I said...."

Striker pushed the phone further forward.

"Look at the fucking picture! I asked you a question. I have a nineteen year old girl lying dead outside this fucker's flat, so when you've finished playing the hard arse, you can give me an answer."

Sandra took the phone from the detective and studied the image.

"Yeah, that's the twat."

She almost threw the iPhone back.

Striker recovered it and slipped it into his pocket.

"So tell me what happened."

"I already told Twinkletoes there." She gestured toward Tag, who was doing his best not to look sheepish.

"Tell me."

Sandra knew she was dealing with a very different animal to that of the young uniformed officer. She sighed theatrically.

"He was in the Indian. I was pissed; he offered me a lift; I went to his flat to shag him and he fuckin' strangled me, okay?"

Striker's limited patience evaporated.

"I'll finish the fuckin' job if you don't start to co-operate, girl."

"You don't frighten me, you Paddy prick."

Striker leaned in. "No? You sure? Well how about I nip to your grubby little flat on Oxford Road and give it the once-over; then a short trip to your three useless bastard sons' gaff on Farrington Park. Say then I finish my nice trip around town with your three places of work; let's see Bowkers on the docks, you clean there, Mondays eh? Palmer and Harvey, Tuesdays and Fridays, isn't it? Then finally, that little one you don't tell the tax man about, Crystal Cleaning, cash in hand there, eh?"

Sandra was furious.

Tag was impressed.

Striker got his detailed information.

The two cops ambled back to the car with Sandra's tirade of abuse fading into the early morning air.

"How did you do that?" asked Tag.

"What?"

"Find out all that information about Sandra so quickly?"

Striker stopped by the passenger door and tapped the side of his nose with his finger.

"Trade secret," he said, and eased his massive shoulders into the car.

They drove back to Avenham, the car silent for a while, until Striker broke it.

"What made you join the job, son? You don't seem the type."

"I'm not," agreed Tag. "In fact I'm resigning as soon as I can get hold of my shift inspector."

"I see."

"Me joining this job, well, it was a bit rash," Tag continued. "My father had a job lined up for me; he works in the City of London, a banker."

"Popular man, then?"

Tag smiled," He's a rich one."

"But you chose this?"

"Like I said, a rash decision; when I left university, I'd had enough economics to last me a lifetime, I fancied a bit of excitement, saw the advert, the rest, as they say, is a mystery."

Tag turned into Oxford Road and pulled the car to a halt outside the crime scene. He looked to Striker for the next move.

"Have you done with me now, Striker? My job list has grown a bit since our jaunt."

Striker was back to his furious typing on his iPad. "You haven't got a job list, son, and that resignation letter you have in your pocket can stay there for a day or two, until we get to the bottom of this one."

Westland eyed the detective suspiciously.

How did he know I had the letter in my pocket?

Striker didn't look up from the iPad, he just tapped the side of his nose again.

Striker and Westland stood outside Penrith House and donned paper SOC suits and overshoes. They walked slowly to the block, both men deep in thought for different reasons.

Tag followed reluctantly; he still had the flashbacks of blood and dead teenage girls running through his head.

Striker just had that tingle again.

They signed in with the uniformed officer guarding the scene. The guy was about retirement age. He nodded at Striker and gave Tag a derisory look.

Tag thought he might just get used to the negativity, just before he resigned.

They stepped into the corridor. To his relief, Ayesha's body had been removed and most of her blood had been cleaned away.

They stood at the door of 307. Striker nodded at Westland. "Go on, son."

"What?"

"Well it isn't gonna open on its own now, is it?"

Westland considered that Striker could do a far better impression of a battering ram than he ever could, but obliged by throwing his shoulder into the door.

It didn't budge, the substantial mortice refusing to give way.

Striker watched in mild amusement, and simply gestured for Tag to try again.

At six foot two and a tad under two hundred pounds Tag was no lightweight, but after three attempts to break down the stubborn door, Striker had seen enough. He removed a silver coloured box from his jacket pocket and selected a metal implement that looked like a cross between a key and a surgical device, inserted it into the lock and turned the mechanism first time. The door swung open. Tag rubbed his bruised shoulder.

"Your idea of a joke, Striker?"

"I like to keep the atmosphere light."

The detective dropped the box back into his jacket and his face changed.

"Heads up now though, son."

Tag switched on his Maglite until he found the light switch. The hallway smelled like a hospital.

Off to the right was a small kitchen-diner; to the left three further doors, leading to a lounge and two bedrooms.

They made a quick sweep of all the rooms, not expecting them to be inhabited, but better safe than sorry.

In the lounge was a sofa and a television; each bedroom contained a single bed, stripped of all bedding and an empty wardrobe. The kitchen too was bereft of any cutlery; in fact Tag considered that Sandra had the wrong flat, not a single soul had inhabited this place for some time. More to the point, Tag had never seen a place so clean since his mother had visited his digs at university.

"Weird," he said.

Striker had his head inside one wardrobe.

"Professional, son."

"What is?"

"The place has been cleaned, and I don't mean by Mrs. Mop. I mean 'cleaned'. No prints, no DNA, we're wasting our time here."

Tag stepped into the kitchen, and opened several cupboards.

"Know what you mean there, Striker…but?"

"But what?"

"But how do they get rid of rubbish then?"

"Who?"

"The residents, you know, how do they empty the bin?"

Striker walked over and grabbed Tag by the chin and shook it playfully; he thought he would break his jaw.

"You are a clever fucker, Westland. Come on."

Now when Tag made the rashest of decisions to join the police force, he had considered that he *may* have to occasionally complete unpleasant tasks. You know, look at dead people and the like. However, he had not considered that he would be forced to climb into a dustbin the size of a small country, by a man who would scare Boris Karloff out of his Frankenstein suit.

"Just get in there, son," Striker urged.

"It fuckin' stinks!"

"Of course it stinks, Westland, it's a dustbin."

"Jesus Christ, Striker, I've just stood in something really bad."

"Don't be a girl."

Westland poked his head over the rim of the bin, his white paper suit soiled by unknown substances.

"Do you want a fucking go?"

"Privilege of rank, son; now get on with it."

"What exactly am I looking for?"

"Evidence."

"That being?"

"Use your head, son, that wasted university education of yours, any utility bills with 307 on them?"

"There's nothing in here that isn't covered in shit," Tag wailed.

Westland disappeared from view and there was more thrashing about and cursing, including, derogatory Irish, red-head and American comments.

A minute or two later, he reappeared, his paper hood had slipped from his head, and his hair had flopped forward into his face; he also sported a broad smile.

"Tell me you love me, Striker."

Tag Westland threw a clear evidence bag containing a pair of black patent stiletto shoes onto the floor.

"Bingo," said Striker.

CHAPTER TEN

Striker sent Westland home to shower and get some sleep as he wanted him back on duty by eleven a.m. That was followed by a heated conversation with a certain Inspector Thompson, who insisted on using the term 'feckin' every other sentence. The inspector told Striker, in no uncertain terms, he couldn't have Westland as he was already desperately short of manpower. Striker told him otherwise.

The forensic science laboratory in Chorley, Lancashire was only five minutes' drive from Striker's house on Buckshaw village. Sandra Mackintosh's right shoe had a bloodstain on the heel, and hopefully her attacker's fingerprints elsewhere. Prints would only take hours to identify. DNA would be days. Striker was convinced he didn't have days to play with.
The package that had been recovered from Ayesha Chowdry's hand contained a circuit board. It would be many more precious hours before the anti-terrorist branch had any further information as to its possible use.
Why leave it for us to find? Did she bring it with her? Was it planted?
So many questions.
Striker entered the reception area of the lab and produced his ID to a tired looking G4S security guard.
He was waved through to the next level of the interior, where he was met by a white-haired man he knew very well. The man sat at a desk surrounded by evidence bags and samples.
"I might have known it would be you, Striker," said the man.
"Only you and the fucking birds are awake at this time in the morning."
Striker shook the man's hand.
"It's a rush job, Stevie."
"It always is when I see you, pal."

Abu Al Zachari had finished his prayers. He washed his hands and feet, dried them carefully and sat cross-legged on the floor of the small room.

With him were two other men; both wore Arabic national dress and sported lengthy beards.

The conversation was hushed and in the mother tongue.

"The situation is grave, my brothers," he said. "We have a new enemy. This time it comes from within the infidel community. It is not the security services who have caused us this setback."

"Are you certain of this?" said the first.

"Most certain, my brother; I believe it comes from a man who has aspirations of great power; a man who would see all Muslims banished from the shores of this country, a man who would make war against all our people."

"The infidels are too soft for this, my brother; too moderate; they have no stomach for the fight," said the second. "We have heard all this rhetoric before from the BNP, the EDL, and what? Nothing; they are shouted down by the mainstream parties. This could never again occur in Europe. The far right is a spent force."

"You are wrong, my friend. This man has charisma; he will bring the moderates out onto the streets, there will be much bloodshed. The police will lose control soon. We cannot stop our own people from taking revenge; Mosques will burn, people will die; our people."

"The courier," said the first. "The boy Abdulla, could he have betrayed you?"

Zachari shook his head. "He has never seen my face, he only knows me by code-name."

"And the hardware we required?" said the second.

"That will be replaced within forty-eight hours," replied Zachari.

"Then, God willing," said the first, "we will continue as planned and deal with this other threat you speak of when we have achieved our goal."

"Agreed," said the second.

At ten a.m. another meeting was taking place in the office of Detective Chief Superintendent Errol Graham.

Seated around the table were three other men; Det. Supt. Chris 'Slick' Jemson of the Anti Terrorist Branch, Det. Ch. Insp. William Potts of the Operational Support Unit, and Ewan Striker.

A laptop sat on the desk, plugged into a small HD projector. A white screen had been erected in one corner; it was filled with the images of the two murder scenes. That would not have been unusual, except that they had been taken from a website that had been in the public domain since nine a.m.

Graham rubbed the top of his head; he had not slept for over forty-eight hours.

"Run this by me again, Slick."

Jemson was close to retirement, he'd seen and done it all in his time; but the internet and social networking were definitely not his forte. Fortunately he had Striker on his team, who had briefed him fully.

"This site ceased to exist at exactly nine-fifteen this morning, so it was technically live for just fifteen minutes. Somehow, and we don't know how yet, it was programmed to send its own web address to the social networking site, Twitter. We don't know how it selected the members, possibly just randomly, and as yet we don't know how many; not that it matters now. The site was downloadable from the moment it was live to when it closed itself down. Essentially it meant that every person who subsequently viewed it was able to copy and paste all the material, pictures, text etc. Then, of course they could post it elsewhere. It hit the first 'voyeur' blogs within minutes."

Graham looked puzzled. Striker explained.

"Blogs and sites that post beheadings, executions, that kind of material; 'Gruesome' were the first to re-post. It's had over a million hits this hour."

"Jesus," said Graham.

Striker scrolled through the material.

At the top of page one, was a fluttering Union Jack. A header scrolled left to right through the Ensign. It announced 'The Fight Back'.

Beneath was a colour photograph of a very dead Abdulla Mohammed Hussain, hanging over the inspection pit; the sign around his neck proclaiming his alleged crime, 'Terrorist'. Standing either side of the body were two figures, dressed completely in black paramilitary uniform, their faces obscured digitally; both held firearms.

Under the photograph was a single line of text.

'This man was about to murder your children.'

"Those look like police weapons," said Graham.

Striker shook his head. "Similar, sir, but no; they are MP7's, used by the Special Forces, particularly in the US. Very quiet, very accurate, and the round will defeat body armour."

If it were possible, the second image was even more disturbing, even more powerful.

The once beautiful Ayesha Chowdry lay on her back, the single bullet wound to her forehead weeping her blood. Her clothing had been arranged to show her hijab off to the full. The small mystery package was clearly visible in her hand, again the sign proclaimed her alleged crime. 'Terrorist.'

Beneath was another single line.

'She carries the death of your families in her hand.'

'Slick' Jemson nodded to his sergeant. Striker tapped at his iPad and began.

"The site used a server somewhere in northern Europe; the Netherlands is the favourite so far, not that it will do us any good chasing that line, it will probably turn out to be an internet cafe. Whoever designed it is a pro, no doubt. It will leave a footprint somewhere, but they are long gone.

It will spread worldwide; when the rest of the USA wake up it will go viral. We can't stop it; we need our press people working on this ASAP; damage limitation. Thankfully, the images are so graphic that they won't make the TV; but it won't stop edited versions making the screen along with descriptive and the usual surmising. Once the public see the TV, they too will search the web for the images, like drivers passing an accident."

He tapped some more.

"As you know, victim one is Abdullah Mohammed Hussain, nineteen years old; worked as a clerk for his cousin Tariq Hussain QC. Abdullah was an educated guy from a middle class family; his parents live in Pakistan and run a successful business there, exporting clothing worldwide including the UK. The family is clean as far as we know. Abdullah was not. He was a radical and had attended three training camps in Pakistan in the last year. He was red-flagged.

Victim two is Ayesha Chowdry, again nineteen. She studied at UCLAN and worked part-time as a receptionist at the Royal Preston. Her family are wealthy, both mother and father are doctors, the father being a consultant surgeon. There is no intelligence to suggest any criminal activity within the Chowdry family. As of this moment, there is nothing to connect the two deceased. Ayesha appears to be a completely innocent victim. That said, Ayesha appears to have been going to deliver a package to 307 Penrith House. I don't believe the package was planted. I think that whoever this vigilante group are, they either wanted us to find that package to show us that there is a genuine threat, or they were disturbed by a local beat cop investigating a separate incident. Our tech team is working on identifying exactly what that package contained; as of yet, other than the fact that it is some kind of circuit board, it's a mystery. The registered tenant at 307 is one Khalid Mustapha. We know that he sexually assaulted a woman called Sandra Mackintosh at that address on the night of the first murder, after picking her up in his taxi. She was lucky to escape alive. Uniform were investigating, but she refused to make a complaint. The flat was searched last night; it had been visited by a professional clean-up team; draw your own conclusions from that. I believe whoever Khalid Mustapha is, he is a major player in this plot. If these guys know his identity, he could be next on the list."

Graham nodded. He still didn't like Striker, but he had to admit he was good.

"Could they already have the guy? Could they have cleaned the flat?"

"Unlikely, it would take several hours to do a job like that. I think the clean-up was to cover the assault. Mackintosh was never intended to escape, but when she did, the assailant was forced to act.

Ayesha was found very shortly after death; uniform came very close to stumbling on her killers. I think we scared them off, before they could check the flat."

Graham tapped the desk.

"So we need to get this guy circulated before these crazy fuckers get their hands on him. There must be a picture of him at the taxi firm."

Striker handed his iPhone around the room.

Graham raged, "How long have you had this?"

"Few hours."

Jemson came to his sergeant's aid.

"If we put this out there in the present climate, we will have every right wing nutter in the country topping anyone who looks vaguely like this guy and posting his corpse on Facebook. Let my guys do their job for a day or two."

After a few moments, Graham nodded. "Forty-eight hours, Slick," he pointed at Striker, "And no more."

William Potts had remained silent during the exchanges.

Rather than investigate the murders, his role was to quell the ever-rising tide of violence that was sweeping the county "You know what will happen now these pictures are out there, don't you, boss?"

Graham nodded.

"I've already asked for another forty support units from other forces, Will. That's another four hundred and eighty cops; you realise the cost of that? It's astronomical. This could bankrupt the force. I'm counting on you to keep a lid on this."

Will Potts was a tough guy. He stood and nodded his respect at the detectives.

"Better say your prayers tonight, guys," he said.

Tag Westland had slept fitfully; images of the dead girl flashed into his subconscious, waking him. Twice he had slipped downstairs, only to sit shivering on his sofa drinking tea.

He showered and dressed in jeans and a sweatshirt; Striker had insisted on plain clothes. He drove the short hop into the city, doing his best to clear his head. He'd tried to ring Scarlet twice, but it had gone straight to voicemail; he opted to send a text. *Hope you are okay? x.*

Striker was sitting in a small cafe named Brucianni's on Fishergate. He waited impatiently for the young cop. The building had been a coffee shop since the 1950's and, despite the arrival of the big chains, it was still the coolest place to hang out. The decor hadn't changed since it opened; dozens of black and white photographs of Hollywood stars adorned the walls. Tag wondered if any had actually visited. The staff all wore traditional black skirts and blouses, with white aprons. A very pretty girl was serving behind the counter. Tag smiled at her and she blushed charmingly. It was eleven oh three a.m.

"You're late, son," barked the detective.

"Didn't sleep too well, Striker, some of us are human."

Striker felt some sympathy for Tag, but tardiness would not wash. He handed him a ten-pound note. "Get yourself a coffee and a sandwich."

Tag took the money and offered a weak smile. "Thanks."

"And a fucking alarm clock," he added.

After placing his order with blushing girl, Tag sat and played with his food, added sugar to his Americano and stirred it. He was in no mood for wisecracks, even from Striker.

"So what is the plan then?" he said flatly.

Striker sighed. Tag considered it a strange sound coming from the man; it was hurt in a solitary breath, as if the world was against him.

"I'm going to break some rules with you, Westland. I'm going to brief you, tell you what I know."

Tag looked up from his cup. He wanted to ask, why? Why him? After all, he wasn't exactly qualified, was he? That, and Striker knew full well about his intentions to resign. Despite his misgivings he was curious. This was what he'd joined the stupid job for after all. In the end, all he could manage was a very tired, "Okay."

Striker fired up his iPad.

"First, I have some questions for you, son, and then, I'm going to tell you a little about me."

"Go on."

"The taxi driver who took Mustapha to Burnley, who was he?"

Tag took his pocket book from his jeans and thumbed the pages. "Erm...Iftikar Mohammed Din."

"Badge number?"

Tag looked at the page, willing the information to be there.

"I didn't get that, sorry."

Striker made a 'humph' sound and tapped away.

"Address?"

"Eh?"

"The address of the taxi driver? And the address he took our rapist-terrorist to?"

Tag was already feeling inferior; his day was getting worse. "I didn't get the address of the driver. All he could remember, was he took the guy and a young girl called, erm...Ismi, to Burnley, near to the football ground; picked them up outside the flats; they had bags."

Striker gave Tag a look that would cut steel.

"Anything else?"

"Erm... yes...he...erm, the guy, Mustapha, he made a phone call from the public booth before he got in the taxi."

Striker was back to his keyboard. "I already knew that."

"What?"

"The phone call, I knew he'd made one. He was ringing Abdullah Hussain's mobile. I answered it."

"Fuck," said Tag.

"Exactly," said Striker. He stopped typing and turned the tablet to the young cop. "Not something you might want to see whilst you're having bacon; but you need to see this all the same."

Tag scrolled.

"Oh Jesus Christ."

Striker nodded. "It went live at nine o'clock this morning, was downloadable for fifteen minutes. It hit Sky News just before I left the station."

The detective pulled the screen away before Tag was sick.

"I need to tell you something about me. Before we go any further."

Tag looked up, not knowing what to say, so he stayed silent.

"I was born in the States; my dad was a Navy Seal, a real tough old boy. He met my mom in Ireland and they moved to the US, Chicago. I went to school there. My dad taught me all the things he knew; shit, I was a black belt before I was nine, it was just how the guy was, you know?"

Tag nodded, surprised at Striker's sudden openness.

"I was good at sports, I was a line-backer, but despite everything, I never really fitted in."

Striker rubbed his locks.

"This didn't help; I got all the 'ginger' jibes; that and the fact that I was always so well 'turned out' for school; Jesus, I even pressed my boxers, still do."

"You iron your underwear?" Tag was incredulous.

The detective pointed a thick finger. "If you breathe a word of this I'll rip your head off and shit down your neck."

Despite Tag feeling like a train was changing points in his head; he couldn't help but smile at the revelation. He did his best to remain solemn and made a small cross against his sweatshirt.

"God's honour, mate."

Striker glowered menacingly.

"Anyway, what I'm saying is, I kinda rebelled. I was always into computers. I spent more and more time holed up in my bedroom, playing with them; sent my dad crazy. By the time I was fifteen, I could hack just about anything."

Tag's eyes widened.

"You're a hacker?"

"Was."

"That's how you find information so quickly! Is that how you found out so much about Sandra Mackintosh?"

Striker allowed himself a smug smile. "That was easy; Mackintosh and her sons all have form, she has a couple of convictions for soliciting, the sons are a fucking walking crime spree. I checked the collators system for addresses; her last antecedence notes gave me her three places of work; then I cheated a bit and used my other skills and looked at her benefit claims."

Tag's eyes were wide.

"You hacked a government site?"

Striker shrugged as though it was the most natural thing in the world.

"Most fifteen year olds can hack government sites, son. She claims housing benefit, because she's low paid; she also receives working tax credits. That's how I found that she only disclosed two places of work; seemed common sense that she wasn't declaring the third income; like I said, easy."

Tag sat back and sipped his coffee. "Well, Striker, you old dog, I'm impressed."

The detective waved away the compliment.

"The reason I'm telling you this little tale is because you don't fit in either. You don't act or think like a cop, you don't play the cop game, you don't socialise with cops, and I'll bet a pound to a pinch of shit that the reason you want out is because you think all cops are arseholes."

Tag nodded towards Striker, "Present company excepted."

"Of course," he said. "That's the reason you're sitting here now, because you don't think like a cop, you're not tarnished by the institution of the police service, and I need someone who thinks like you do."

Tag was doing a fair impression of a goldfish.

"You do?"

"I do; now let me tell you what I think is going on."

Wilson sat on the bench outside casualty and smoked a cigarette he had bummed off a visitor.

In his other hand he held a clear plastic bag that contained his worldly goods; his driving licence, his appointment card for out-patients, his 'Help for Heroes' badge and eleven pence in cash. He stubbed out his smoke under his shoe, took out the badge, clipped it to his chest and pondered his next move. He felt better than he had in a while, he'd managed a couple of showers and a shave, and a kind nurse had found him a decent pair of jeans and a sweater to wear. The co-codomol pain killers seemed to keep most of his discomfort at bay, he'd even managed to keep down some cornflakes and milk, just before his discharge.

The trouble with planning your next move when you are jobless, homeless and have eleven pence to your name is that you have limited options; and there lay the reason for Wilson's lack of movement from the bench.

He wasn't waiting for anyone, he was just waiting.

Wilson had lost track of time when Sandra Mackintosh appeared at his shoulder.

"They let you out too then, eh?" she said.

He turned his head.

Sandra was dressed in the clothes she had been admitted in, minus the black tights. Again a kind hospital worker had found her some footwear; but a red boob tube, black miniskirt, bare legs and sneakers, were not the look she was probably hoping for. Some men would have described her figure as 'ample,' others would not have been so kind.

She had managed to apply some make-up, hiding some facial bruising, and her hair was tied back in a ponytail. The lesions around her neck seemed even more prominent than before. She made light of her appearance.

"I'm looking good, eh, Wilson?"

"Always did look good to me, Sand," he said.

"Aw, you always was a sweet talking bastard, weren't ya?"

Wilson smiled. "Suppose I was back then."

Sandra sat down next to Wilson and grabbed his hand.

"We had some good times, didn't we? Remember that weekend in Blackpool, eh? Fuckin' hell, I was so sore I couldn't walk for a week after."

Sandra guffawed at her own quip and slapped Wilson on the back. Even with the meds, he felt it and winced with the pain.

"Oh sorry, love," she said. "I forgot about your ribs. Them Paki bastards have got a lot to answer for eh? Between me and you, eh?"

"I'm okay," said Wilson. "What about you though, love? How are you now? Nasty business that."

Sandra stuck out her ample bosom. "Take more than some Abdul with a BDSM fetish to knock me back, Wilson. I'm fit as a flea now."

Wilson turned and looked at his old lover.

"Yeah, I suppose it would; you always were a tough bird."

Sandra took hold of Wilson's hand again. For a moment, twenty years dissolved into twenty seconds.

"We were great together, me and you, weren't we? You, the hard man of the town, and me, fit as fuck on your arm? Good times, real good times, mate."

Wilson studied his shoes, what was left of them.

"Yeah, love, good times. Good job the wife never found out, eh?"

Sandra smiled and let her mind wander back those years. "Yeah it was, lover." She put her arm around her old friend; this time her touch was gentle.

"Where you stayin', Wilson?"

"Me? I'm in Fox Street."

"The mission?"

"One and the same."

"Jesus, love; I didn't think it had come to that."

Wilson scratched his once jet black moustache, which was now prematurely pure white. "Got kicked out of my flat three weeks ago, landlord said I was a fire risk."

"What?"

"I put a pizza in the oven when I was pissed and forgot to take it out the box; made a mess of the kitchen, eh?"

Sandra gave her trademark belly laugh.

"Bloody hell, Wilson, you're a health and safety risk!"

He looked at his shoes again.

"Suppose I am."

Sandra's tone was tender; not something that came naturally to her.

"Listen, mate; it's been a long time, eh? Who would have thought that you and me would bump into each other in an A and E?"

Sandra touched her bruises with her fingers. "I suppose we've both seen better days, ain't we?"

Wilson nodded, "Too true, love."

Sandra turned. "Well why don't you stay at mine for a bit; just till you get yourself sorted out, eh?"

Wilson looked into the once pretty face of Sandra Mackintosh. It was still there, somewhere, hidden behind years of hard graft and harder drinking.

"You sure, love? I'm not the man I was, I'm a piss-head. The juice has got me nailed, Sand."

She squeezed his hand. "We all love a good drink, love, don't we? I'm not sayin' move in permanent or anythin', just till you get a place, that's all."

Wilson couldn't believe his luck; he'd had enough knockbacks to last a lifetime; this was the gift horse.

"Aye, go on then, love; that would be great."

CHAPTER ELEVEN

Scarlet opened the washing machine, lifted out her father's bedding and dropped it into the waiting plastic basket. She looked out of her kitchen window, into the small back yard of her house. The sky was clear blue, without a single cloud, yet a northerly breeze kept the temperature down and the air fresh. It was a good drying day. Scarlet had not ventured to work for the last couple of days, calling in sick. Her father's home help, Zakia, had not dared to leave her house on Deepdale, due to the violence on the streets.

Scarlet could still hear the fear in Zakia's voice.

I cannot come today, Scarlet. My house is damaged; burned. They have thrown a petrol bomb at my door. My brother is in the hospital, they have thrown stones at him, the police are everywhere, they say not to come outside.

Scarlet shuddered; she couldn't believe what was happening to her town. Vicious thugs roamed the streets looking for anyone they considered fair game, anyone with brown skin.

She picked up the basket and stepped into the yard. The breeze felt good on her face; she breathed in mouthfuls of the cool air and started to peg the washing.

"Maureen!" her father shouted from his room. "Maureen, I want you!"

Scarlet looked up to her father's window.

Maureen, Scarlet's mother, had left them five years ago; disappeared off the face of the earth with only a brief note proving that she ever existed.

Sorry, Scarlet. I just can't live with him anymore. Mum x

Five years without a word; five years without her mother;

"Coming, Dad!" she shouted.

Scarlet dropped the sheet back into the basket and climbed the narrow staircase to her father's room.

He was sitting on a commode, his trousers around his ankles, his once powerful legs now withered to little more than spindles.

"I don't want you!" he spat angrily. "I want Maureen! Where has she gone? I told her not to be so long at the shop."

"Mum isn't here, Dad. You know that," Scarlet said gently.

"Fuck off!" he bellowed, before bursting into a hacking cough that doubled him over.

Scarlet waited for the attack to stop, before carefully lifting her
father from the chair. She cleaned him as she would a child,
restored his limited dignity, and sat him on his newly made bed.
He looked at her, all anger instantly dispersed, turned off like a tap;
recognition returning fleetingly.
"You're a good girl, Scarlet, aren't ya? Dad's good girl?"
Scarlet managed a smile; she had cried so many times over the last
year and a half, that there didn't seem to be any tears left.
"That's me, Dad, your good girl." She stroked what was left of her
father's hair. "Now, do you want me to get you some breakfast?
Some toast and eggs, poached the way you like them?"
The man smiled, open mouthed, and nodded.
"You lie here for a minute then; I'll put Radio Two on for you,
whilst I get the eggs on, eh?"
Scarlet didn't get a response; her father had disappeared again,
back to the place only he knew.

James Kavanagh, Scarlet's father, had been what the police called a
career criminal. The trouble had been that he wasn't very good at
it. He had spent almost half of Scarlet's childhood behind bars.
Scarlet's earliest memories were dominated by visits from surly
detectives at five in the morning, dragging her father out of his bed
and searching their home, tipping out drawers, turning over
mattresses, laughing between themselves.
As Scarlet grew older, and her understanding developed, she came
to hate those men, the men who took her father from her, the men
who wrecked her bedroom and damaged her things.
She hated the police. Even though she knew what her father did
was wrong, he was still her hero.
She remembered good times too, times when her father was at
home, when he would spoil her, take her to the cinema, the park,
even to Blackpool on the rides sometimes. She always had nice
presents at Christmas and birthdays, although she had them taken
away once when it turned out they were stolen.
Her dad always had a scam or plan up his sleeve, the next job was
always going to be the big payday, he was a dreamer.
On release from prison, he would promise Scarlet and her mum
that it was the last time, but within weeks, he would be back in
with his old mates, planning the next big burglary.

His real downfall was meeting a man called Billy Edwards. Scarlet met him once and he scared her, but her dad looked up to Billy, he was 'big time', he said.

Edwards recruited Kavanagh to drive a getaway car on a post office robbery. They were all caught.

When James Kavanagh was sentenced to seven years in jail, Scarlet's mum had seen enough. The following morning, Scarlet found her mum's note on the dresser; she was sixteen.

Four years into his sentence, James was diagnosed with Alzheimer's and was given parole. His deterioration was swift. Six months later, the doctors found a growth in his left lung. Despite chemotherapy, his condition remained terminal.

Scarlet cracked two eggs into boiling water; her phone vibrated in her pocket and she checked the screen and read the text.

Hope you are okay x

Striker and Westland walked along Fishergate toward the multi-storey car park that served St George's shopping centre. It was a good day for the time of year, blue sky, warm sunshine.

Westland broke the silence. "You married, Striker?"

The detective shook his head.

"Ever?"

"Nope."

"You got a girl, then?"

Striker turned to Westland and pointed at his chin.

"You think anyone could love this face?"

Westland shrugged. "There's someone for everyone, so they say."

"That so?"

"Yeah, that's what they say."

Striker turned down the edges of his mouth and shook his head. There was a brief shadow that drifted across his face, but he shook it off.

"Nah, not so far anyhow; we ain't all like you, kid, all smooth talking and twinkle-toed."

"I think you could do alright, if you weren't so...so...grumpy."

Striker stopped walking.

"I'm a pussycat, son, you have me all wrong."

Westland took a step back, light on his feet, and a smile on his face.

"More like a fucking bulldog."

Striker pulled back a fist.

"A bulldog that bites, you cheeky little bastard."

The banter continued until they reached the opening to the shopping precinct.

Westland looked across the road.

"What's going on there?"

A small group of people were gathered outside Aslam's Clothing, a small independent retailer. Some held placards, one had a megaphone. Two uniformed officers in full riot gear, stood nearby, but didn't appear interested in taking any action. Striker and Westland stopped to see what the commotion was about.

Fishergate was the main shopping street, and despite the unrest in the city, it remained remarkably unscathed. Business seemed to be going on as usual, the majority of the violence had been contained within the predominantly Asian areas of Preston.

Striker looked at the small group and let out a low growl.

"I know who's behind this," he said.

The placards being waved about were not handwritten, but printed; a red white and blue design was on top of each banner, displaying the emblem of the Justice for Great Britain Party

Tag stood at Striker's shoulder. "Who?"

"A sleazeball called Alistair Sinclair, the Right Honorable MP for Nelson."

Westland read the various captions. They all sported the same rhetoric. *STOP Muslim Racism, BOYCOTT Racist Stores, Play YOUR Race Card.*

The man with the megaphone was in his forties with greying hair; he wore a smart suit and tie. Tag was also surprised by the appearance of the other demonstrators. White, middle-aged, all female, all equally smartly dressed. They looked more like a contingent of the Women's Institute, than ultra right-wing nutters.

"Weird," he said.

Megaphone Man started his rant.

"This business behind me is owned and run by a racist. Aslam's Emporium has five stores in the north west of England, and employs over thirty young people. They manufacture clothing right here in your town, not five miles away. The factory employs twenty-eight men and women. Aslam's also has a warehouse and distribution centre in Bamber Bridge with eighteen staff.

Out of all those people, how many are white?

None! Not a single member of Aslam's staff is white. Not only that! All of them, every employee, are of Pakistani origin!

Forget white! At Aslam's there are no Indians, no Afro Caribbeans, no Arabs, no Hindus, and no Jews! No Catholics, no Protestants!

And what is our government, our council, doing about this? Nothing!

Boycott this business! Don't buy from these racists!"

There was a screech of tyres as a blue BMW car pulled up.

"Here's the cavalry," said Striker.

Five Asian men alighted from the vehicle, all young, all wearing street clothes; jeans, hoodies, training shoes.

The driver seemed to be in control of his crew. He was a big guy, with powerful shoulders and arms. He sported a thick gold chain around his neck and had intricate patterns cut into his close-cropped hair. He approached the two cops first. "Why are you not stopping this shit, man?" He pointed at the group who were all walking in a small circle and chanting their slogans.

"Move them or we will!"

The cops tried to placate the man; tried to explain the letter of the law; he was having none of it. He got into the face of one cop.

"Fuck you, man! You're all as bad as these fuckers here!"

He turned to his crew and motioned them into action. There was some pushing and shoving; the cops moved forward, one got straight on his personal radio. Megaphone Man started up again.

"See what happens to ordinary people when they protest about racism. This is a peaceful protest, a legal protest."

The big guy grabbed at the megaphone and it squealed sonic feedback.

"Get off me!" shouted the man.

Another of the crew had torn a placard from the hands of one woman. She looked scared but stood her ground defiantly.

Then it got nasty; one of the Asian group pushed a little too hard and a woman fell to the pavement, she was knocked unconscious.

He was grabbed by a cop, and within seconds, it became a mêlée.

Some members of the public looked on, some joined in.

From nowhere, a cameraman and a female reporter appeared.

Striker shook his head.
"He got exactly what he wanted there, eh?"
Tag looked both bemused and concerned. "What do you mean?"
A full PSU drew up and twelve riot cops started to restore order and make arrests.
"Sinclair," said Striker. "It was just for the cameras. That will add more fuel to the flames tonight. You can see the headlines now, can't you?"
The two men turned and walked into the shopping precinct.
Tag looked at Striker.
"They do have a point, though."
"As in?"
"Well, if it was a white business, and it didn't employ any minorities, or say, all the workforce were Catholic, there would be an outcry."
Striker was losing his short temper.
"Listen, Westland, you should try being Catholic in Belfast; try getting a job in some firms there."
Tag was not backing down. "I know all about the divisions in Ireland, Striker, but things are changing there, just as they are all over the democratic world. It will take years, but it is changing."
Striker stopped by the car park payment machine and pushed coins into the slot.
"And you think that by raising the temperature on the streets of Preston, it will achieve anything, son? This is racism disguised as peaceful protest, this guy Sinclair is fuckin' dangerous."
Tag looked a little crestfallen. "I just think they have a point, that's all."
Striker grunted to signal he was tired of the conversation.
"Let's get to J and G cabs."

Errol Graham slept in his favourite armchair. He'd been to bed, but sleep wouldn't come. In the end he'd trodden the stairs, made coffee and spread the various files relating to the two murders in front of him. They now covered the carpet at his feet as he snored quietly.
His wife Emily touched his arm gently to rouse him.
"It's one, dear, you asked me to wake you at one."

Graham opened his eyes and yawned; two hours sleep in forty-eight was not a good return for a man just turned fifty.

"Thanks, honey," he said, rubbing the stubble on his face with both hands.

Emily gave him her worried look, the one that said he was doing too much. "Would you like some breakfast, Errol? I can rustle up some bacon and sausage. I've got those nice pork and herb ones from the market."

Graham dropped his hands to his stomach, decided it wasn't time to start his diet quite yet and nodded. "That would be great, Em; I'm famished."

His wife turned on her heels and he heard the familiar sounds of food being prepared in the kitchen. He leaned forward and collected up the papers from the carpet. On the arm of the chair was a thick notepad. He had scribbled a 'to do' list before he'd fallen asleep. It ran to four pages.

Errol lifted himself from his chair and felt his back complain. He stretched it to no avail, found the remote and switched on Sky News.

Shaky camera shots of a small demonstration were rolling. A middle-aged woman lay unconscious on the pavement; angry Asian men were struggling with police. Errol turned up the volume. A woman anchor provided a voiceover.

"A small, peaceful demonstration turned ugly this morning in Preston, Lancashire, the scene of two apparent vigilante style murders and recent race riots. A group of supporters of the Justice for Great Britain Party were protesting about the alleged racist employment practices of a local retailer, Aslam's Clothing Emporium, when they were seemingly attacked by local Asian youths. Reports say the police were slow to react to the fracas and one woman, forty-nine year old Marie Henderson, was seriously injured."

The producer cut to the studio where an attractive blonde with a serious expression picked up the story.

"I'm joined in the studio by Mohammed Bashkir, spokesman for the Muslim League of Great Britain and MP for Nelson, and the leader of the Justice for Great Britain Party, Alistair Sinclair. I'll come to you first, Mr. Sinclair. Exactly why were your supporters protesting in Preston this morning?"

Sinclair was doing his best to look concerned. "Well first, Annabel, let me say that our thoughts and prayers go out to Marie Henderson and her family at this time. Marie is a valued member of our party, and we wish her a speedy recovery after this vicious and unprovoked assault. But to answer your question, we have conducted an investigation into the employment practices of several businesses in the Lancashire area, Aslam's being just one; we have found that a shocking feature of their business model is to only employ Pakistani, Muslim workers. Not only that, but only to buy materials and goods from Pakistani Muslim suppliers. Our party is outraged by this practice and thought it essential that we bring it to the notice of the public and government."

Annabel turned to Bashkir. "What do you say to these claims, Mr. Bashkir? Sky News understands that Prime Minister David Cameron is to make a statement today in the Commons, calling for an investigation into this allegation."

Bashkir did little to hide his disgust for his fellow panelist. "This is pure bigotry and lies. The Justice for Great Britain Party is a fascist movement disguised as a mainstream party. This incident today is designed to take the spotlight away from the vicious murders of two innocent Muslims in Preston, a nineteen-year old boy and teenage girl. What are the police doing about these terrible crimes? Nothing! Our people cannot leave their homes due to gangs of white men trawling the streets in search of violence. Mosques have been burned, businesses and homes wrecked. Why is Cameron not talking about this?"

Graham hit the mute button, he'd heard enough. His wife walked into the room holding a plate with an oven-gloved hand. She looked at the screen; Sinclair was speaking, hands gesticulating.

"He scares me, Errol," she said flatly.

The chief detective nodded solemnly.

"He scares me too, Em. He's the worst kind of bigot. He feeds on people's fear, it's like the bad old days."

Emily gestured toward the plate. "You want this at the table or are you going to eat and work?"

Errol gave a tired smile.

"Table, I think it may be a while before we can sit together again."

Striker and Westland's visit to J and G taxi's was swift. The owner was much more co-operative. However, he did stay firmly behind the protective grill in the office; obviously concerned that Striker may decide to encourage his collaboration by half strangling him for a second time.

They exited with the address of Iftikar Mohammed Din.

The parade of houses that made 88 Broadway a quiet and pleasant place to live looked over the river Ribble. The water ran deep and brown most of the time and was not a place for swimmers or fishermen.

Nonetheless, with the sun shining and the trees swaying gently, it made for a pleasant change to the grim scenes not a mile away.

Din's house was a three-bedroomed pebble-dashed semi. The front garden was enclosed by a low wall, and cast iron railings. They looked newly painted. The garden itself was awash with colour.

All manner of plants and shrubs that neither Striker nor Westland could name had been lovingly nurtured to make the space a picture of green-fingered pride.

Two taxis were parked outside the house; both were in great condition and as clean and tidy as the house itself. Mr. Din was not averse to polish.

Westland knocked.

The door opened and Iftikar stood and inspected his visitors.

Striker produced his ID.

"Police, sir, Lancashire anti-terrorist branch."

The man looked at Westland, most people would not have recognised him out of uniform, but after a few seconds, a light came on.

"You are the policeman from last night?"

Westland nodded. "Yes, sir, that's me. Constable Westland and this is Detective Sergeant Striker."

Iftikar stood back. "Please come in, officers."

Westland thought the house smelled delicious. Cumin, coriander, garlic and massala filled his nostrils.

They were led to the front of the home, a comfortable lounge that was filled with family pictures.

"Please sit," said Iftikar. "Would you like some tea?"

Striker dropped his considerable frame onto a large sofa. "That would be nice sir, thank you."

The man turned and walked into the kitchen where his wife was preparing the curry that had made Westland's mouth water. They spoke Urdu to each other, Iftikar explaining who the men were, and that his wife was not to be alarmed. She did not question her husband, simply accepted what he had to say and hurriedly found a hijab to cover her face, as she was not expecting male visitors.

Iftikar returned to the lounge and joined the officers.

As he sat there was a rumble of small feet that careered downward from upstairs. The din was mixed with giggles and stage-whispered conversation.

Iftikar raised a black eyebrow.

Striker could tell that Din was a serious soul, not given to outbursts of emotion, but Din was unable to hide his amusement at the noise that was approaching them.

Before he could speak, two young girls, dressed identically in bright green and gold trousers and tops barreled into the room, howling with laughter.

Both landed at Striker's feet.

"My daughters," said Din, as sternly as he could muster.

Din's wife rushed into the room covering her face with her hurried addition and ushered the children from the room.

One of the obviously twin girls complained briefly, but it was short-lived.

Iftikar himself was a tall, lithe man, dressed in traditional white trousers and shirt. Striker noticed that they were as immaculately clean and pressed as his own shirts.

Iftikar's handsome face was angular, almost Roman. He sported an impressive beard, and had close-cropped hair that was covered by an intricately designed skull-cap. His voice was deep and although he couldn't hide his first language, had the strongest Preston accent.

"Allah, in his wisdom, gave me girls. They are devils, no?"

"They are children," said Striker. "You must be very proud of your family."

Din revealed a set of perfect teeth that a dentist had manufactured, rather than nature provided. Striker felt the man was as much of an anomaly as he had encountered in a while.

There was no doubting Westland's first impression; Din was indeed a devout Muslim, but Striker couldn't take his eyes from those dentures. Although the Qur'an states that any wealth acquired through business was to be used for the support of the family, he considered that some of it went on Din's vanity, rather than charity.

"I am a modern man, sir. I believe in education for all. My daughters will use their God-given intelligence, it is a religious activity for any Muslim."

"They are very pretty," stumbled Westland.

Din smiled again, he nodded at Westland.

"They are, officer. It will be a trying time as they grow up in western society."

Striker stood as Din's wife walked in with tea.

"Ah, thank you," he said. "Very kind of you."

Westland pushed himself further into his armchair and concentrated on not spilling anything.

Quiet settled on the room as each sipped black sweet tea from small glass cups. Din broke it.

"So you are here about the man called Mustapha."

Westland sat up.

"I am not a fool," said Din, shooting a surprisingly hard glance at Tag. "I may be a taxi driver, but I am educated and I know people."

Striker leaned forward and placed his tea on a decorative tray.

"What do you know about this man?"

Din jutted his sharp chin.

"The Qur'an forbids the worship of idols. This man was obsessed with women, white women. He could not take his eyes away from bare flesh, both real and photographed."

Striker pressed on.

"His passport says he is Iraqi?"

Din shook his head. "I don't think so, detective. I think he spent time there, but he is Syrian.

I am Shi'a, 'Ashariyah,' or 'Twelvers' in your language. Our religion separates us from the majority of Muslims in this country; over eighty percent of the Islamic population is Sunni."

Westland couldn't help himself.

"Didn't the Shi'a form Hezbollah in the Lebanon, the anti Jewish group?"

Striker was both annoyed and slightly impressed. He turned and gave Westland his best 'shut the fuck up' look.

"Go on, sir."

Din turned to Westland. "That is true, young man. Every religion has its fighters. I think you will find your own fair share in the Christian world. Nonetheless, the Shi'a and Hezbollah have recently attached themselves to the Syrian regime and would now appear to be fighting alongside government troops. It has put them back in the news again, I'm afraid. The man you seek though would be firmly in the rebel camp with the other side, with the Sunni, with Al-Qaeda. Do you not find it strange that our Prime Minister Cameron wishes to support the rebels, and therefore Al-Qaeda?"

Tag had seen the news, had seen the dead children allegedly gassed by the Syrian government. It was a humanitarian and political mess. He didn't answer, he didn't have one.

Din leaned in. "Believe me, this man is not called Mustapha, he is not Iraqi and the child he travels with is not his blood. He is Syrian, he is Sunni, he is Al-Qaeda, and he is a dangerous man."

Striker couldn't decide if Din was simply perceptive, or his own religious bigotry was clouding his judgement. Striker was well aware of the origins, developments and deep rooted divisions within the Muslim faith. It seemed to him that every religion thrived on division. When there was no enemy to fight from outside, they would fight each other within.

He changed tack. "Where did you take this man?"

Din smiled. "That is a strange coincidence, Mr. Striker. I took him to Lebanon Street, ironic, isn't it? It is near to the football ground in Burnley. I can't say if he went to a house there, or someone collected him and the child. He waited on the pavement until I had left."

Minutes later the detectives stood outside Din's house, the sun was warmer than ever, yet their mood was dark.

Tag dropped into the passenger seat of Striker's Audi police car. "You think Din is right?"

"Possibly, I spent some time in the Middle East when my dad was posted there. You get to recognise the features of the different races, you can spot Lebanese, Iranians, Saudis, it isn't that hard.

Our man doesn't look Iraqi, and Din is right about one thing, Mustapha is a sexual predator."

Tag looked at his feet. There was something else on his mind and it troubled him.

"My dad," he said. "He's a reasonable educated man. He goes to church, calls himself a Christian, yet he hates the Jews. Always has, we fought about it a lot when I was at university. He blames them for everything that is wrong in the banking world. Din is a good guy, yet hates Mustapha more because he is Sunni than because he could be a terrorist. What is wrong with the world?"

Striker started the car.

"Fear," he said, pushing a CD into the player;

Billy Holiday sang 'Strange Fruit.'

Southern trees bear a strange fruit,
Blood on the leaves and blood at the root,
Black bodies swinging in the southern breeze,
Strange fruit hanging from the poplar trees.

"Fear," he repeated.

Sandra Mackintosh was banging about in her bedroom whilst Wilson sat on her sofa inspecting the disorder in the small lounge. Considering Sandra cleaned for a living, it didn't seep into her own home life.

The ashtray overflowed with butts, and empty cans of Special Brew were carelessly discarded on the carpet. Clothes, including some racy items of underwear, were draped over the solitary chair adding to the general picture of mess.

Sandra almost bounded into the room. She had changed into jeans and a roll-necked sweater that covered her injuries; applied some further make-up and brushed her hair.

"Will I do, then?" she chirped.

"Aye, love, you look grand," said Wilson, standing to leave.

Sandra placed her arms around Wilson's neck and kissed him on the mouth. Her hand slipped downward and squeezed his crotch.

"We don't have to go out just yet you know, we could stay here and get a carry out."

Wilson had gone without any sexual activity for some considerable time, he didn't even know if he was still capable. He was sure of one thing though, he needed a drink more than he needed sex. He held Sandra's breast in his hand, more from habit than lust and gave it a gentle squeeze. She moaned quietly.

"Mmm, it's been a long time eh, hun?"

"It has, love, but I could go a beer or two first."

Sandra looked slightly upset, but considered that she did have a man in her house, and for the first time in a while, he wasn't going to walk out straight after he'd got his oats.

"Alright, love; I could go a vodka or two myself. There's forty quid in that jar on the mantle; that will get us in the mood eh?"

Wilson walked over to the pot ornament and removed two twenty-pound notes.

"Come on then, it's happy hour at the Blackamoor's Head."

The pair walked slowly into town, along Lancaster Road to the old pub that had been servicing clients since 1861. It had been given its unusual name due to it being in close proximity to Turk's Head Yard, the site of a boarding house run by an Egyptian trader in the 1840s. He had installed a stained glass window in the snug bar depicting a Moor dressed in a turban and fine silk clothes. Preston had been home to black people long before the mass immigration of the 1960s. It seemed that the population was far more welcoming back then.

The pub was busy enough with a mix of wizened older drinkers and younger men dressed in street clothes. A full sized England flag, that should have been a poignant focal point but instead shouted bigotry, was draped along one wall; a television flickered in one corner showing horse racing with the sound down.

Wilson licked his lips as he approached the bar, felt for the two crisp twenties in his pocket and ordered a pint of Stella Artois for himself and a large vodka and coke for Sandra.

The barmaid gave him a hard look, but softened when she saw currency appear on the counter.

"Five quid, love," she said holding out a hand devoid of noticeable fingernails.

Wilson paid and grabbed the glass. He drank greedily, devouring half the beer, feeling the alcohol hit his system almost instantly; he had been sober for almost two whole days.

The barmaid handed over his change.

"Ready for that, were you?"

Sandra sidled over and took her own drink. "Yeah, he was, love, we've both been in the Royal Preston ain't we, Wilson?"

Wilson nodded, more interested in finishing his beer than making small talk.

The barmaid raised a brow.

"Oh dear. Nothing too serious I hope."

Sandra pulled down the neck of her sweater to reveal her bruising. The woman behind the counter let out a low whistle.

"Fuckin' hell, love, what on earth happened?"

"Some Paki bastard did it."

Sandra's voice was loud enough to carry across the room; several heads were raised from their racing papers. One shaven headed twenty-something couldn't help but comment.

"String the fuckers up, I say; think they own the fuckin' town these days."

"Too right," added another tattooed thug. "'Bout time we did somethin' about the black bastards. That bloke that's been on the telly has the right idea."

"Who's that?" said the barmaid.

"That Sinclair fella," said Tattoos. "He knows what to do with 'em. Started that new party, Justice for England or somethin' like that. He's gonna send 'em all back where they came from, stop 'em from takin' our jobs an' that."

"You've never had a job, Craig," cackled the barmaid. "Yer fuckin' bone idle."

"Fuck off, Mary," said Tattoos. "There's no jobs out there 'cos of them Pakis an' Poles an' that."

Wilson finished his pint and waved his glass at the barmaid. "The Poles are alright, lad," he said. "They fought with us in the war."

"Yeah, right," scoffed Tattoos. "What war was that then?"

Wilson took a long drink from his new pint.

"The second World War, son; that's why there are Polish clubs all over the place. The Poles hate the Germans, and the Russians for that matter; but you're an ignorant twat and know fuck all."

Tattoos stood up and flexed his considerable muscles.

"Listen, granddad, if you know what's best for you, keep your gob shut."

"Wind your neck in, Craig," bellowed the barmaid. "Or you'll end up barred again."

Wilson turned and faced the lout for the first time.

At twenty-five years older and with broken ribs, Wilson would have his hands full and he was sober enough to know it. Even so, he didn't like the lad one bit and he had never been one to back down.

"Sit down, son, or I'll break your jaw."

Tattoos walked forward and balled his fists ready to fight.

Sandra stepped between the aging gladiator and the young pretender.

"Now then, lads, come on, it's them Pakis we should be fightin', not each other, eh?"

"That's right, love," added the barmaid, grabbing her mobile and waving it at the lout. "Now sit down, Craig, and drink your beer or I'll call the cops."

Tattoos looked across the room for any support for his cause, but found none. Wilson may have been a drunk, but he was still well known in the town for his vicious temper. Reputations were long-lasting when it came to street fighters.

"Ah, fuck the lot of yer!" he shouted, turned on his heels and barreled out of the door.

Wilson shrugged his shoulders and resumed his pose at the bar.

Sandra placed a beefy arm around his waist and eyed him admiringly.

"No bottle these kids eh, love? You've still got it, Wilson, ain't ya?"

Wilson didn't reply, just drained his beer and waved his glass again.

Westland had tolerated the dismal music in Striker's car for almost thirty minutes when they pulled up in Lebanon Street, Burnley. After Billy Holiday had finished, there'd been a procession of tracks by people he had never heard of, a mixture of wailing saxophones, screaming trumpets, strange time signatures and indeterminable melodies.

Striker called it 'jazz fusion'. Westland had another name for it.

The area around Turf Moor football ground, the home of Burnley FC, is one of contrasts. To the north is a shopping area with a large supermarket and a bus station, to the east there are smaller shops, mixed with fast food outlets that serve the football crowds in the daytime and the drinkers that frequented the pubs to the south of the stadium at night.

Lebanon Street sat to the east, and formed part of a larger block of streets containing private and council dwellings.

Both men stepped from the car.

Striker rubbed his locks and scowled.

"This doesn't add up."

Tag understood immediately. Red and white England flags adorned almost every house. Bunting was stretched across the street in the red, white and blue of the ensign.

"Doesn't seem the kind of area that our man would hide out in." Striker fumbled in his trouser pocket, removed a pack of gum, offered Tag a piece and nodded.

"Just the kind of place that would welcome him with open arms, son," he said, sarcasm dripping from each word.

Tag looked around and set off walking toward the eastern side of the ground.

"Where you going?" asked the detective.

"Not far," he said. "Come on, I need to get that bloody music of yours out of my head."

Striker caught him up.

"You don't like jazz?"

"Punk is my thing."

"Punk?"

"Yeah, y' know; Dead Kennedys. Green Day, Dropkick Murphys, that kind of thing."

"Shite," muttered Striker.

Tag smiled, not expecting anything else from the bullish cop.

"Bet you've never been in a mosh pit in your life, have you?"

"Nope."

Tag looked at Striker's massive frame doing its best to burst from his leather jacket and judged it was probably a good thing for any fellow moshers that he hadn't.

"Each to their own, Striker," said Tag. "Each to their own."

They strolled along Harry Potts Way and onto Brunshaw Road. On the corner of Albert Street, Tag stopped and inspected a building.

"What's that, Striker?" He read the sign. "KSC110 Club?"

"The Knights of Saint Columba, son; I thought you were educated? It's an Irish thing, even though it was founded in Glasgow, a Catholic fraternal organisation, named after Saint Columba. Some say they are the Catholic equivalent of the Masons, but that isn't quite true, they're not a secret society, more like a charitable club." Tag nodded at the door toward three burly drinkers enjoying a cigarette in the sunshine; they looked like off duty doormen and they viewed the cops with suspicion. The KSC was not the only venue to have a presence outside its doors. There was no sign of rioting or trouble in the area, but every business that remained open was taking no chances.

"They don't seem too welcoming, if you ask me," said Tag. "Anyway, I'm a Protestant."

Striker moved on.

"That's not the only reason you couldn't be a member."

"Oh yeah?"

"Yeah," he said. "They don't allow women."

Sandra Mackintosh sat in the window of The Greyfriar, a JD Wetherspoons house on Friargate, which sold cheap drinks to anyone who could stand a round. Wilson was at the bar purchasing drinks with the last of her forty pounds. After the Blackamoor, they had visited two other hostelries and she was well on her way to being pissed.

Wilson sat heavily and spilled a little of Sandra's vodka in the process.

"Hey, come on, Wilson! That's the end of the fuckin' cash, mate, don't spill me last drink."

"Sorry, love."

Sandra, quickly found her good humour and draped an arm over Wilson's shoulders.

"No worries, lover, we've had a good day, ain't we?"

It had been a good day; for anyone else, it would be time to go and sleep off what had been a very boozy afternoon, but for Wilson, he had just about got the taste. His mind wandered to how he was going to finance more drink.

"We're skint now, then?"

Sandra took a large gulp of vodka.

"Well I am, lover; that forty was my shopping money for the week. What you got?"

Wilson felt the tiniest pang of guilt.

"When I last looked, eleven pence."

Wilson knew that Sandra was a product of the system. It wasn't a system that was given much airtime on the BBC. She may use bad language, but she wasn't a bigot or a racist. Not in the sense that the politicians might suggest. Sandra would never dream of hurting someone because of their creed or colour. She might do you damage if you threatened her family or friends. She might if she was drunk and you upset her; but she wouldn't give two hoots what colour you were, or where you worshiped your God.

That said, she had been brought up on a Preston council estate in the nineteen seventies, one of five girls. In her lifetime, the paper shop had become the Paki shop and the chippy had become the Chinki. It was just how it was. It was natural progression.

Her father was a good honest working man, some would have called him a 'navvy', a term given to Irish labourers who came to England to dig the maze of canals that fed factories and ports during the industrial revolution. The nickname came from the word 'navigator'. It is now considered offensive.

Seamus Murphy was an Irish Catholic who like many in the 1960's settled in Preston to work on the roads and motorways. He worked hard, fought hard and drank harder; but there was always food on the table and coal for the fire. Despite everyone knowing Seamus well, all the drinkers in the local club called him 'Paddy'.

To them, all Irishmen were Paddies.

It was a term Wilson had used himself, just as his own father had. Education didn't come into it.

Sandra's mother didn't have an opinion on the various races and creeds that filled their town, until she had a drink in her; unfortunately, that was most of the time.

From an early age, Sandra had always liked bad guys, even at school, the boy who had taken her virginity, Mickey Brown, had been a villain and been to prison; she loved him, they had gone behind the art block, it hurt her, but it was the best thing ever. To Sandra he was a god, he had power over people, they were scared of him, and that meant they were scared of her. She was just thirteen.

After Sandra's mother died suddenly, her father found life impossible. He couldn't juggle sixty hours a week on the graft and five teenage girls. Less than a year after her first sexual encounter, Sandra was briefly taken into the care of the local authority as a 'wayward girl'.

There she mixed with girls of the same age, with the same issues or worse. It was an accident waiting to happen.

By the time she was sixteen, she was pregnant and had disowned her father, changing her name from Murphy to Mackintosh, by deed poll.

Seamus dropped dead on his spade at age forty-seven.

Sandra didn't go to his funeral.

Wilson eased himself from his seat and rummaged in his jeans for change.

"What you doin' now?" asked Sandra.

"Bandit," he said.

"Waste of money, love, that's why they call 'em bandits."

Wilson pushed the last of Sandra's pound coins into the machine; it whirred and clicked, each reel dropping into place with an audible electronic ping. It took Wilson a second or two to realise, but once the steady chug of coins started to rattle into the bowl, he turned to Sandra and beamed.

"I've dropped the fuckin' jackpot, love, a hundred quid!"

CHAPTER TWELVE

Tariq Hussain QC had returned from chambers and was studying a brief at his desk in his Preston office. He found it hard to concentrate on the subject matter, the events of the last days played on his mind.

His children hadn't been to school, his wife refused to leave the house. Even though they lived fifteen miles away from the troubles, they were virtual prisoners in their own home.

Not because they were at risk, but because Tariq's wife perceived the risk.

That was enough.

Fear had locked the doors and bolted the windows of their beautiful house.

He checked his watch, closed the brief and stood.

He shouted in the direction of his temporary secretary's office.

"I'm going to prayers, Hilary. I'll be back around five."

"Okay, Mr. Hussain."

As Tariq trod the stairs to the street, his mind turned to Gina, his devoted ex employee. He missed her wit and efficiency. He turned over that shocking morning's events in his mind, Abdullah's murder, the brash detective, Gina's tears.

He cursed his own mistake. He should have denounced the protesters that had disrupted the homecoming parade.

Hussain had little time for British or American foreign policy, especially when it came to the Middle East. However, he valued the democracy that ruled in the UK. Unlike the corrupt regimes in India and Pakistan, and the dictators that headed the royal families in the Emirates and beyond, his country had a free and fair electoral system.

The people of the UK had the ability to protest, the freedom to speak out, it was a basic human right, but to inflame tensions between communities, who had so far lived peacefully together, was folly.

Whoever had made the decision was foolish in the extreme.

It had given the far right the opportunity they had been waiting for. Now, a far more formidable source of bigotry and evil was amongst them, in the shape of Alistair Sinclair.

Tariq walked in the sunshine, until he reached the private underground garage that served his offices. Ten steps found him in the dim coolness of the six-car unit. He stretched out his arm and pushed the remote that opened the doors and boot to his black Mercedes car, then dropped his briefcase in the cavernous space and slammed the lid. He ran his hand lovingly along the sleek paintwork, removed his overcoat, folded it neatly over his arm, opened the driver's door, draped the coat on the passenger seat, and sat inside.

He loved the smell of the leather interior. He had promised himself a car just like this one when he was still studying law. Now he had it. He had a fabulous home, a beautiful wife and two healthy children. He charged more money per hour for his services than some people earned in a month.

He was a success, and he enjoyed his accomplishments by rewarding himself with the car of his dreams.

What is the problem with that?

Hussain fumbled for the ignition switch, found it, and the engine roared into life. It was as he leaned to select the drive gear that he felt the ligature curl around his neck.

Tremendously strong hands gripped the leather belt that forced his head back against the seat, cutting off his air supply and causing his eyes to bulge grotesquely in their sockets; he had mere seconds to stay conscious, the lack of blood-flow to the brain shutting everything down inside his head, he couldn't think, couldn't move. Black clouds were circling his head, shrouding his vision in a darkening fog, his chest burned as he fought for a single breath that would never come unless he was freed.

His bladder gave way, he was aware of the warmth engulfing his groin, but rather than embarrassment, he found it strangely comforting.

His hands flailed uselessly against his throat, all strength drained by the lack of circulation.

Then there was light.

He could breathe again; his heart pounded and he felt both dizzy and sick in equal amounts.

The belt was loosened, replaced by a powerful hand that gripped his hair. There was warm breath against his ear. The man had a gruff voice, deep and throaty, a smoker's voice and a smoker's smell.

He spoke in strongly accented English.

"It is good to be alive, isn't it, Tariq? Dying is not all heaven and virgins, you know.

It's emptying your bladder all over your car seats; it's praying that you can just have one more chance. One more breath."

The man wrenched his hair again, tearing some from the root.

Tariq shook with fear. He wanted to be brave, wanted to fight his assailant, but he couldn't find the strength. He felt like an animal in a snare.

"What...what do you want? I don't have money...I don't have anything...no...Sorry, I do have...erm...my watch, take my watch! It's a Rolex, worth thousands...."

"Shut up!"

The voice bellowed in Tariq's ear. It shocked him, made him physically jump.

"Okay...okay...I'm sorry, what do you want?"

The voice dropped to a whisper again.

"What I want is not important, Tariq, it's what our people want."

"I don't understand, just...just let me go; I won't tell anyone," blubbered the lawyer.

Tariq could feel himself start to sweat. Fear had overtaken reasoning or principle. The man gave a short sinister laugh.

"That's right, Tariq, you won't tell a living soul."

Abu Al Zachari released his grip and pushed a 9mm pistol into the QC's neck.

"Now drive carefully, if you draw any attention to us I will kill you. Then I will take this obscene car to your house and behead your wife and children."

Westland stepped into the Kashmir takeaway and ordered a chicken tikka kebab with salad, extra chilies and garlic sauce. Striker went with a double portion of plain grilled chicken, a portion of lamb shish and salad, no sauce, no bread.

"No bread?"

Striker shook his head. "Carbs are the enemy, man."

"And your body is a temple, eh?"

Striker just gave him a look that had 'be quiet' all over it; Westland took the hint and studied the shop's posters, read the local headlines from a two-day-old paper and sent another text to the lovely Scarlet one 't'.

Fancy a drink tonight?

He still hadn't had a response from his previous attempt, so he was starting to doubt his pulling powers with the elusive miss.

Ten minutes later both stood on the pavement outside, hungrily pushing food into their mouths.

Westland licked sauce from his fingers;

"So, I've counted seven CCTV units from the drop off point to here. Four outside cameras, and three interior cams that point out to the street; I reckon that our man would have walked this route, rather than into the estate. If he was picked up, this would be a far more likely area. All we need to do is get permission from the owners of the shops, and that KSC club place, to view the footage."

Striker chewed the last of the mountain of meat he had ordered and dropped the empty tray into a bin.

Westland looked at his own food; he had managed barely half.

"You eat like a pig, Striker."

"I like meat," he said. "You eat like a bird. Come on, finish up, we'll start at the KC Club. I'm feeling persuasive."

Westland took a last bite and reluctantly dropped the remains of his deliciously-spiced kebab into the trash.

"I hope that doesn't mean you are going to strangle people again."

Striker pointed at his own chest. "Me? I'm a pussycat, son," and strode off in the direction of Albert Street.

They arrived at the door of the club to find their path blocked by the same three bouncer types they had passed earlier, all chain smoking, black bomber jackets, beer bellies and bad attitude.

As Striker strode toward them he removed his own coat and draped it over his shoulder, holding the neck with one thick finger.

Westland had never seen Striker in a t-shirt.

Arnie in his prime would have been impressed. Tag had fully expected the detective to have muscles; what he wasn't prepared for, was to see that both Striker's massive arms were covered in intricate full sleeve tattoos.

"Keep your warrant card in your pocket, and your mouth shut, son," he said out of the corner of a smiling mouth.

The biggest of the three men stepped forward and held out the classic 'you have to be a member' hand.

To Tag's further astonishment, Striker opened his mouth, and out came Ian Paisley on acid, he couldn't have sounded more Northern Irish.

"Y'all right there, lads, now?"

The big guy stood his ground, but Tag could see that the other two were already intimidated by Striker's appearance. It wasn't just the muscles and the attitude, it was that stare of his.

Just think Roy Keane reading Sir Alex Ferguson's book, mixed with Robert de Nero in Cape Fear, or Al Pacino in Scarface laced with a touch of Anthony Hopkins as Hannibal.

The lights were on, but no-one was home.

Blend that with his awful attempt at smiling and he scared Tag more than a girlfriend holding a pregnancy test.

The big guy remained solid, squared his shoulders and spoke in a thick Lancashire accent.

"Members only, pal. This is a private club."

Striker stopped short of the man.

"And what makes you think that we wouldn't be members there?"

The big man stepped in close.

"Well, we don't know you. So you're not members," he turned his head toward his two mates. "Do we, lads?"

Both shook their heads solemnly. One walked over to Tag, stood in his personal space, prodded him roughly in the chest and said, "No, we don't, Willy; and we don't like pretty boys in here either."

The man smelled of cigarettes and whiskey. Tag stepped back, considered a retort, but thought better of it. Striker had the plate, best see how things panned out.

"No need for that, lad," said Striker, continuing his Belfast boy act. "Me and my mate here just want to have a quick word with the steward of the club is all."

"Well you can't," said Willy. "Now fuck off."

It was Striker's turn to go on the front foot. He looked at Tag. "That's not friendly now, is it? The boy isn't that pretty, and he's my guest." Striker took a step away from Willy, to give himself some room for manoeuvre.

The big man wasn't the sharpest knife in the drawer, but he knew why Striker had stepped away, you can't fight without space. He screwed his face into a sneer.

"You sure you want to do this, pal? You're outnumbered."

Striker nodded at Tag, who knew exactly what he wanted.

Westland bounced lightly on the balls of his feet, dropped his shoulder, exactly the way he'd been taught since age eight, and gave Fag Breath a sharp left jab. The man looked more startled than hurt, but with lightning speed, Tag followed up with two more stinging lefts, the second blow opening a cut on the bouncer's brow.

The man staggered, wiped his eye and inspected the blood on his hand.

"You fucker!" he spat, and launched himself forward like a marauding bull.

Tag was ready, the man was too fat, too slow and too old. The split second he was in range, Tag threw a perfect right cross that landed squarely on his jaw.

Fag Breath went down like a sack of potatoes and hit the tarmac with a nasty slap.

Striker's sinister smile returned to his face, and he gave a knowing wink.

"I reckon that evens things up, Willy. What d'ya say? Do we get to see yer man, or do we finish this out here?"

After the standard macho staring match, Willy broke it and looked over at his remaining standing mate. He didn't like what he saw. The man was pale faced, sweating and hopping from foot to foot.

Willy had bottle, but he knew when he was beaten. The big guy alone looked like he could take on most of the town that was before Carl Froch had turned up.

He stepped away, gave the slowly rising Fag Breath a derisory look and muttered, "Steward's behind the bar, name's Paddy."

Striker pulled on his coat, and pushed past the man.

"That's a fuckin' surprise."

Tag followed the detective into the club, rubbing his knuckles. Hitting someone with boxing gloves on was one thing, bare-fisted was quite another.

"So you box?" said Striker as they approach a rotund, red faced man who was serving pints behind a small bar.

"Since I was a child," said Tag absently. "I was bullied at boarding school, my dad sent me to a club to toughen me up. It was his way."

"Sounds like my old man," said Striker and leant on the bar. "You want a drink?"

Tag nodded. "Why not, I'll have a Jack and Diet."

"You don't drink on duty, son."

"I don't usually knock people unconscious either." Tag held up his grazed knuckles. "Make it a double."

Tag got a fresh orange juice and Striker treated himself to water.

Within minutes Striker had convinced the club steward to allow them access to a small cluttered office that contained the club's CCTV recorder.

He sat at the screen of the surprisingly modern system and turned to the beetroot-faced barman.

"Give us a minute, mate," said Striker.

Word had already reached the steward's drinking clientele that the two men had easily got the better of Willy and his bullyboys. He decided not to argue.

"Don't be long," he managed.

Striker tapped at a dusty keyboard and entered the times he was interested in into the unit.

Four camera shots appeared simultaneously onto the screen; Striker selected the outdoor camera and wound the scene forward at double speed.

Tag watched over his shoulder. Within seconds he heard himself say,

"There."

CHAPTER THIRTEEN

If Wilson was drunk, Sandra was incapable.

They held onto each other as they staggered down Glovers Court. Sandra had fallen over twice since leaving The Greyfriar. Wilson had helped her to her feet and they had laughed so much their sides hurt.

It had been a great day.

They wobbled past the multi-storey car park on Avenham Lane and headed for the pelican crossing that would take them onto Oxford Road.

Sandra fumbled for the button to change the lights to red. Wilson looked behind him and spotted the off-licence.

"Just a minute, love," he slurred. "Let's get a carry out, eh?"

Sandra did her best to focus.

"I don't want another, love." She rummaged in her bag. "I could do with a pack of fags though."

Wilson pushed his hands into his pockets and pulled out notes and change.

He folded two twenties together and handed them to Sandra.

"That's the housekeeping that we spent. You keep hold of that, love, I'll get the fags and a few tins for tonight."

Sandra looked up into Wilson's weathered, scarred face and felt the old stirrings from the past.

"You're a good man, Wilson. Fuckin' salt of the earth, you are."

She leaned forward unsteadily and kissed him on the mouth.

Wilson held onto her and allowed himself the simple pleasure of being close to someone.

Two skinheads walked by, both had their faces covered by scarves. One held a baseball bat.

"Dirty old bastards!" one shouted.

"Fuck off!" countered Sandra.

"Go on, slip the old cow one!" barked the other.

They laughed and sauntered off in the direction of Deepdale.

Wilson studied them. His brain was working overtime; fighting the effects of the alcohol, then he remembered the parade, Charlie's parade, the trouble, the riots.

He shook his head.

"You won't fix this mess with a bat, lad," he said, under his breath.

Tariq Hussain had driven his car to Burnley. Throughout the journey his legs had shaken uncontrollably. His urine had chilled the fabric of his trousers; he felt like a naughty child, embarrassed at his inability to control his bodily functions. More so, he cursed his lack of bravery, his lack of guts that might enable him to stand up to the monster sitting behind him.

He had tried to force himself to think logically, to formulate a rebuttal as he would in a court of law, but his fear controlled his thought process, he was unable to rationalise his lot. He couldn't think any further than the cold muzzle of the gun resting against his neck.

Zachari had remained silent except to give directions. Tariq didn't know what scared him more, the silence or that evil gruff tone. He'd been marched to the door of a small grubby first floor flat, close to the football ground. His legs gave way halfway up the stairs; Zachari rewarded his faltering steps with a punch to the back of his head that left him nauseous and terrified.

He was pushed onto a square landing. Zachari handed him two keys and ordered him to unlock a sturdy door. His hands shook and it took him three attempts to turn the mortice and then remove a large padlock. The moment the door was open he was propelled into a foul-smelling room, darkened by heavy drapes.

"Sit," spat Zachari, and pointed his pistol at an ancient wooden chair that occupied a corner of the tiny space.

Tariq did as ordered, but as his eyes adjusted to the gloom he couldn't look away from a filthy, sheet-less bed that took up almost half the area. He felt his stomach lurch; it was if he was falling from a great height, he was helpless to prevent his last meal spraying from his mouth, covering his trousers in vomit.

"Oh my God!" he spluttered.

He retched over and over. He felt like his very stomach was trying to enter his throat.

More vomit dribbled from his chin. He could taste acid in his mouth. Then came the tears.

A young girl, ten, maybe twelve years old was lying on her back on the mattress. Her head was tilted at the most unnatural angle, black bruises circled her neck, her staring eyes burned into Tariq's memory. She wore one-piece Mickey Mouse pajamas; they had been ripped open.

Zachari sneered at the lawyer's weakness. He couldn't fathom why a man, a Muslim man, someone of wealth and power, should baulk at the death of a female.

"What is wrong with you? You empty your guts over a dead girl? I thought you understood the difference between value and worthlessness? You should be grateful you are capable of helping our glorious cause."

Zachari grabbed Tariq by the chin. His grip was so strong that Hussain cried out in pain.

"Look at you," Zachari mocked. "You're a disgrace, a coward. You have defended many of our soldiers in the infidel courts; yet you could never be a solider yourself. You have no guts. The elders in the council tell me they are indebted to your skill. You have ensured our freedom fighters avoid the shame of British prisons. They tell me you are one of us."

"Never," whispered Tariq. "I will never be..."

Zachari cut Hussain off in his tracks. He raised his gun and pointed it expertly at Tariq's head. The safety catch clicked. Tariq thought he might faint.

"Be quiet! Take off your clothes," he whispered. "All of them."

The QC heard the command, but his arms wouldn't move. His eyes darted between the gun and the child, a child no older than his own twins. From somewhere deep inside his gut, he felt anger overtake his fear. It boiled over, releasing massive amounts of adrenalin into his blood. He shook, but this time it was not fear that caused the tremors in his hands and legs.

He locked eyes with his captor.

His voice was steady; his previously high-pitched fearful tone replaced with the deep note reserved for the courtroom jury.

"You evil bastard, you have murdered a child, taken her life, for what? You are disgusting. You wear the robes of a Muslim, the beard of a holy man, yet you kill an innocent. You are going to tell me this is in the name of Allah, aren't you? Excuse yourself your evil, hide behind a faith that would denounce you as a cold-blooded killer."

Tariq looked at the torn clothing of the girl and then back to Zachari.

"A killer and a paedophile; a rapist, a..."

Tariq was cut short by the blow from Zachari's pistol. He was quick, tremendously strong, and professionally brutal. He smashed the butt of the weapon into Tariq's face over and over, demolishing his eye socket and cheekbone. Seven blows, eight, nine; blood spurted from Tariq's face and splattered the dirty wallpaper; the floor, even the dead child.

Hussain lolled forward in the chair, barely conscious, blood dripping from his eye and pooling at his feet.

Zachari leaned close. He pushed his thumb into Hussain's damaged eye socket. Over the screams of the terrified man, he bellowed. "Take off your clothes!"

He removed his thumb, and slid it slowly up and down against the lawyer's lapel. Streaks of claret soaked into the Savile Row suit.

"Now," he said, his breathing frighteningly normal, belying his violent exertion. "All of them."

Tariq fought to stay conscious, the pain was almost unbearable; he robotically obeyed, his brief attempt at rebellion quelled by the instantaneous violence of his captor.

Once naked, he sat shivering; he'd allowed Zachari to bind his ankles and wrists to the wooden legs of the chair without resistance, he was beaten and he knew it. Now, he watched as Zachari searched the pockets of his bloodstained suit. The suit his wife had bought him for his birthday.

His face was agony. He was convinced he would never see from his left eye again.

Zachari threw down Tariq's jacket in frustration.

"Where are your keys?"

Tariq looked up. Rivers of pain shot down the side of his head. He licked his dry lips.

"What keys?"

Zachari towered over his victim. He was exceptionally tall, standing six feet six inches, with broad muscular shoulders. His head was shaved, but he sported a full black beard. He had the nose of a boxer. At some time in his life the septum had been surgically removed after some traumatic injury. He had numerous facial scars around his eyes that sat deep and black under a flat forehead. The lobe of his right ear was missing.

Despite all of his historical injuries, he was a handsome man, who had attracted women all his life. Evil infidel whores, who taunted him, forced him to defile them.

His arms were unnaturally long, even for a man of such great height, and his forearms poked out from his shirt where most men's wrists would be.

He had the biggest hands Tariq had ever seen.

Zachari sat on the disgusting bed, seemingly unaware that Ismi, the girl he had raised as his own daughter for the last eight years, lay slowly decomposing next to him. His face was close enough to Tariq for him to smell the sourness on his breath.

Zachari lit a cigarette and inhaled deeply.

His voice rasped away, little more than a whisper, he inhaled his smoke every few words.

"I need the keys to your Nelson business, that and the combination to your private safe in the upstairs office, the one used by your incompetent and cowardly cousin."

"Abdullah?"

"Yes, Abdullah. It seems cowardice runs in the family, eh?"

"I...I don't understand," stammered Tariq. "What has my cousin to do with you...with this?"

Zachari blew smoke from his nostrils. It was of little consequence that he might divulge information to the lawyer. Tariq would die this day, no matter what. He could spare himself suffering, he could avoid the death of his wife and family, but he would die here in this stinking flat.

"Your cousin has been holding some items that are of extreme importance to the cause. On his last visit to one of our training facilities in Afghanistan, he brought five very important items home with him. He was a courier, a mule. He considered they would be safe in your office. Unfortunately, it was his job to deliver one of the items to me."

He raised a huge finger and wagged it.

"Just one, just the one, and keep the rest safe until we required them. Not a difficult task. Instead he gave the job to a mere girl."

Zachari stubbed his cigarette and immediately lit a second.

"You know the girl's family, I understand? Chowdry, yes? The father is a fine surgeon is he not? Ayesha, of course, was the apple of her father's eye. Shame Abdullah had been fucking her, rather than concentrating on the task at hand; that and his forthcoming marriage."

Hussain grimaced.

"Oh, you don't know about that? About your young cousin's dirty little secret?"

Zachari laughed, it was a hollow sound, devoid of any emotion, even sarcasm.

"He could have lain with dozens of the cheap whores who hang around handsome young Pakistani boys. But no, he had to break the rules. His mind was not on the job; he became careless. And, more importantly, he was being watched.

A vigilante group, with connections to the security services, knew of his secret. They caught him, took him to a back street garage and dangled his cowardly body from a hook until he told them all he knew. He spilled his guts to the infidels."

Hussain did his best to focus on his captor.

"He told them about Ayesha?"

"The child walked to her death because of his lack of courage. She was shot in the head, my brother."

Zachari stubbed out his second cigarette and blew the last smoke from his lungs. "More importantly, the item was lost."

Tariq was open-mouthed, drying blood covered one side of his swollen face.

"What item? What could be so important?"

Zachari shrugged. "The what, this is of no consequence. The important matter is to replace it, and the replacements are inside your safe."

With his right hand, he pointed his pistol at Hussain. It was a casual gesture, as if aiming a loaded gun at a man's head was the most natural act in the world.

With his left, he picked at his teeth, some morsel of food had suddenly annoyed him. He spoke through his thick fingers, as he fought with the rogue piece of meat.

"You have two choices, Tariq. Give me the keys to your office; I'll need the combination to your safe of course, and then, I shall return."

He found the annoying item and spat it on the floor.

"Then I will kill you swiftly, without pain. Do you understand that?

He stood.

"Alternatively you could cross me, give me the wrong code, and I will return and kill you slowly. Believe me, I know many ways to keep a man alive through agonies you could never imagine. Then, of course there is your family. That pretty wife of yours, your children."

Tariq could take no more. His shoulders began an uncontrollable spasm. He wept.

"Please," he begged. "Not my family, take what you want from me. The keys are in my briefcase in the car."

"And the code?"

"97984...no...no...97985."

Zachari turned, tore one last strip of tape and secured it to Tariq's mouth. "Pray to Allah that you have remembered well, my friend."

Tariq heard Zachari turn the key in the padlock, before his heavy footsteps faded ever further as he trod the stairs to the Mercedes. His ankles and his wrists were numb; the more he struggled against the gaffer tape, the more it seemed to cut into him. The room was silent except for the rumble of traffic from the street below. The curtained window ten feet to his left muffled the sound.

The air smelled of blood and death.

He considered trying to shout for help despite the tape, tried to weigh the consequences of crossing Zachari against what would undoubtedly happen once he had the mystery items he needed. He'd never gambled, but he didn't like the odds of both bets.

CHAPTER FOURTEEN

Grant Bliss walked the perimeter of the rally site. It was just over an acre of spare land that sat adjacent to the council offices on West Paddock, Leyland. It would have been built upon, had it not been for the small matter that below the grassy surface lay an underground lake. The police had tried to stop the event with a legal injunction, but the might of the party's legal team had overturned the order, and over four thousand people would pour onto the field to hear Alistair Sinclair speak this night.

The party faithful had been canvassing, handing out flyers and posters and telling anyone who would listen about the flagship event.

A huge stage had been erected, with a two hundred foot backdrop that would depict stills and video behind the speaker in perfect sync with his dialogue. A lighting rig and public address system on the scale normally reserved for outdoor rock concerts, was being tested. Dozens of workers were applying the finishing touches to what would be the first live televised speech by the leader of the Justice for Great Britain Party.

The BBC, Sky News, CNN and many others would feed the country and the world with the leader's words. Miles of cables were being laid between mobile transmission vehicles. Attractive anchors and battle-hardened Westminster commentators were recording sound bites, or interviewing local politicians from the other major parties.

The EDL and BNP representatives were doing their best to both distance themselves from the event, yet agree with the basic premise of Sinclair's policies.

The small Lancashire town of Leyland, previously known for motor manufacturing, would be catapulted back into the limelight, for an altogether different reason.

Bliss looked upward to the clear blue cloudless sky and smiled. Even the weather was with them.

Bliss was not a big man. Average, would have best described him. Average height and average build. His character, though, was anything but.

Bliss had joined the army as a boy soldier aged sixteen to escape the mean streets of Clapham, London. He was attached to the Royal Engineers and took an apprenticeship in mechanics.

At twenty years old he was posted to Northern Ireland. Within a year he was approached by 14 Intelligence, commonly known as 'The Det.'

Working in plain clothes, on some of the most dangerous streets of Belfast, Bliss had seven kills to his name in as many months.

He served his country until he was thirty-five and was decorated for bravery on three occasions.

Now, twenty years on, he ran his own private security company that turned over five million pounds a year. He employed ex-servicemen from four different countries who all had one thing in common. They would do anything for money.

He'd met Alistair Sinclair at a dinner in Knightsbridge three years earlier. They quickly found that they held the same political beliefs. Within a year, their friendship had developed and the outline of the Justice for Great Britain Party had been formed.

Bliss did not crave political greatness; Sinclair could have all that. Bliss simply wanted to see every enemy of his country where they should be.

In a box.

Bliss had contacts in high places. The information that had led to the capture and assassination of Abdullah Hussain had come from the very top end of the security services, from a man just like himself, a man tired of the red tape that tied the hands of the great and the good.

All his informant had given him was a name and a flight number; that and the certain knowledge the target was preparing to commit an act of terrorism on British soil.

The fact the victim lived in the north of England, not twenty miles from Sinclair's political heartland, was pure luck. The decision to publicise his murder at a time of social unrest had been political genius.

Bliss and his most trusted men had followed Hussain from Heathrow. The tireless work Danny Slade and his surveillance team put in over the weeks that followed was little short of heroic.

They eventually discovered that the boy was nothing more than a mule that had carried a package back to the UK from Pakistan. Despite their disappointment at their seemingly low level target, they kept the nineteen year old under surveillance as he played out his teenage life.

Thousands of man hours went into the round the clock observation, but the package Hussain had smuggled into England remained untouched in the safe of a local barrister. Worse still for the team, there was no sign of the mysterious recipient.

On the very day the violence erupted in Nelson, the surveillance team lost their boy for four hours.

By the time they relocated him, Sinclair and Bliss had made the decision to act. The timing was just too good to miss.

Hussain was snatched from outside his house in Preston.

In the chaos that raged in the area, no one noticed three men break into a backstreet garage and drag a boy inside.

Hussain had been tougher than Bliss had expected, but as any soldier knows, they all talk in the end.

Even Bliss had grimaced as his men forced the meat hook under Hussain's collarbone. Despite a rag being forced into the boy's mouth, he had screamed so loud that Bliss thought he might be heard in the street outside.

They had let him dangle from the hook for thirty minutes without posing a single question.

As Hussain moaned in agony, Bliss had casually prepared the sign to go around the boy's neck and set the camera for the money shot. The sign had been Sinclair's idea.

He was a man for finishing touches.

The boy had told them all about Ayesha, the drop and the codenamed recipient, before the fire was lit under him, but Bliss knew it was best to be sure; besides, it would look good in the photograph.

The girl had been a major bonus. When the tap on Abdullah's mobile messaging first revealed the affair between them, little did they know that the boy would use her for the drop itself.

She may well have been an innocent party, but this was a war; and collateral damage happened in conflict, ask any soldier.

The images of the dead girl were priceless. They had ensured that the violence on the streets had festered, infected and inflamed the very hearts of the Muslim community.

The police would soon lose control, and out of anarchy would come order, the kind of order that Bliss understood perfectly.

Finding Ayesha Chowdry was simple. Bliss himself shot her, watched her bleed. He had removed the package from the girl's bag and slipped it into her lifeless hand. Then he posed her, not just the small square box, but also her clothes, her limbs, until they were just…perfect.

She was beautiful in death. Had Slade not been there, he would have been tempted to touch her further.

He would treasure those photographs for years to come.

They were disturbed by a nosey beat cop and had been forced to leave the package. It would have been nice to know exactly what it was. His mole at MI6 had stayed as firm on that snippet of information, as he did about the identity of the man Abdullah had called, 'The Fisherman', the intended recipient of the item.

The spooks could have the address of their Fisherman as payment in kind. Let them have him. Bliss had achieved exactly what he'd wanted.

Half the north of England was on fire.

Bliss reached the back of the stage.

Danny Slade was bawling commands at three of his temporary guards who were erecting barriers.

Bliss didn't interrupt, rather he waited until Slade noticed him.

His right hand man barked another set of orders, before turning and loping over.

Slade nodded his acknowledgement.

"Boss."

"Danny, how're things progressing with the stage?"

"On time, sir. Everything is as planned."

Bliss smiled, "Good…good, Danny, that's what I would expect from you."

Slade nodded again. It was a measured movement, from a man who calculated everything he did. Nothing was left to chance. He was a methodical planner with an exact eye for detail. He considered every possibility; born into the family of 'what can go wrong will go wrong'.

On the very rare occasions that things did go out of kilter, Bliss knew Danny Slade would fix it the only way he knew how.

With extreme violence.

Daniel Charles Slade had been a corporal, attached to 14 Intelligence Unit. Bliss had been his commanding officer. Ireland had been their battleground.

To Danny, loyalty was the most important thing in life, not just loyalty for the sake of it, but earned loyalty.

Grant Bliss deserved every drop of devotion a man could squeeze from himself.

To Danny, he was a hero. When other officers shirked their responsibility, Bliss did not. If a man deserved to die, Grant Bliss ensured life extinct.

Grant placed an arm around Danny's shoulder and spoke quietly. Even outside, you had to be careful.

"What news do we have on the device, Danny?"

Slade was taller than Bliss by three inches, and as the song goes, 'meaner than a junk yard dog'.

"Still waiting for the tech fuckers to work out the detonation system, boss."

Bliss grimaced, "And why is that, so close to zero hour?"

Slade knew his stuff. "Because we have to be able to throw the rucksack over a fence, it has to be totally stable. That isn't a big problem, C4 is very reliable in that way as you know, but because it is so inert, it's a fucker to set off, especially with a mobile signal."

Bliss pursed his lips. "I'm sure you won't let me down, Danny."

"No, sir," he said.

"That's what I thought…and the delivery system?"

"I think I have that in hand, sir."

Bliss slid his arm away.

"Good man, Danny, good man."

Slade was much more than a soldier of fortune, much more than a man of violence, and much more than a meticulous planner. He was a judge of men. He could find the right man for the right job.

As he walked back towards the small group of guards erecting the security barriers, he checked out one man in particular.

A small wiry guy with a widow's peak was working his bollocks off and berating his two workmates for being slow.

Slade approached him.

"What's your name, mate?" he asked.

The man wiped sweat from his receding hairline. He looked surprised to see Slade.

"What...me? Err... Barry, boss."

He held out a dirty hand.

Danny Slade took it and shook firmly. "Barry?"

The guard took a moment for the question to sink in. "Oh, Barry Williams, boss, sorry."

Slade released his grip.

"Good stuff, Barry. I like a man who isn't afraid of hard work."

Barry smiled revealing uneven, tobacco stained teeth.

"That's me, Mr. Slade; I'm a grafter, me."

"I can see that," said Danny thoughtfully. "Good man, keep it up."

Barry wanted to keep the conversation going. After all, it was never a bad idea to keep in with the head honcho, but Slade had turned on his heels.

"Thanks, boss!" he shouted after him.

Danny stopped in his tracks, as if he'd forgotten something.

He strode over to Barry and dropped his voice.

"Tell you what, Barry, I like the look of you. I bet you're the kind of man Mr. Sinclair would like around him."

Barry beamed, couldn't believe his luck.

"Oh aye, boss, I mean, yeah, that's me. I think Mr. Sinclair has got it right, me. Got them Pakis on the run, hasn't he?"

Slade smiled, exposing ten grand's worth of dentistry.

"Yes, I suppose he has, hasn't he?"

He dropped his tone further. "Look, Barry, I need lads like you, hard-working, call a spade a spade type of lads, ask no questions kind of lads." Danny tapped his nose conspiratorially," Know what I mean?"

Barry's chest was going to burst. He could feel it.

"Deffo, boss, that's me, that is. Ask no questions get told no lies, eh?"

Slade chuckled. It didn't suit him to laugh. He didn't have the face for it, too many battles, too many injuries. He had a face that scared small children and grown men in equal quantity.

"Exactly that, Barry." He rested his hand on Barry's shoulder. "Tell you what, matey. You nip and see me tonight, straight after the rally. I'll give you a little job to do. Earn you an extra five hundred quid. Maybe earn you some cred with the big man too."

Barry was definitely going to explode.

Wait while Gina hears about this!

He almost asked what the job was, until he remembered he wasn't supposed to ask questions.

He tapped his own nose, mirroring Danny's earlier move, but only managed to look like a pantomime villain.

"You can count on Barry, boss."

Slade walked away, the firm dry ground beneath his feet, the late afternoon sun warm on his back and a massive smile on his face.

The tech boys needed to come good, and come good soon.

Tomorrow was going to be a big day.

CHAPTER FIFTEEN

Wilson stepped out of the shop and into the last of the evening sunshine. He wore a puzzled expression.

Sandra was leaning against the traffic light post waiting for him to return with cans and cigarettes, doing her best to focus.

"What's up, love?" she slurred.

Wilson scratched his head. "Bloke in there won't serve me, says I'm pissed already."

Sandra laughed out loud. "Well yer are pissed, you old bastard."

"I am a bit, but I could still do with another couple just to, you know, just to, finish off like."

Sandra wobbled toward him and took his hand.

"Never mind, love. We'll walk up past mine and go to the Paki shop up Frenchwood." She let out a loud burp. "He'll serve any fucker, him."

They negotiated the crossing and ambled up Oxford Street.

"Do a left here," said Sandra. "You can nip through, past St Augustine's school and onto Manchester Road, shop's just up from there."

Directly across from the Catholic primary school was Jamea Masjid. Sandra had walked past the mosque hundreds of times, had chatted to the guys entering or leaving, or simply watched the kids running about in the playground of the school opposite.

Her own boys had attended St Augustine's, she had stood with the other mums waiting for her kids, chatting shit and swapping stories of ne'er-do-well husbands on the pavement outside.

The mosque and its visitors had been as much a part of the landscape of Avenham as the pub or the newsagents.

As she and Wilson turned the corner from Oxford Street, Sandra was shocked at what she saw.

"What the fuck is going on, Wilson?"

The troubles had passed Sandra by. She had been out drinking herself to oblivion when the rioting had started, then she had her run in with the taxi driver, been hospitalised, met Wilson, and gone straight back on it. The fact that the town centre had gone unscathed had meant that Sandra and Wilson had walked around the bars that afternoon in relative calm.

Wilson smoothed his moustache with a thumb and finger.

"It's about the parade, I reckon."

A makeshift barricade blocked their path. Around twenty Asian men manned it, some had their faces covered, others carried sticks or clubs. As Sandra and Wilson drew closer, the men turned toward them, one raised his hand.

"Go back!" he shouted.

"What d'ya mean, go back? I fuckin' live here!" bawled Sandra. She focused on the youth; despite his face being partially covered by a scarf, she recognised him.

"That's you, Jala, init? For fuck's sake, I've known you all your life, yer dad 'n all."

Jala pulled down his scarf; he was young and despite his macho bravado, he looked scared. His mouth was turned downward.

"We're protecting our mosque, our houses. There are no cops over this side. Just go back. We don't want trouble."

A second, bigger man, with a full beard, pushed Jala to one side. He held a section of scaffolding pipe in his hand.

"Do as you are told, woman. Go back to other side. Go and wallow in your filth with the other infidels!"

Sandra squared her shoulders; her head had cleared enough to know when she was being insulted.

"Oh yeah, and what are you gonna do about it if I don't?"

The man ignored Sandra, turned to Wilson and raised the pipe.

"Take your whore away, before I cave in your skulls."

Wilson was sobering quickly. He grabbed Sandra by the arm and pulled her back. She struggled to free herself, but Wilson was too strong.

"Get the fuck off me, Wilson! I'm not scared of a few Pakis."

Wilson glared at the man with the scaffold pipe.

"Neither am I, love; just step back."

"Go!" shouted the man.

Wilson stood his ground.

"Why don't you put that scaffold down and come and fight me, big man? Instead of havin' a go at a woman, eh?"

The crowd behind the barrier was starting to get restless. Some began to shout words of encouragement to the bearded man. Some were on their mobile phones, making calls or videoing the stand-off.

Sandra taunted the man.

"He won't do that, Wilson, he's no bottle, just like the rest of the Paki bastards."

More men were arriving by the second. The crowd behind the barricade had grown from twenty to forty. They poured from the mosque and the streets behind.

Wilson's head was full of booze and anger. He thought about his son, about Charlie, about how brave he had been, about how he had been blown to pieces by the Taliban. Men with beards just like the man that faced him now had cowardly left a bomb on the road, didn't dare to face him; to fight him.

Wilson took off his coat and rolled up the sleeves of his shirt, just as he had done hundreds of times before, when he was about to punch his way to a prize.

"Come on, son. Are you a man or what?"

The crowd began to chant.

Sandra folded her arms defiantly, seemingly oblivious to the massive danger in front of her.

"Knock the fucker out, Wilson," she said flatly.

The man dropped the pipe to the floor and the crowd cheered.

Wilson had fought the gypsies in Ireland, been the only Englishman there, taken their money and walked away. What was the difference?

He felt the old thrill of excitement, felt the adrenaline flow through him, his only focus was the man about to climb the barricade in front of him.

He was much younger than Wilson, fitter, quicker and sober.

The bearded man vaulted the barrier, turned to the crowd and raised his arms like a champion entering a boxing ring.

What had been a quiet defiance, intended to protect homes and families, had turned into a baying mob.

Wilson looked into the eyes of the man that faced him and saw the merest hint of fear. He stretched his neck and shoulders. He felt no pain in his ribs; the alcohol had seen to that.

He clenched his fists, tucked in his chin and circled his opponent the way he had done all his life.

His foe was taller and wiry. Wilson had the bulk of a heavyweight gone to seed. It was like a greyhound facing a bullmastiff.

Wilson beckoned him on with a wave of his fist.

The man lurched forward and launched a kick to Wilson's groin, catching him on the thigh. Wilson responded with a head-butt that glanced off the man's eyebrow and followed it up with a vicious left hook to his ribs.

He felt impact flow through his knuckles, wrist and forearm and knew he had done damage.

The man cried out and stepped back, dropping his right arm and sucking in air.

Wilson showed the man his left again, never intending to throw it, just to move him toward the devastating right hook, which was his trademark.

The man stepped into range and Wilson threw the right. Ten years ago he would have connected and the fight would have been over. Today, however, he hit thin air and knocked himself off balance in the process.

The man was on him, wind-milling punches into his kidneys and the back of his head.

The crowd was screaming, and had grown in size, maybe a hundred strong. Some younger men attempted to climb the barrier, but were pulled back by the more senior spectators.

Despite landing several punches the man had no technique, and Wilson simply tucked up, dipped at the waist and regained his balance.

The man tried to grab Wilson around the neck and pull him to the ground. Wilson ducked away again and caught his opponent with an uppercut. It wasn't as sweet as he wanted but was enough to send the man reeling backwards, blood pouring from his lip where he had bitten through it.

Despite the noise of the crowd, Wilson could hear Sandra shouting encouragement somewhere off to his left.

He locked eyes with the man for a second time. This time he knew he had him. Wilson may have been older and slower, but his pure technical prowess and bull strength meant this was a no-contest.

He beckoned the man toward him again, but he stayed put, flashing looks over to the baying mob behind him, unsure whether to run back over the barrier to safety and shame, or face Wilson and certain physical damage.

Wilson made up his mind for him. He stepped forward and threw three sharp punches at the man's head. He managed to dodge two but the third caught him square on his cheekbone; Wilson felt the tell-tale bone on bone reverberation, all the way to his elbow. The one he always felt when he had caught an opponent clean. The man went down.

Wilson stood over his unconscious opponent feeling as wired as he had ever felt in his life. He wanted to stamp on his head, turn his face to mush, take his revenge for Charlie.

He was so engulfed in his own fury, he didn't notice the first men climbing the barricade and running toward him.

Westland yawned as he stepped into the last of the shops that had cameras facing the street. It was a video rental store, which appeared to have more 'top shelf' titles than top shelves.

He considered that this detective lark was all very well on the television, but in truth it was pretty boring. All it seemed to entail was walking door to door, asking the same questions and hoping to see yet another few seconds of footage of the man they were looking for. All they had managed to see so far were shots of him walking further toward the town of Burnley, dragging his luggage and a young girl behind him.

Striker, on the other hand, seemed immune to tiredness or boredom. The man was a machine.

What had been a sunny day had turned to chilly dusk and Tag had zipped up his hoodie against the cold. As he stepped inside the shop, he reversed the process as the place was sweltering.

Striker introduced himself and showed his ID to a small pug-faced man with glasses that were thick enough to start the great fire of London if left in the wrong place.

"Police? No problem with police," said the man, in an eastern European accent. "Everything legal here, no young girls, no funny stuff, all good."

"I don't care about your smut," said Striker flatly. "I want to look at that." He pointed to the ancient camera that poked out over an awning outside the shop.

The man shrugged. "Broken," he said.

Striker turned to Westland. "Go and stand outside, son."

Tag was about to complain about the temperature, considered it futile and walked into the chill, muttering more Irish, American and ginger jibes.

Striker leaned over the counter to get a better view of the back room of the shop. A prehistoric tube television sat on a desk, surrounded by old VHS boxes and soft porn magazines.

Westland appeared centre stage on the screen. The picture was blurred, but it was the young cop, no doubt.

Striker struck like a viper, grabbing the proprietor with a ham of a fist, lifting him from his feet.

"Broken, eh?"

"Let go me! I complain! You can't do this!" spluttered the man.

Westland ran back into the shop as Striker was starting to shake the shopkeeper like a terrier with a rat.

"Sarge! Put the guy down, eh?" He walked over, stood precariously between the men, and played good cop.

"Sorry about that, mate," he said, brushing down the flustered shopkeeper.

The man was pale. "He crazy!"

Westland nodded. "Yes, sir, he is. He's not quite right." Tag tapped the side of his head. "Best you let him see the tape."

Striker glared at Tag. "Crazy?"

Westland smiled meekly. "Come on, boss. Let's get this over with."

The shopkeeper stood aside.

"When I say broken, I mean machine broken, no times, no search, just record."

Tag continued with his placating tone.

"That's okay, mate, we'll just have a quick look and be out of your way."

The pair walked into the cluttered room. Striker had not forgiven his prodigy.

"Crazy?"

Tag shrugged. "Well come on, Striker; I've known you what? Thirty six hours, and you've tried to throttle two people already."

Striker snorted and started to wind back the tape.

"No search facility," he said.

"That's what the guy was trying to tell you, Rocky."

"Shut up and watch, we'll have to wind it back in play mode until we see him."

Tag slumped into a flea-bitten armchair. "That will take forever."

"Just watch," barked Striker.

The old machine whirred away as the two cops watched dusk turn to daylight, cars reverse along the road, and people walk backwards along the pavement. An hour passed. Pug Face was starting to get restless.

"I need close," he shouted from a safe distance. "There is trouble tonight here."

Striker was having none of it. "Shut up and watch your porn," he said.

"No! I cannot. Trouble coming; English and Pakistan fight."

Striker hit the 'rev x 3' button to speed things up, but stopped suddenly.

He hit forward then paused the frame.

"What is it?" asked Tag.

"A Mercedes," said Striker. The black vehicle was clearly visible, as was the private plate. "Tariq Hussain's Mercedes."

Tag looked puzzled.

Striker turned in his chair and laid his hands out palm up.

"Tariq Hussain QC? Abdullah Hussain's cousin?"

A light came on in Westland's head. "The dead kid in the garage?"

"One and the same," explained Striker, pulling the tape from the machine.

Tag scratched his head.

"So let me get this straight, we think Abdullah gave this mystery package to Ayesha. She was to deliver it to the guy we know as Mustapha the taxi driver; but he wasn't there, he'd done a runner, he'd been compromised by letting Sandra escape."

"Yes," said Striker.

"This mystery vigilante group tortured Abdullah until he told them of the drop, and they shot Ayesha Chowdry."

"Correct, two points," said Striker. "Actually, I think you turned up and scared them off. Either way, Mustapha had been long gone. Remember he took Din's taxi about nine in the morning and that clean up on his flat would have taken hours."

Tag pointed at the old VHS tape in Striker's hand.

"So we have a professional terrorist, waiting for a delivery of a package. This piece of circuit board is so important, two people are dead just for touching it, yet the shooters left it for us to find. And what has the lawyer got to do with all this? Where does he come into it? How come his car is in this area? Coincidence?"

Striker stood.

"I don't believe in coincidence, son. Come on."

Errol Graham sat in his office, lights out, head bowed, exhausted. His investigation was going nowhere. Despite thousands of man hours, hundreds of interviews and the best forensic teams working around the clock, they had nothing.

Abdullah Hussain had walked out of his house and disappeared into thin air, before turning up dead.

One witness had reported a dark-coloured saloon in the area of the lock up garage around the right kind of time-frame, no registration, no description of the occupants.

Useless.

A forensic search of Hussain's laptop had revealed he visited some pretty radical websites. Then again, he had a fervent interest in lesbian pornography. Did that make him lesbian?

The girl was as clean as a whistle, hard-]working, good grades. Other than the fact that Ayesha had met Abdullah once at a family wedding, there was no evidence that they even knew each other.

Graham rubbed his face; he needed a break, something to work with, anything.

The knock on his door was sharp and demanding.

He clicked on his desk lamp.

"Come," he said.

The officer that stood framed by the doorway looked pale. Graham didn't recognise him.

"Yes?" he demanded.

"Sir, you are needed in the control room. It's urgent, Mr. Potts sent me to get you."

Potts was the officer in charge of the public order side of the incident. He was probably under even more pressure than Graham. The cost of policing the violence was astronomical and the support from neighbouring forces was depleted, as they too were feeling the force of the social unrest in their own areas.

Every officer they could muster was out on the street, the cells were full, the hospitals were full and there seemed no end to the anger and brutality between the communities.

"Tell him I'll be right there," said Graham.

The cop turned on his heels and Graham searched his pockets for aspirin. A band was playing marching tunes in his head.

He stood wearily and headed for the lift.

Within seconds he was standing in the control room;

He found it a dimly lit centre of activity, each controller moving teams of officers around the city with calm voices. Large white-boards with lists of call-signs and hours of duty were constantly updated by the control room inspector, together with inventories of reserve support units awaiting deployment.

The second list looked extremely thin.

These operators worked blind, using telephone and radio communication to complete their tasks.

To the left of the room was a separate area that contained eleven television screens. Here, streamed images from the city's CCTV systems were constantly scrutinised by specially trained civilian operators. The remote cameras, mounted around the hot spots of Preston could be panned and zoomed at will, and the footage used to deploy officers and subsequently prove guilt or innocence of offences.

William Potts was hunched over one screen. Graham stood at his shoulder.

"You wanted me, Will?"

Potts turned, he had the look of a beaten man. His voice was level, but underneath Graham could sense the note of fear in it.

"Jesus, Errol. You need to see this."

Potts wound back the footage, before hitting play.

The images were crystal clear. They came from a camera mounted high on a building on the corner of Oxford Street and Charlotte Street.

A group of men were erecting a homemade barricade in front of a mosque.

"That's the Jamea Masjid," said Potts. "The locals must have been feeling a bit vulnerable. We haven't had any incidents in the area until now, but the rioting has been moving ever closer. I've had mobile PSUs keeping an eye, but I had to take them off about three hours ago to relieve the lads on Deepdale."

Potts wound the footage forward. The barricade had grown, as had the crowd manning it.

"Watch now," he said, pointing toward the bottom of the screen. "The two figures here, the man and the woman walking up to the barricade."

Graham looked in his top pocket and removed his reading glasses. He peered at the two people, definitely a man and woman. They looked in their forties, and from the way they walked, a little worse for wear.

There was an altercation, the woman was arguing with a man, there was some waving of arms and the small crowd seemed agitated. Then a man jumped the barrier and there was a fight. As the contest between the two men commenced, the crowd grew further.

The older drunken man was a boxer. Even from the high vantage point that the camera gave the viewer, you could see that he was a fighter, the way he moved, the way he threw his punches.

What Graham couldn't understand, was why on earth anyone would undertake such a crazy exchange in front of what had quickly become a mob.

The fight lasted less than five minutes, but in those minutes the crowd behind the barrier had more than doubled.

Then, as the younger man went down, the crowd broke ranks and poured over the makeshift structure they had erected.

They surrounded the man and woman; some had sticks or bats. They engulfed the pair, raining down blow after blow. Graham could see the man vainly trying to get to the woman, swinging punches wildly, throwing people off him, deflecting the dozens of strikes.

The more he fought the more the crowd came upon him.

Then the woman was struck by what appeared to be a scaffolding pipe. A spurt of blood erupted from the crown of her head, the sight of which only seemed to inflame the throng further.

Her arms flailed upward, she went down and the mob fell upon her. There was a flash of steel.

Graham spoke without thinking. "Oh my God, they're going to..." He didn't finish his sentence. He wanted to turn away from the screen, but he couldn't. He was a hare in the headlights, glued to the shocking images unfolding in front of him.

A man was kneeling on the woman's chest, hacking, sawing. The throng surrounding what Graham prayed was the woman's corpse was jumping up and down, screaming, baying for more, the pack instinct had taken over, the most basic of human instincts had prevailed.

The unstoppable hunger for violence had to be fed with blood. Graham had lost sight of the man; he too had fallen to the floor under the mêlée.

The detective had seen so many things in his life. So many things he would rather forget, things that only ever came to him in his darkest nightmares, yet he had not been prepared to witness what unfolded in front of him.

A man, no a boy, no more than sixteen or seventeen, was standing on an oil drum; playing to the crowd, a smile on his face.

In his left hand he held a knife and in his right, the head of Sandra Mackintosh.

To the left of the boy, the crowd parted and the corpse of William 'Fighting Billy' Wilson was being dragged along the tarmac by a rope around his neck. Minutes later, he was suspended from a lamp post as the crowd danced around it in victory, hung like an animal after slaughter.

Graham realised he had his fist in his mouth and he had drawn blood on his knuckles.

"Where the fuck were our boys, Will?"

Potts barely mumbled his answer, a mixture of shame and defeat in his voice.

"Just out of shot, six constables and one sergeant, at the junction."

Graham was incredulous. He pointed at the screen, hand shaking.

"And they watched this? Stood by and fucking watched this?"

Potts kept his voice as calm as he could. "What the hell did you expect them to do, detective? Do you want to see seven more bodies hanging from the fucking lamp posts? They had no support! We don't have any more cops! Understand? No more fucking cops!"

Graham flew into a rage. The other controllers stopped their work and turned toward the outburst of anger and frustration.

"Well, get me some! Turn out detectives, get them some kit, they're coppers too, Will. They've all done the training, check the pen pushers sat on their backsides in offices, anything and anyone who can hold a shield and a baton, then ring the Chief and demand some more support. I want this street cordoned off now and I want arrests made. I don't give a flying fuck who we upset. I don't care if you have to storm the mosque, I want those fuckers who did this locked up within the hour. Am I clear?"

Pott's voice remained low and level. He wasn't a man prone to temper. He was tough and streetwise, but anger never got anybody anywhere.
"You know what will happen when we go in there, don't you, Errol? It will be like a warzone."
Graham looked at his long-time friend and ally from under a furrowed brow. His temper had subsided slightly, but he spoke through gritted teeth.
"If we don't, the troops will. Do you want to see that? Imagine how the Paras will deal with this, Will. This will make Bloody Sunday look like a picnic. Find me some people before it's taken out of our hands."

Striker strode off toward the junction where the Mercedes had exited onto the main road. Tag hurried behind and shivered against the chill.
They turned the corner into a narrow street.
Twenty yards further down, Striker stopped and looked at the ground. As darkness had fallen and the air temperature had changed, shiny dew had formed on the tarmac. The road beneath Striker's feet was lighter in colour; a dry oblong was obvious to see.
Striker felt the age old tingle, the hairs on his neck standing proud to attention.
"It was parked here," he said.
Tag stuffed his hands into his pockets, a look of disbelief on his face. "Of all the parked cars in the street, this space just happened to be the Merc? Jesus, Striker, I didn't realise you were related to Tonto. What next, you put your ear to the ground and tell me when the Indians will arrive?
Striker ignored the sarcasm. He'd heard all the comments before, but he was rarely wrong. He stood dead centre on the dry patch of road and turned to his right.
"Where are you?" he muttered.

"You talking to the wind now, Striker?" chirped Tag, keeping a safe distance from the detective, just in case his comments weren't taken in good humour.

"Very funny, Westland, but our man was here, no doubt."

Tag shook his head.

"Okay so what does your spider-sense tell you to do now?"

Striker pointed to a half glazed door, directly across the street. It appeared to be an entrance to a first floor flat above an empty shop.

"There," he said. "Let's have a look in there."

Tag followed behind the detective. He was starting to feel like a lap dog, attached by an imaginary leash, to a raging bull crossed with a Marvel comic hero.

"This is someone's flat," said Tag. "We can't just go wandering in..."

Striker pushed the unlocked door open. Behind it was a set of uncarpeted wooden stairs. Weeks, maybe months, of junk mail filled the square space at their feet.

Tag was about to speak, but Striker put a thick finger to his lips and gave him the hard stare.

They started their silent climb. Tag's feelings changed instantly, from his comic lack of understanding to the first pangs of nerves. He could feel his heart start to race; hear the blood pump in his ears. Whatever Striker had felt, he had no way of knowing, but there was something very wrong at the top of those stairs.

At the summit was a single formidable door, secured by a padlock. There was barely enough room for the two men to stand side by side.

This time Striker didn't wait for Tag to use his body strength to attempt a break in. Instead he threw his own massive bulk at the door. Not only did the padlock give way, but the hinges splintered from the frame and the whole door slammed to the floor.

Both men piled through the opening, ready to face whatever lay in wait.

Tag lurched to the left, Striker to the right.

Both were stopped in their tracks by the scene that faced them.

Tag heard Striker whisper.

"Oh Jesus, Mary and Joseph."

Westland's eyes adjusted to the gloom of the room, but it was the overpowering smell that filled his senses.

There was a naked man, tied to a chair; his head lolled forward, his face covered in blood. Then he turned to the bed in the corner.

He put his hand to his mouth, convinced he would puke. He couldn't take his eyes from the dead girl. He was frozen, locked in a world of death and violence, the like of which he had never encountered. First it was Ayesha, now a young innocent child.

He would never forget the staring glassy eyes, the angle of her slender neck, the grey colour of her skin. He felt his stomach lurch. He wasn't going to be able to control himself.

Striker grabbed him by the shoulder and pulled him backward toward the exit.

"Not in here, son, spill it outside."

Tag stumbled back down the stairs, bile in his throat. He lost his footing and slid the last three risers, landing with a thump on his back. Junk mail slid from the hall and into the street as he attempted to find purchase and scrambled to his feet. He managed three more steps to the pavement and threw up his lunch.

The young cop wiped his mouth with the back of his hand and took deep breaths of clean air. He rested his hands on his knees, like a marathon runner who had just crossed the finish line.

"Fuck, fuck, fuck!" he said, spitting out pieces of half-digested kebab.

Tag heard footsteps and Striker appeared in the doorway.

"The guy's alive, son, it's Hussain, the lawyer, our man was in the Merc."

Tag pushed his frame upright and managed a nod.

Striker held out his mobile.

"When you've finished throwing your breakfast everywhere, ring for the cavalry, will you?"

The 'cavalry' arrived in the form of a paramedic unit, local detectives, a sprinkling of uniforms and a forensic unit.

Striker sat in the back of the ambulance with Tariq Hussain. A medic was cleaning the wounds to his face. Tariq's body shook. The once confident QC was reduced to a shivering wreck.

The man in green turned to the detective.

"He needs a doctor, and soon. He has a fractured eye socket. He's in shock."

"Yeah," said Striker. "Go for a quick walk, son. I need a chat with your man here."

The medic shook his head, dropped his swabs in a bowl and stepped from the ambulance.

"Remember me?" said Striker.

"How could I forget?" winced the lawyer. "You're such a people person."

Striker shrugged.

"So he took you from your office?"

Tariq nodded, but before he could answer, a light came on in his head. His voice was sharp, insistent.

"You must get some people to my house, my wife, my family."

"It's done," said Striker. "They're safe."

Hussain seemed to deflate, the weight of the world lifted off his slender shoulders. He considered his words.

"He's a terrorist," he said. "He killed the girl."

"I know."

Hussain looked up, a movement that hurt him and he winced. "But you don't know, he wanted something from my safe, my office, in Nelson, something Abdullah was supposed to deliver to him, a replacement."

"What was it?"

"The same item Ayesha was taking to him."

The medic edged his way to the back of the ambulance.

"We need to get this man to hospital, detective."

Striker twisted his body and eyed the man.

"Two minutes," he spat.

The medic was fifty, maybe older. He'd seen enough shit to last him a lifetime.

"Now," he said. "Talk later, big fella, at the hospital."

Striker paused, took a look at Hussain and nodded.

"Okay, I'll send an officer to take a full statement. There's a team on its way to your office now. Don't worry, Hussain, we've got it covered."

He stepped down from the ambulance and strode over to Westland, who was standing shivering on the pavement outside the flat.

"You alright now, son?"

Westland nodded. "Suppose so, it isn't every week I find two dead bodies. I'm beginning to think you are bad for my health."

Striker pulled a pack of gum from his pocket and offered Tag a strip.

"If you want to head home, son, you can. I'll take it from here. It will only get worse from now on."

Tag unwrapped his piece and pushed it in his mouth. He shook his head. "I've come this far, Striker. I was never one for doing the sensible thing."

"Good lad," Striker slapped him on the back. "You've done okay, son."

Tag didn't feel like he had done much of anything, apart from puke and cover himself in shit, but he took the compliment.

"What about the Merc?"

"Circulated, along with the best pictures I could get from Mustapha's fake documents and the CCTV we collected tonight."

Tag gestured toward two men exiting the flat door in white paper suits. "They got anything?"

Striker shook his head. "Nothing we don't already have so far. It will take them most of the night to complete a full fingertip search."

The pair strolled toward their car.

Parked directly behind Striker's Audi was a black BMW M3 saloon. It glistened in the streetlights. Leaning casually against it was a man who smoked a small metal pipe. It was the kind Tag had seen for sale in the various 'head' shops in Amsterdam.

The guy didn't look like a pot smoker. He was of small, wiry build; mid fifties with short, salt and pepper hair. He had a weathered face, with deep wrinkles on his forehead. Tag considered he could have been a trawler-man. Either way, he had spent many hours in the elements. The guy was casually dressed in a leather bomber jacket, that would not have been out of place in an eighties cop show, faded denims and CAT boots.

As they approached, he tapped the contents of his pipe out on the heel of his boot, checked it was empty and pushed it into his pocket.

He straightened. Tag did not like the look of the guy. He wasn't big, by any means. He was probably twice Westland's age, but he had trouble written all over him.

As they drew level, he spoke.

He had a thick Glaswegian accent, guttural and flat, calm.
"You'll be Striker then?"
Striker stopped.
"And you are?"
The Scot extended a hand.
"A friend of the family," he answered.
Striker didn't take the hand. The man shrugged and pushed it back into his pocket.
"Please yersel'."
Tag took a step back, there was something about this guy he didn't like. His eyes were cold, yet they flashed between Striker and Westland, alive and sharp.
"Dinnae worry, son. I'm no here to cause ye any bother."
Striker spoke to Tag, but didn't take his eyes from the man.
"He's the Firm, son, MI6."
"No exactly," said the man. "But I am here to help you and the big man here."
Striker walked on.
"We don't need your kind of help."
Striker pointed the remote at his Audi and there was a double blip-blip as the doors were released.
The man turned slightly.
"So ye won't want t' know what was in the wee package Ayesha Chowdry was carrying t' yer man's flat, then?"
Striker stopped dead.
"Are you fuckin' me around, sunshine?"
The man raised his hands.
"Not at all, big man, I'm serious, gen up."
Striker turned back.
"I'm all ears."
The man zipped his coat.
"It's a long story, and at my age, I'm starting to feel the cold. Is there anywhere a man can get a good pint of Guinness around here?"
Tag opened his mouth without thinking. "There's a KSC club just around the corner."
Striker shot him a death stare and he made a mental note to keep quiet from now on.

The man smiled to reveal perfect teeth. He noticed Striker clock them.

He touched them with his forefinger.

"Nice, eh? I needed some new pegs after the old ones were removed in unfortunate circumstances."

"Shame," said Striker.

The man ignored the sergeant, and turned to Tag.

"So show me where this club is, son, they'll welcome a good Catholic boy like me."

"I'm not too sure about that, mate," muttered Tag. "It's this way."

The three men walked onto the main road and back toward the club. Police support units, mini buses with metal grills on the windscreens, filled with helmet-clad officers, cruised past small groups of Asian youths forming on each street corner.

"Looks like they're expecting a wee bit of bother," said the Scot."

As they reached the KSC, the same three bouncers were standing outside. This time they had added pickaxe handles to their armoury.

"So do these boys," added Tag.

This time there was no challenge other than a cold stare from the men; Striker, Tag and their mystery guest were allowed access without an issue.

They stepped into the warmth of the bar. The national smoking ban didn't appear to be enforced, and every table appeared to be occupied by chain-smoking beer drinking men, dressed in various levels of working clothes and hi-visibility jackets.

"Just my kinda place," chirped their guest, rubbing his hands.

Tag bought the drinks. This time he got his Jack and Coke, a pint of Guinness for the Scot and Striker's customary water.

They huddled themselves into a corner, as far away from the cigarette smoke as possible and sat.

The Scot guzzled at his pint, quaffing half of it in one go. Then, much to the disgust of his company, removed the pipe from his pocket, and started to fill it with tobacco.

"Do you have to?" snapped Striker.

The man looked across the table at the bulk of Ewan Striker, lit the pipe and exhaled smoke over his shoulder, away from the men.

Tag noticed his eyes again. If there was anything at all behind them, it wasn't on show.

"Live and let live, big man," he said. "After all, isn't what this is all about?"

Striker leaned in.

"Let's just get on with this, shall we? Time is money."

The Scot nodded, took another drink and stowed his pipe. He extended his hand for a second time.

"Des," he said.

This time Striker took it and shook. Then it was Tag's turn. The man's hand was like sandpaper.

"Westland, Tag Westland," he said.

"Pleased to meet you, pal," said the Scot.

He settled back in his chair, and began.

"My father gave me some good advice when I was a wean, in my early teens," said Des.

"He told me that there were only two kinds of men, wankers and liars. You know what I mean, by wanker, Striker, you being a Yank n'all?

After all, you guys over the pond use 'jerk off', don't you?

It doesn't have the same ring to it, does it?

The Greeks have a word for it, malaka.

That has a good guttural sound to it, eh?"

Striker had lost patience with Des already.

"Just fuckin' get on with your tale, son. I'm not interested in your early formative years, or how many words you know for wanker."

Des leaned toward the detective. He voice was quiet and measured.

"If you keep on trying to intimidate me with your muscle, son, you will need the same dentist as me. Understand?"

Tag turned referee.

"Come on, guys, let's just play nice, eh?"

Des shrugged. "The boy might look a bit of a ponce, but he's clever, Striker, knows what side he's on."

Striker sat back smoldering.

"Get on with it... Jock."

Des drained his pint.

"I think you'll find that is racist terminology, Striker." He turned to Tag, "Get us a wee half there, son. My throat's dry."

Tag rose warily, expecting fireworks at any moment. Des continued, unconcerned.

"As I was saying, what my dear old dad was trying to instill in me, was that we all do things we think we shouldn't do, things we are ashamed of, Catholics, Protestants, Hindus, Jews and Muslims. All of us, see? And before we understand that it is a normal part of growing up, we experience guilt after the event. You're a Catholic, Striker, just like me, you must have suffered a good old dose of Catholic guilt, eh?"

Striker remained silent.

"Well, anyway, our man suffers from that guilt, has suffered from it for years. He just deals with it in a different way to the rest of us. We fault ourselves for our weaknesses; he blames the object of his desire.

Where we may feel a pang of shame at our actions, visit the confessional and promise to be a better boy next week, Abu Al Zachari strangles the life out of his victim at the point of orgasm. It cleanses his soul; he convinces himself he is ridding the world of the evil of the sexual female."

Striker sat up. "Abu Al Zachari?"

"That's your man," said Des." Age forty two, born in Syria to a wealthy family, radicalised and trained by the Afghans, he killed eight American soldiers before he was twenty one."

Tag returned with a half pint for Des, he didn't understand that the Scot meant he wanted a whiskey.

Des eyed the glass.

"Cheers, son," he said with a hint of sarcasm.

"Anyway, Zachari travelled to Iraq in early 2000 as a soldier of the Al Qaeda insurgence; fighting against Sadam's Ba'athist party. He added a few more bodies to his tally, but his liking for rape and murder had already started to get the better of him."

Des took another sip of his beer, felt for his wee pipe, but thought better of it.

"He was arrested by the Iraqi police in 2001, and jailed for an attack on a western journalist, a woman called Tabatha Freeman, an American. She was thirty-two, just his type, heavy-set, brash. He posed as a taxi driver, something he has continued to do his entire career, he raped her, but was discovered by locals before he could finish her off.

He was sentenced to ten years.

Trouble was when the American invasion started in 2003, and Sadam was deposed; one of the first things the Ba'athist regime did, was release every prisoner in captivity. They considered that it was best to let the American soldiers deal with the scum of the earth. Zachari was free.

Quite how he found the girl we now know as Ismi, the poor soul you just found in the flat around the corner, we don't know. He probably selected her at random, maybe even killed the mother. She was maybe two when he took her.

What Zachari did do, was use the girl as a passport to travel. He posed as a refugee fleeing the war zone. We believe he crossed the Turkish border and somehow made it to Greece.

From there he was in the EU and he could move about at will. The nice people in Italy gave him a visa, a passport and refugee status, he settled in Pescara using the name Mustapha.

Whilst there he contacted his Al Qaeda chums and restarted his work. His job has always been quartermaster. He has the talent and guile to source and stockpile weapons, ammunition and explosives. He also has the capability to fight, both on a physical level, the guy is huge, and a weapons expert. He was attached to the Abu Hafs Al Masri Brigade, the team allegedly responsible for the 2004 Madrid train bombings.

The French secret service firmly believed Zachari sourced the plastic explosive used in the attack. They were sure he'd bought it from Spanish miners, it was a civilian type PE called GOMA 2 ECO. Once he got his hands on that, he constructed thirteen IEDs. Ten detonated, killing a hundred and ninety-one people and wounding over two thousand others, it was the biggest terrorist atrocity in Spanish history."

Des took a drink.

"But the big fella has always been unable to control his urges. His DNA was found at the scene of two rapes and murders, one in Rimini, and another in Bologna.

Before he made it to the UK, we believe he was responsible for sixteen sexual attacks on women across Europe. None survived. Interpol had matched all the DNA evidence found in Europe, and realised they had a serial killer on their hands; it was just that they were unable to put a name or a face to it. DNA records were not team followed the container, the other half stayed UK-side and kept tabs on the boys who had loaded the merchandise.

Two days later we lost all contact with the team on the Belgian side. The port police found them in a disused warehouse a week later. They'd been beheaded. The knife used to kill them had been left for us to find. It had Abu Al Zachari's fingerprints on it. He was taunting us."

Striker shook his head. "And the Stingers?"

Des shrugged.

"What about the terrorist boys on our side of the pond?" asked Tag?

Des drained his half-pint and wiped his mouth with the back of his hand.

"That sweet little bunch currently reside in Bellmarsh prison. They have never spoken a word. It took us a year to even identify them."

Striker's mind was working overtime, digesting everything he had heard in double quick time.

"So the minute I dropped Sandra Mackintosh's shoe into the forensic lab, all the bells and whistles went off on Canary Wharf?"

Des nodded. "This is the closest we've been to him since that day."

"And the items he's so keen to get from our lawyer friend?"

"The missing link, it's a ROM chip. The Stinger is a pretty old piece of kit. It locates its target via infrared proportional navigation, pretty much point and shoot kind of stuff. The chance of hitting a modern day aircraft is about eight to one. The chip that was removed was fitted to a later model. That enables a second navigation mode that directs the missile towards the target airframe instead of its exhaust plume. Basically, you can't fuckin' miss. Zachari probably had copies made in China. They were delivered to Pakistan and collected by Abdullah Hussain. The kid was no more than a mule."

Striker considered this last snippet.

"So you are here to find Al Zachari?"

"Not exactly," said Des, standing to leave. "But two heads are better than one, eh?"

"What about the crew that killed Abdullah and the girl? Where do they fit in?

The Scot shrugged.

available for the first offence in Iraq. It wasn't until 2008, when a grainy picture of Al Zachari was published in the States as a suspect for the Madrid bombings, that his first victim, the journalist Tabatha, came forward and identified him. Unbelievably, she had kept a blouse she had worn on the night of the attack, unwashed and untouched."

Des took another drink.

"All very Monica.

From that day, the CIA had the DNA of the most wanted terrorist in Europe."

Striker's head was spinning with information.

"But he remained at large?"

Des removed his pipe and filled it. This time no one complained.

"In late 2010, after months of work, MI6 got a man on the inside of an Al Qaeda cell based in Bradford. His cover was that of an Algerian arms dealer. He would provide six MANPADS to the team. We didn't know at the time, but Al Zachari was part of that little band of happy clappers, once again acting as quartermaster."

Tag looked puzzled.

Striker bailed him out. "Man portable air defence systems."

Westland was open-mouthed. "You mean rockets?"

Des nodded. "Six FIM-92 Stingers, to be precise."

Striker was incredulous.

"So let me get this straight in my head. You and your boys at MI6 thought it was a good idea to let a bunch of terrorists, living and active in the UK, get close to six surface to air missiles?"

Des held up a hand.

"Listen, Striker, decisions like those are made way above my pay grade, I'm just a messenger here, believe me it gets worse. The plan itself was sound. The man on the inside would deliver the six MANPADS, one was fully functional and was used to demonstrate the capability of the unit, the other five had a key component missing from the guidance mechanisms. They were pretty much useless. Once the deal was done, the plan was to follow the dud packages to their destination and make the arrests."

Des lit his pipe again, exhaled and announced, "Piece of piss, eh?"

"I sense a big fuck off 'but' coming," said Striker.

"Too right, pal. The five Stingers were concealed in a container that was to leave Hull and dock in Zeebrugge. Half the surveillance

"Now that is a mystery. Enjoy your evening, chaps. See you around."

Des made his way around the table, thought better of it and turned to the two cops.

"If ye do catch up with the big lanky bastard Zachari, take care of yersel, lads. He's one mean son of a bitch."

Tag didn't know why but he stood and offered his hand.

"Thanks, Des," he said.

The Scot shook, but was looking over Tag's shoulder. "Jeezo," he muttered.

Tag turned to see Sky News on a large screen. The KSC normally reserved it for the football. A customer shouted to the barman to turn up the volume.

Two mugshots filled the screen.

"Fuck," gasped Tag. "That's Sandra and Wilson."

The photographs were replaced by footage taken on a mobile phone. The channel had digitally hidden some of the film, but it was clear to see that Sandra and Wilson had been murdered in the street. Tag recognised the mosque as being on his patch.

The footage then switched to a live feed. Hundreds of police officers were fighting running battles on Avenham and Frenchwood. Petrol bombs rained down on them; bricks, bottles, anything the rioters could find were thrown at the blue line.

The cops had surrounded the mosque and there was a standoff. The crowd inside the KSC was getting restless. Some shouted at the screen,

"Fuckin' murdering Paki bastards!"

"Let's kill them fuckers!"

The barman was trying to calm his customers, but most were drinking up and heading for the street outside.

Tag felt Striker's hand on his shoulder. "Time we weren't here, son."

Tag turned. Des had disappeared.

"Yeah, okay, let's go."

CHAPTER SIXTEEN

It was turning very ugly on the street outside. Tag felt a twinge of
guilt at not being in one of those PSU vehicles, the lads were
definitely going to be up against it.
"Poor fuckers," he said, as the pair pushed through a thickening
crowd.
"You'll see action before long, son, don't beat yourself up yourself
on that," said Striker, pulling his keys from his pocket.
They reached Striker's Audi but Tag stopped before opening his
door.
Striker could see the lad had been struggling since finding Ismi.
He'd worked Westland too hard, the crime scenes had affected
him, only natural, but this was something else, it was the
something that Striker knew was eating away inside the boy.
Westland was far too shallow for his own good, he'd had it easy in
his life, no doubt.
Good family, big house, private school, blessed with natural rakish
good looks and the ability to either talk or fight his way out of just
about any situation, all the toys a boy could wish for.
Women fell over themselves to share his bed, and the worse he
treated them, the more they seemed to like it.
Man about town, it's the way he rolled.
So, having the world at his 'dipped in shit' fingertips, he decided to
piss everyone off in the Westland household by becoming a
Lancashire cop on twenty grand a year.
Westland loved his parents, so why had he hurt them by leaving?

Striker knew.
Beneath the shallow facade, lay another Trevor Arthur George
Westland.
You just weren't allowed to see it.
As the two men faced each other over the roof of a cop car, the
other Tag Westland was fighting to get out, right there and then.
Tag rested his arms on the roof of the car.
"You know why I really joined this job, Striker?"
"To piss me off?"

"Hah, very funny, sergeant, can't anyone have a serious conversation around here? I'm...I'm trying to talk to you about...erm...something... you know; something important?"
Striker opened his door. "So get in the car and talk."
Westland was not for moving.
"No, I want to talk now, here and now."
Striker slowly pushed the door closed.
"Okay, son...shoot."
Tag took a deep breath, slightly surprised he had got his way.
"Right...well yeah...as I was saying, the reason I joined this laughable career path, this fuckin' joyful job, is err...is err...well I wanted something that was mine, you know? Something that my dad hadn't arranged for me, I wanted to prove that I didn't need his money, his influence, I wanted to show him that I could succeed on my own."
Striker let him rant. This had been coming, and Uncle Jack Daniels was helping him on his way.
"So I joined this...this... stupid job, where people fuckin' hate you all the fuckin' time, even if you're trying to do the right thing."
He waved his arms left and right. He was incredulous.
"You work in a station where half the cops don't give a fuck and the other half can't wait to get off the street into an office. Your boss can't say a sentence without the word 'feck' in it; and if you don't join the fuckin' masons you can kiss your arse goodbye to any kind of career. Oh but there's worse, and I mean worse! I've been shat on!"
Tag pointed at his head.
"Fuckin' shat on, Striker!"
The sergeant did his best to hide a smile.
"Oh that's right, Mr. fuckin' perfect, Mr. fuckin' yes sir, I've ironed my boxers, sir, I've got big muscles so I'm fuckin' right all the time sir! Have a good laugh at the posh lad! Go on, snigger away that he's bitten off more that he can chew, eh?"
Tag held his palms together, and for the first time Striker saw fear in his eyes. There was the merest shake in his voice.
"I've been in this job six months, six fuckin' months, Striker, I might as well have been delivered to you from a fuckin' spaceship for all I'm worth. When I met you I had my resignation in my pocket. I'd already decided that I didn't have what it took to be a

street cop. I couldn't stand to see the futileness of it all. To stand by and watch man's inhumanity to man on a rollercoaster with the brakes failed."

Tag managed a smile, which verged on hysteria.

"Then all this happened. I went from what I thought was hell, to the gates of Hades.

In less than two days, I've seen two dead bodies, crawled around in a skip, punched people unconscious, been sick, and I'm pretty sure the guy we just shared a drink with is some kind of spy."

Striker held up his hand, before Tag had a panic attack.

"I know you're upset, son, so I'll forgive the boxer short comment."

The detective opened the door for a second time and met Tag's eyes. He waited for calm.

"Take it from me, you're good enough."

Tag stayed put. There was one other thing.

"It's shit about Sandra and Wilson. I can't believe that happened."

Striker nodded.

"Life is shit, son; get in the car."

Within ten silent minutes they were on the M65. Jaco Pastorious played Portrait of Tracy. Tag was looking absently out of the window. "You really think I'm good enough?"

"Really."

Tag turned. "That guy was a spy, wasn't he?"

"Probably."

"I knew that," said Tag, and the car fell silent again.

Striker pulled onto his drive. "Home sweet home."

"Nice," said Tag. "It's a sort of post modern, Victorian, Bellway, Barratt development moment."

"Not everyone can live in a seventeenth century house in the country."

Tag laughed. "I rent a three bed semi with no central heating, as my landlord considers it a luxury."

Striker unlocked the front door. "I can run to heating."

Tag didn't quite know what to expect from Striker's house.

Clean and tidy, organised, definitely, one look at the guy and you would expect that.

What else?

Well the entrance hall was all clean lines, wood floor and white walls. The unexpected additions were the three photographs that hung to Tag's right. All were works by the American photographer, Richard Avedon. His stark style dominated the senses the moment you stepped inside; black and white single portraits on white backgrounds, Louis Armstrong, taken 1955, Oscar Levant, shot 1972 and centre stage was Chet Baker, a close up face shot taken 1986.

Tag couldn't take his eyes from the Baker image. So much emotion and life experience condensed into one single facial expression. Tag waved a finger at the stunning image, but couldn't find the words.

Striker stood behind him.

"Seen it, bought the t shirt, eh?"

Tag smiled. "Hell yeah, that is exactly it. I saw this shot in New York at an exhibition when I was on gap year."

"Lucky boy," said Striker. "I saw it in a book."

"And I had the silver spoon, blah blah blah, don't rub it in, sergeant," said Tag, inspecting the stretched canvas.

After a few seconds, he turned to the detective and pointed his thumb over his shoulder. He had a big daft grin on his face. "These ain't cheap, Striker."

The big man pulled off his coat, ignored the comment and stupid face.

"I don't do cheap, son. Now I have to send some reports by secure line, the coffee machine is through there, I'll take a double espresso."

Tag shrugged and found the kitchen. It was as the builder had designed it, no new units or surfaces, pretty much the show-home style on the budget the buyer could afford. There was one notable exception. Where a microwave had once sat, was a built in Bosch Espresso machine.

Tag let out a low whistle. His mother had whined for months at his father to purchase the very same item. At thirteen hundred pounds for a coffee maker, Dad had remained firm.

Two silently-delivered espressos later, Tag wandered right and negotiated a spiral case, before finding a surprisingly cosy lounge.

Wood burner, fat couches, lots of books, hundreds more long players.

Pride of place was a Linn hi-fi system.

The Kilmax Exakt DSM system is built and personalised to your own room.

Tag rested the coffee cups in a safe location before approaching the Rolls Royce of all hi-fi systems.

He ran a finger over the controller. Tag knew his hi-fi. It was something close to his heart. He wouldn't have chosen the sergeant's unit, but if you were a classical or jazz fan, it was just perfect.

It was also the price of a small saloon car.

Well you are a dark horse, Striker.

Tag found his cup, sat in a comfy chair and took stock. No sign of a television, a small pile of newspapers and magazines sat neatly on top of a leather topped coffee table; The Telegraph, Chicago Tribune, Modern Jazz, Computing Today, no surprises there.

He studied the considerable bookcase. Everything from Booker Prize winners to pulp fiction was ordered together alphabetically. There was plenty of escapism on the shelf. Heroes and villains, cowboys and angels, all rubbed shoulders with political history and sporting biographies. There was no sign of literary snobbery, just a single guy with a taste for the written word, rather than the moving image.

There was no doubt Striker had expensive taste, the pictures in the hall, the coffee maker, the fabulous hi-fi.

Not an easy thing to achieve on a sergeant's pay.

Had Tag been able to see into Striker's garage, he would have been even more impressed. The Audi was a police vehicle, but tucked away in the centrally heated integral garage under several layers of protective sheeting was a classic 1972 Porsche 911 turbo with less than ten thousand miles on the clock.

Striker appeared and broke Tag's thought process. He'd changed into joggers and was pulling a backpack onto his shoulders.

"Pass me my coffee, son."

Tag did so. "Nice place you have here, Striker."

The detective ignored the comment, drained his espresso in one, found a bottle of water in his pack and washed it down.

"I'm going for a run, and then I'm going to get my head down for an hour. There's a guest bed and shower on the top floor. You look beat, kid. Use it."

Tag rotated his neck. He felt the tendons complain. "Yeah, thanks, Striker. I'll do that. What's the plan later?"

Striker untangled a set of headphones and pushed them in his ears. "I've done all I can with the information we have. It's out there, we just have to see what turns up."

Tag nodded; whether it was the warmth of the room, or the sudden release of tension, he didn't know, but he felt a rush of fatigue wash over him. He stretched.

"Okay, I'll get some sleep, if you're sure it's alright."

Striker nodded. "I need to clear my head first. I'll wake you." He checked his Omega. "Three hours tops, okay?"

CHAPTER SEVENTEEN

Striker stepped out into the darkness and began his run, taking his usual route. The wind was picking up. He looked skyward and saw clouds beginning to blow across the full moon. An aircraft with its landing lights blazing into the heavens banked hard right towards Blackpool.

A storm coming, in more ways than one.

He pushed himself toward the town, over the motorway and railway bridges. He felt himself relax and drop into his stride, increasing his pace as his muscles warmed to the task. He passed Balshaws high school. To his surprise, cars were parked on both sides of the lane.

Before he could make the ancient cross, a traffic cop, filtering cars onto the supermarket car park, barred his route.

He jogged right, taking him behind the Tesco store. As he approached Towngate, he was forced to slow, as hundreds of people were being funneled along the shopping street toward the town hall.

Striker stopped and felt in the pocket of his combats. He found what he was looking for; the flyer he'd been given by the bruiser outside the Ship Inn a couple of nights earlier.

The crowd was heading to the Justice for Great Britain rally. The numbers surprised Striker. In stark contrast to the atmosphere he had left in Burnley, and what was being televised in Preston, the crowd had a carnival feel to it. Burger vans and balloon sellers were doing a brisk trade.

What shocked Striker more, were the customers. Rather than the knuckle-dragging, swastika-tattooed thugs he'd expected, the throng was made up of families, men carried children on shoulders, middle aged, middle class, middle ground voters waved small Union Jacks, as they strolled toward the showground opposite the council offices.

Striker joined the crowd, pulled his iPod from his ears and walked alongside an elderly couple.

The man was a full foot shorter than Striker. He wore a regimental tie.

"You think this bloke can change things, chum?" he said, linking arms with his wife.

Striker looked over the heads of the hundreds in front of him. They were less than two hundred meters from the venue. Massive spotlights beamed into the night sky, rousing music boomed from a powerful public address system, giving a Churchillian feel to proceedings.

"Do you?" questioned Striker.

The man shrugged.

"We moved here to Leyland last year, mate, we had to get away from it, we'd lived in Haslingdon all our lives, there isn't a shop left there where people speak English, that or they refuse to, our club, the Legion, shut down 'cos all the folk who liked a drink have moved or died. No one on the council wanted to look after people like us, pensioners who'd worked and lived all our lives in the town. My missus didn't feel safe anymore. Somethin' needs to be done, them folk in big houses who don't live next to 'em don't understand. My home town isn't mine anymore. It's like bloomin' Pakistan."

"I think people should be careful what they wish for," said Striker.

"That's what I told him," chirped in the man's wife.

"We need to see what this chap has to say though, Maureen," said the man tapping his wife lovingly on the hand. "I like the sound of him."

It seemed to Striker that thousands of others felt the same way. The jovial atmosphere followed the crowd all the way to the site. It was unbelievable that five miles away, Preston was burning, yet here, over four thousand souls were squashed onto a patch of land, eating hot-dogs and candy floss. The media were lapping it up, the press and TV were everywhere.

The detective clocked some private security guys keeping a watchful eye on the crowd, but it was low-key. Other than the traffic cop he'd seen earlier, he couldn't find a single officer.

He did, however see a black face. He was standing dead centre of the massive stage.

The music died down and the backdrop changed from pure blue, to the logo of the Justice for Great Britain party.

The man held up his hands and approached the mic.

"Ladies and gentleman! Welcome! Welcome to our rally! My name is Glen Jonson.

I was born in Preston, Lancashire.
My parents travelled from Jamaica, to settle here in 1962. They
have lived and worked alongside the people of this county for over
fifty years.
I am proud to be a black man, I am proud to be British.
However, I am not a liar, so will not tell you that life has always
been easy, that my parents and I have not suffered racism at the
hands of the white man.
Yes, we have suffered, we have fought against the racists, and will
always fight against the curse of racism in our community.
I am not here to support a racist.
I am here to support fairness."

The huge sub-woofers either side of the stage started a low rumble.

"I am here to support Justice!"

The noise grew to deafening proportions. The crowd was expectant
and began to cheer.
The announcer was starting to sound like a man about to introduce
the world heavyweight champ at a boxing match.

"I am here to support the Justice for Great Britain party!
I am here to support... Al...is...tair Sin...clair!"

The crowd erupted; pyrotechnics exploded from somewhere
behind the stage, firing strips of shiny red white and blue paper
high into the air. Lasers twisted and flicked into the night sky,
Land of Hope and Glory blasted the crowd.
Sinclair took to the stage.
He wore dark trousers and a white open-necked shirt, his sleeves
rolled up to his forearms, man of the people, ready for work.
The music stopped, but the fervent crowd did not, they cheered,
whistled, and chanted his name.
It was a full five minutes before he spoke.
Finally he raised his hands.
He started with a booming tone. "I stand in front of you this
evening as leader of the Justice for Great Britain Party, as a

democratically elected member of the British government, as a British citizen.

The good people of east Lancashire turned out in their thousands to vote for me and my policies, therefore, it is my right, as it is the right of all of us, to speak out against violence, intolerance and discrimination.
To speak out for a free and fair society."
He settled into his rhythm. No notes, no teleprompter.
"The right to free speech is an intrinsic part of our civilization. Tonight, I will make no secret of my beliefs, my thoughts, or my fears. I speak as I find. There is no hidden agenda.
I lead the Justice for Great Britain Party; a party that is growing every day."

A huge graphic blazed behind him showing membership figures.
"As of tonight, my friends, our membership has outstripped that of the Liberal Democrats as the third biggest political party in the UK."
The crowd cheered; it was almost a minute before Sinclair could continue.
He was the epitome of middle class reason. "We are not the EDL or the BNP.
We are not thugs with tattoos; we are ordinary people. We are not a racist organisation; nor do we affiliate ourselves to any establishment that shows intolerance to any minority, to any religion.
Our party is the champion of fairness!
Our party is the champion of freedom!
Our party is the champion of faith!"
Our party is the champion of Justice!"
More cheers and whistles.

Sinclair slipped a touch of anger into his tone.
"The gutter press, the left wing BBC will tell you a different story. They will say that I am a monster! The new Hitler! The new Mussolini!
They say that anyone who supports our party is a misguided, uneducated bigot.

But they are wrong.
I am new, I'll give them that. I have new and bold ideas, but I am neither dictator nor despot. I am not a radical or racist. I represent every race and religion."

The massive backdrop behind Sinclair changed to footage of the rioting on Avenham.
He waved his arm toward the flickering images.
"Not five miles from where we stand tonight, a grave cancer is spreading across our country. Not five miles away, buildings burn, the police have lost control of our streets, vicious thugs roam our towns, the Christian community is at war with the Muslim.
Within the last four hours, reports tell us the dreadful news that an innocent woman has been beheaded on a Lancashire street, yards from her own home!
So-called community leaders hide these criminals in a mosque. They harbour the perpetrators of this vicious and senseless killing. They hide them in a house of God! Our police have lost control and are under attack from hundreds of their supporters. Supporters of this horrible crime; the thin blue line is pinned down and powerless."

Sinclair dropped his voice.
"It is not a question of funds. The police have had all the financial support possible.
In just thirty-six hours, the cost of policing the unrest is estimated at two point six million pounds. Countrywide, the cost is ten times that.

Despite the brave men and women of our police forces, hundreds of angry Muslim men from all over the country will travel to make war against the Christian population of Preston.
The violence is escalating. Rioting has now been reported in Birmingham, Luton, Bradford and Bristol.
Cameron sits on his hands and watches Rome burn, but even someone as inept as he, must see what is needed here. He must know who must surely intervene in this horror that is upon us."

Sinclair's voice rose to a crescendo.

"We need British troops on British streets to quell this violence, now!"

The crowd erupted again. Striker looked around him, studied the faces that gazed admiringly at the man delivering the rhetoric. *God help us.*

Sinclair was just warming up.

"If we don't act, and act quickly, the world will see that Britain is a broken country.

Our economy will go into meltdown.

Foreign investment will fall.

Jobs will be lost; your jobs."

The backdrop changed again and footage of 1960's Lancashire filled the screen. Sinclair dropped his voice.

"Forty five years ago, a Conservative MP gave an infamous speech to parliament. He was denounced for his views.

He claimed that the ethnic changes to working class communities would lead to 'rivers of blood' flowing through our towns.

He claimed that the Race Relations Act being pushed through Parliament would create imbalances to our very society.

He claimed that the 'black man would hold the whip over the white'."

Sinclair held up an apologetic hand.

"Old fashioned language, my friends.

Language that would not be used in our modern and enlightened times, but true language, nonetheless."

The hand became a warning finger.

"Another great orator, another man denounced for his views, said: 'I have a dream that one day right there in Alabama, little black boys and black

girls, will be able to join hands with little white boys and white girls as sisters and brothers'."

There was a ripple of applause from the audience.

Sinclair was commanding. He had the charisma to carry the crowd with him. He raised his voice again, using his natural deep baritone to its maximum effect.

"Well I have that same dream, my friends.

I have a dream, that the closed communities which have developed in our towns and cities will open their arms and embrace the British way of life.

I have a dream, that someday a little white girl will happily attend her local primary school and play with little Asian girls and boys without having to cover her head and face with black cloth.

I dream of an end to segregation, just as Reverend King dreamt of freedom from the shackles of southern repression.

I dream because here in the city of Preston, not five miles from where we stand, is a segregated community.

The immigrant population has created their very own apartheid, where white people are not wanted or welcome.

We have opened our borders and our arms to people from all over the world. We have given homes and shelter to hundreds of thousands of the poor and needy.

Now we are seeing the cost.

Martin Luther King said:

'It is time to lift ourselves from the quicksand of racial injustice'.

I agree with him. We must stand together. We must ride out this terrible storm, but first we must quell the violence that is spreading on our streets.

So I call on Cameron; call on this inept and sluggish government."

The backdrop picture changed again. Three Queens Lancashire Regiment soldiers stood to attention. Sinclair stepped back and swept his arm toward the image.

"Send in the troops now! Reclaim our streets! SEND IN OUR BOYS!"

Tag had showered. The warmth of the water on his back had eased his aching neck, but sent him ever closer to sleep.

He dried himself, pulled on his boxers and fell onto a single bed. Within seconds he was asleep and snoring quietly.

He'd managed forty minutes of blissfully dreamless slumber, when his phone bleeped and shocked him awake.

He checked his messages, doing his best to focus.

How about now?

Tag sat up and read it again, then checked the sender. Scarlet had replied.

How about now? Of course, he'd sent the 'drink sometime?' type text earlier.

For fuck's sake, he thought. Of all the times a girl could pick. Tag swung his legs over the bed and wiggled his toes on the thick carpet at his feet. He stared at the screen some more and did his best to formulate a plan.

He had no clean clothes, *slight issue.*

He had no transport, *police car on drive, keys in hall.*

Striker would kill him, *maybe, maybe not.*

It was worth the risk.

Tag rushed to the bathroom and checked himself in the mirror. He needed a shave. He rooted in a vanity cabinet and found a new toothbrush, toothpaste, razor, foam and aftershave.

"Striker, you're a star."

Ten minutes later, he was stumbling down the stairs, whilst spraying aftershave under the arms of his sweatshirt.

Keys? Where did he leave the keys?

They were sat just where they should be, on the table by the front door.

Tag snatched them into his palm and kissed them.

"Thank you, Lord!"

Moments later he was adjusting the seat of the Audi and trying to find a decent radio station. He reversed off the drive, paired his phone to the Bluetooth hands-free and dialled the delicious Scarlet 'one t.'

"Well hello, Scarlet," he said using his best chat up voice.

There was a brief silence, before a very quiet tone on the other side asked, "Who is this?"

Tag was somewhat deflated, but wasn't the sort to give up so easily, especially after he'd taken the risk of stealing the psychopath of the year's police car to enable this rendezvous.

"It's Tag," he gushed. "You just texted me about that drink?"

"Oh yes," she said. "Sorry, I didn't look properly."

"No problem, erm...I'm just in Leyland, where would you like to meet?"

Her voice was almost a whisper. "I can walk down to the Tickled Trout, that is probably best, away from the trouble..."

"I can get you from home, honey, I don't want you taking any...."

"No!"

Scarlet's voice raised so much it made Tag jump in his seat.
"Okay, okay, hun, no problem, the hotel is fine," soothed Tag.
"Sorry," countered Scarlet. "It's just, my dad, he's not too well
and...Well, he just isn't..."
She trailed off without further explanation.
Tag put his foot down and the Audi responded willingly. "Like I
said, no problem, honey, I'll be at the hotel in ten minutes or so."
Tag thought he heard Scarlet say 'okay' before the phone went
dead.
He pulled the car onto the M6 and sat back in his seat.
As he did so he looked across into the footwell. Sitting proudly on
the carpet was a magnetic blue flashing light.
He knew he shouldn't, after all, he probably wasn't covered to drive
the Audi, let alone stick the blue light on the roof.
Fuck it.
Tag leaned over, grabbed the light, dropped the driver's window
and stuck on the swiveling beast with a metallic clunk.
He fumbled with the spiral cord attachment, until he managed to
connect it to the cigarette lighter, and 'bingo'.
He had a 'go as fast as you like' light on the roof.
Tag red-lined the Audi, and it responded with a satisfying growl.
He hit eighty before changing up. A broad smile lit up his face.
He fumbled at the dash.
"Okay, where's the noo nahh's?"
What Tag had failed to note was a very clear sticker on the blue
swiveling appendage he had just stuck to the roof of a thirty two
thousand pound police vehicle, a thirty two thousand pound car
that Detective Sergeant Ewan Striker had signed for.
It read, 'Speed limit 70 mph.'
The light did better than the manufacturer's maximum operating
speed, but at ninety five, it broke loose, catapulted backward, was
stopped dead mid air by its cable and bounced against the back
screen. The four-hundred pound sheet of heated screen shattered
instantly, and the light flashed mockingly on the back parcel-shelf
for a second or two.
The neon globe then exited the vehicle for a second time. By now
the cable had stretched sufficiently to allow the three kilogram
lamp to bounce up and down on the boot at three second intervals.

The damage would have been bad enough, but the sight of a police vehicle weaving along the busiest motorway in the country with a blue neon light bouncing around on the boot lid, was not a good look.

The fucking light was still working when Tag pulled up on the car park of the Tickled Trout Hotel.

It continued to mock him, even from the tarmac.

Tag stamped on it in pure truculence, he hadn't thought to unplug it.

The Audi's boot looked like it had been attacked by a hoard of dwarves with those small pickaxes they carry around, except these dwarves were on crack cocaine and steroids.

"Fuck!"

Tag put his head in his hands.

"Fuuuuuuck!"

He released his head, rubbed his face for a moment and looked again. He took a deep breath and remembered a line from one his favorite movies.

"Nothing is fucked here, Donny, nothing is fucked."

Right, think here. It's not that bad. There are lots of riots going on, all over town. I got caught in one, that's all. I had to rescue some poor fucker from the rioting hordes and the bastards trashed the boot of the Audi. Honest, Striker. Scout's honour.

Tag threw the light inside the car and loped toward the residents' bar.

"Fuck it," he said. "I'll worry about it later."

Scarlet had given her father his last medication of the day. He wouldn't wake. Normally, she would just sit in the lounge watching television, until she herself felt tired enough to sleep. Tonight, however, had been different.

Her neighbour, Sandy, from two doors down, had been camped in Scarlet's house all afternoon. Her boyfriend Les had been arrested overnight for looting a late night shop off New Hall Lane. He'd punched a couple of coppers for good measure.

According to Sandy, this meant that Les would be inside for Christmas, again.

Scarlet had listened to Sandy's woes for as long as she could stand it, had read Tag Westland's text message at least twenty times, and eventually arrived at the decision to meet him.

It had meant fobbing off Sandy's lewd questions, but she really wanted to see the handsome cop. She was young and single and she never saw outside her four walls, other than for work and shopping.

And after all, Tag was tall, dark, and funny and seemed to like her.

"There's lager in the fridge, Sand," she said as she pulled on her coat. "Thanks for this, love, I mean it; you've got my mobile anyway, eh?"

Sandy was flicking through the shopping channels.

"Yeah, no worries, chuck, just bring me some fags back with you, eh?"

"Will do," she said, and stepped out into the night.

It took Scarlet less than fifteen minutes to walk from Farringdon Park estate, down Brockholes Brow, to the hotel. She had never been inside the exclusive bar before and felt a pang of instant regret at having picked such a place to meet.

As she peered through the revolving glass doors toward the wood paneled reception, she caught a glimpse of her reflection.

Pretty girl, cheap coat, cheap shoes;

This is a mistake;

Her stomach lurched, who was she kidding, a girl from Farringdon Park, walking into the best hotel in town, meeting a copper?

She turned on her heel and strode back to the car park, hands in pockets, head down.

Scarlet walked straight into Tag Westland.

"Whoa!" said Tag, catching Scarlet in his arms. "Are you running away on me already?"

Scarlet jumped. "Oh... hi... erm... Tag... no.... I was just going to erm..."

"Run away on me," he finished.

Scarlet stepped back, pulled her hands from her coat and pushed a stray piece of hair from her face. She looked up, her breath turning to haze in the chill. She bit her lip.

"If you must know," she whispered. "I lost my nerve, okay?"

Tag was in awe, she was even more beautiful than he'd remembered, her alabaster, flawless skin, framed by the moonlight, her full mouth dark against it, like perfect, purple petals.

Tag was not going to let this happen.

"Okay... so...how about I help you find this lost nerve of yours, as we both made it this far?"

The wind was picking up, and Scarlet lost the battle with her wayward hair. She shot a look toward the hotel.

"You don't know anything about me. I don't belong in there."

Tag held up his car keys.

"There are other places. I can confirm that. I passed a few on my way here."

He gave his best smile and twinkle.

Scarlet wavered.

Tag bent his knees until he was equal height.

"Please?"

She smiled.

"Okay."

"Great," said Tag, linking arms and guiding his prize toward the Audi. "But I do have to mention a little problem with my car..."

CHAPTER EIGHTEEN

Abu Al Zachari was troubled.

Despite an unremarkable journey to Hussain's Nelson office, easy access to the building, the correct code for the safe and the four remaining items he required sitting firmly in his possession, something itched, but he couldn't scratch it.

The 'something' became all too apparent as he approached the safe house where he had left the coward of a lawyer.

A forensic vehicle was parked outside. Its single revolving roof-light covered the buildings with blue neon. Two uniformed cops were standing in the doorway.

Zachari was a man of his word. He would have returned to the flat and killed Tariq Hussain swiftly, but now, well, it seemed he would live. That was not acceptable.

Zachari took a left and simply pulled the Mercedes to the side of the road. There was little point in destroying it, they would know who he was within hours, fingerprints, DNA and now a living witness.

He'd convinced himself that his anonymity was no longer an issue, as he would be back in his homeland within forty-eight hours, away from the brash temptations of the west, away from the vile ways of the infidel.

Anyway, hadn't he taunted them before, leaving the knife? Was he still free?

Fools.

He walked the short distance to Burnley bus station and caught the X 43 service to Prestwich, Manchester.

The bus was half full of people who couldn't afford a car, there was nothing convenient about this service. It would take almost two hours to cover the thirty miles.

Most passengers spent the whole journey either glued to their mobile phones or dozing.

Zachari peered from his window and into the darkness; he watched as the Lancashire countryside was battered by a strengthening wind, and the first fat drops of rain splattered against the glass.

Briefly, he caught his own reflection. Flecks of grey were starting to catch hold in his beard, dark circles formed under his eyes, a sudden wave of fatigue washed over him.
It is time.

Striker stood in the centre of the showground; he watched as the roadies began to dismantle the lighting rig and sound system from the main stage. The crowd began to wander homeward, some clutching flags, some with Justice for Great Britain hats.
Sinclair had brought the house down.
Striker felt sick.
He knew he should leave, he needed sleep.
Instead, he wandered to the side of the stage. A huddle of some two dozen reporters was hurriedly checking mics and recorders. Engineers barked at each other as they rigged temporary lights. The gaggle of press was kept away from a massive motor-home by security barriers and three very stern-looking guards.
Striker took his place at the back, his height enabling him to see everything he needed. The reporters were expectant; they were not kept waiting.
The door of the motor-home opened, and out stepped Alistair Sinclair, flanked by two further guards.
These two were the real deal. Striker could recognise ex Special Forces when he saw them, just as he had hours earlier with Des and his annoying pipe.
The second Sinclair appeared, there was a cacophony of sound from the press. A wall of shouted questions, all aimed at the main man, famous names from radio and TV jostled for position.
The two security guys eyed the crowd carefully, calm, switched on.
Sinclair raised his arm and waited for silence.
When he had control he pointed to a well-known BBC correspondent. "David?" he said.
The man had to shout to be heard.
"You say you want troops on our streets, Mr. Sinclair. That may be easy to achieve, but withdrawing them is another matter..."
Sinclair gave a million dollar smile to a raft of photographers. All he needed was the red carpet.

"We have already drafted our suggestions for the minor military intervention required to quell the current disturbances on our streets. Those detailed reports have been submitted to Cameron and the Alliance. The troops would be on our streets for less than a week."

The BBC man tried to get in with a retort but Sinclair was too quick and slick.

He pointed at a pretty CNN reporter who had forced herself to the front of the melee.

"Jessica?"

"You quote the Reverend King, Mr. Sinclair, yet your manifesto clearly states your belief in the drastic reduction of immigrants to the UK, including the forced repatriation of some migrants already settled here. Surely that is a racist stance."

The crowd of desperate newshounds lapsed into a fervent round of shouted follow-ups before Sinclair raised his arms again.

His suit was impeccable; he'd changed his shirt and added a tie. Somewhere inside that hundred thousand pound motor-home was his stylist, because he was made up for live TV and his hair was perfect.

"Please...ladies and gentleman...please."

Finally he had relative quiet.

"Our policy clearly states that any immigrant to this country must have a guaranteed job to go to that pays a minimum of twenty-five thousand per year and includes private medical insurance."

More shouts from the reporters were ignored as he raised his voice and continued,

"... and that job, that vacancy, cannot be filled by a British! And I mean British worker."

Sinclair wagged a finger.

"I don't care what colour, race, religion, sexual orientation or how able-bodied that *British* person is, so long as they are... British! So you tell me now...how can that policy be racist?"

He was back on his very high horse.

"And to cover your second point, I firmly believe! And in a recent survey, eighty-seven percent of my party members agree. Any immigrant, who has been in this country for less than a year, and commits a crime, should be deported at time of conviction."

A voice from the back shouted,

"Does that include people arrested for stealing food, because they cannot afford to eat, due to the savage cuts in benefits to immigrants already implemented by the Alliance?"
Sinclair's Hollywood smile faltered slightly and there was the merest hint of anger in his eyes.
"Stealing was a crime the last time I looked."
The voice was in again, rising above all others.
"And what would your party do about the vigilantes that have murdered two innocent Pakistani teenagers just this week?"
Finally there was silence from the huddle; everyone wanted this question answered. The press had written thousands of column inches on the story. One red top claimed to have found a witness, who alleged that Ayesha and Abdullah were secret lovers. The woman, only known to the public as 'witness one,' for fear of retribution from the community, suggested that both youngsters were to be the subject of arranged marriages, and that they were planning to run away together. It was a massive scoop.
The Daily Mail had piggy-backed the whole story and slotted it alongside an old piece on honour killings.
It was massive news, as both a political big hitter for the broadsheets and a good old Romeo and Juliet romance for the rest. Sinclair was close to statesman-like.
"The cold blooded murder of two innocent young people is a cowardly and criminal act of violence that will not be tolerated by the Justice for Great Britain party, under any circumstances.
But I must say; that I am now privy to information, via the security services, to suggest that Abdullah Hussain was a radical. He was suspected of having visited terrorist training camps in Pakistan and had acted as a courier for the Taliban."
The crowd went into a frenzy at this information. Striker was as shocked as the reporters by Sinclair's level of knowledge about the case.
The politician hadn't finished.
"And that the item he carried into this country was some form of trigger device for use in a terrorist plot! That item…that very item was found in the hands of Ayesha Chowdry."

Sinclair was uncompromising. "Now, I will reiterate. There is a judicial process in this country, a process that I value above all else. It guarantees our human rights, our right to a fair trial. But is it any wonder, when hate preachers spread their vile language, when bombs are planted in our Tubes and airports, and innocents are beheaded on our streets, that some people will take the law into their own hands?"

Striker had heard more than enough. Sinclair sickened him and frightened him in equal amounts.
He turned to walk away and felt for his phone. Westland could pick him up. He studied the screen briefly, but before he could dial, someone or something walked on his grave.
He twisted and viewed the scene.
Sinclair still spouting, the two ex soldiers eyeing the crowd, the three goons at the barrier.
What was it?
Then he saw him; a small guy, forties, standing off to one side in the shadows, a guy with a widow's peak and bad teeth, a guy that was waiting for something or someone. Striker lifted his iPhone and took a picture.
I don't like the look of you, pal.

Tag and Scarlet ran from the car to avoid what had become a storm.
He pushed open the heavy door that led into the Roe Buck Pub.
It was a small but cosy hostelry, with real ale, real fires and a hearty menu.
He ushered Scarlet forward.
"There's a free table in the corner by the fire. Why don't you grab it and I'll get the drinks?"
Scarlet nodded. Tag had talked incessantly since they left the hotel. He seemed stressed, but rather than being annoyed, she had found his nervous chatter comforting. She felt at ease with him. It was a nice sensation, a feeling she hadn't allowed herself in quite a while.
"I'll have a gin and tonic, please," she said, brushing raindrops from her shoulder.
Tag walked to the bar and ordered. Within a minute he returned with drinks and two menus. "You hungry?"
Scarlet decided to pull off her wet coat. "I wasn't expecting to eat out."

Tag settled in next to her. "Me either, but I sicked up my lunch earlier, so I'm starving."

Scarlet gave him a grimace.

"Oh, I'm sorry," he said. "I was kinda thinking out loud. I'm okay; I'm not ill or anything."

Scarlet took a sip of her drink and then summarised Tag's en route chat.

"So let me get this straight, some rioters smashed up your police car on the way here? You're working on a top secret case that you can't talk about, and you've been sick?"

Tag nodded as if it was the most natural thing in the world, took a gulp of his Coke and offered,

"I saw a dead body."

"And you were sick?"

"Yes."

"Tough guy, eh?"

Tag held out his right hand and showed off his bruised knuckles.

"Well before that, I had to knock a guy unconscious!"

Scarlet did her best to hide a smile.

"Why?"

Tag tried to think of an explanation and opted for the truth. "Well, he wouldn't let us into the KSC Club."

"Us?"

"Striker and me, the guy I'm working with, on this secret job."

"Striker?"

"He's American; he's kinda, well he's a little weird."

"Does he knock people out if they don't let him into Catholic clubs?"

Tag looked at his date. This was not going well. He needed to change tack.

"The oxtail looks nice," he said picking up the menu.

"I'm vegetarian," said Scarlet, stone-faced.

"You are?"

"No," said Scarlet and burst out laughing.

Tag thought it was a wonderful sound. Her face lit up, and if it were possible, she looked even more beautiful. Then a miracle happened, Scarlet rested her hand on his and squeezed it. Tag's stomach did a quick flip.

"Can, I have the chicken, please?"

Tag was caught in her gaze. "Chicken?"

"Yes please, with salad and new potatoes.

"Err...yes...I'll nip to the bar."

Tag strode and ordered.

It was going okay, he could feel it. She actually liked him.

His phone vibrated in his pocket. When he saw Striker's name on the screen, he felt a slight shiver.

Where the fuck are you?

Tag deleted the SMS, but the phone shook in his hand before he could pocket it, and briefly avoid the issue.

And where is my fucking car?

As he shuffled back to the table, Scarlet looked concerned, "Everything okay, Tag? You look a little pale? You don't feel sick again, do you?"

"Err...no...I'm fine."

Grant Bliss handed Sinclair a brandy balloon half full of golden liquid.

"Excellent work, Alistair," he said, pouring himself a hearty measure.

"Thank you, Grant."

Bliss sipped his drink and sat. The motor-home was as secure as anywhere else they could hold a conversation. It had, of course, been swept for any listening devices. It was warm, dry and quiet in its sheltered parking spot at the side of the main stage. The only sound was the howl of the wind outside.

"We were lucky this didn't blow in two hours ago," he added.

Sinclair nodded his agreement, but was studying the screen of his laptop.

"The membership figures are staggering, Grant. We are adding over a thousand an hour." The politician looked up at his comrade in arms. "If this continues, we'll overtake Labour within a week."

"Just what you anticipated, then?"

"Better, Grant, much better."

Sinclair took a large gulp of the fine brandy, and handed the glass to Bliss. "This calls for another."

The head of security didn't mind waiting on his friend. He had the talent and the balls to achieve greatness, and on the back of that success would surely come the changes and subsequent power that Bliss craved.

He handed the refill over. "Did you think it was wise to give out the information about the trigger device?"

Sinclair shrugged. "Your man in Canary Wharf, what's his name? Carrington? Yes? Well he thought it wise to inform us, the second he saw that report from Striker. He was on the blower gloating as to how good his original information had been. He was probably hoping to increase his bloody fee. My little snippet was just a taster for the press. When this Zachari chap blows up whatever he intends to blow up, it will be the final straw. The whole country will implode. We will simply point out that the security services knew of the bomber and the device beforehand. It will only add to the perceived incompetence of the powers that be."

Bliss smiled. "You always were one for the spectacular, Alistair." Sinclair took another drink.

"Talking of which, how are we progressing with our other little matter?"

"It's all in hand, Danny Slade has his patsy. I believe he is meeting him tonight to complete the handover, a guy called Williams, Barry Williams. He'll plant the device."

Sinclair raised an eyebrow. "And then?"

Bliss drained his own brandy and poured a second.

"When he comes to collect his fee, Slade will deal with him."

The pair clinked glasses.

"Excellent," said Sinclair. "Bloody excellent."

Abu Al Zachari stepped off the bus and ran toward the waiting car. The rain was blowing in sheets and he was soaked just from the short hop.

"Salam Alaikum," he said as he sat.

"Alaikum Salam," the driver replied.

The man behind the wheel was young, in his early twenties; African, from the Sudan. Zachari had never met him, but he knew he was a trusted part of the team who would ensure the success of the holy mission. Only Arabic was spoken.

"I am to take you to Longsight, my brother; to a safe place."

"So be it," said Zachari, and sank down into the seat. "But I am weary, forgive me, but I must rest."

The driver nodded. "As you wish, my brother."

Zachari had done as he had said and slept like a baby for the twenty-five minute drive to his new safe house, just off Dennison Road, central Manchester. The building was a mere stone's throw from the road renamed the 'Curry Mile' and the impressive Central Mosque and Cultural Centre.

"We are here," said the Sudanese, shocking Zachari awake.

He sat up and rubbed his face. He eyed the door of a terraced house through the rain-soaked car window.

Within moments both men were inside. Zachari was immediately struck by the smell of cooking. His stomach rumbled as he realised just how hungry he was. When did he last eat?

The Sudanese led him to a downstairs bathroom. Again he used his mother tongue.

"Please, my brother, use the shower. I will fetch clean clothes for you. Ismail, my cousin, is cooking goat. When you are clean, we will pray, eat and talk of the great plan."

"Thank you," said Zachari wearily. "You have my new papers here?"

The young man nodded nervously and disappeared into a small room. Within seconds, he returned holding a Syrian passport, visa documents and tickets. His eyes were wide, small beads of sweat formed on his forehead. His hand shook as he held out the items.

"Here, my brother; we are honored to have such a great warrior in our home."

Zachari ignored the compliment and opened the passport. The photograph showed him clean-shaven. He hated to remove his beard, but God would indeed forgive him this small indiscretion, in order to do his will on a greater scale.

"Do you have a razor? I need to remove my beard, before the jihad."

"In the cupboard, my brother."

"Thank you," said Zachari, studying his tickets. He checked them; a ferry from Dover to Calais, the train to Paris and a flight to the land of his birth. He looked up. "And what is your name, my African brother?"

"I am Okot Mohammed."

"Well, Okot; you are kind and a good host. I will wash myself and then we will indeed pray for our success. Your cousin's goat has a fine smell."

Zachari closed the bathroom door, leaving a smiling Okot standing in the hall. He stripped off his clothes.

Inside the small space was a shower, toilet and basin, soap, and clean towels.

He turned the taps and stepped into the stream of water tumbling from the shower. It was scalding hot, but he relished the pain as the jet bounced off his skin.

He needed to be clean.

Zachari emerged with his shoulders blistering, but he felt alive again. He often challenged his threshold for pain. It was good for the soul. Whatever he suffered now would be repaid in the afterlife, ten times over. The sacrifice would be worth it.

He found a small pair of scissors and a razor and commenced the removal of his beard. Okot knocked and dropped in western clothes; jeans, sweatshirt, training shoes.

A small price; a small sacrifice.

Scarlet scraped the last mouthful of food from her plate. Tag marveled at where such a slim creature could put such a mountain of roast chicken.

"You enjoyed that then?" he said.

"You never got to waste anything in our house. When there was food on the table you ate it. Besides, I'm not the best cook; I eat at the hospital a lot, which is pretty poor, so that was really nice, thank you."

Tag smiled. "You're welcome; I'm glad you came."

Scarlet looked at him, looked into his face, his eyes.

My God, you would do most of anything for those eyes.

"My pleasure," was all she managed.

Tag checked his phone; he'd clicked it to silent through the meal. He now had eleven missed calls from Striker and seven messages. Scarlet didn't notice his reticence.

"I might be going on holiday," she chirped.

"Really," said Tag absently, pushing the phone back in his pocket with a feeling of dread.

"Yeah, depending on how Dad is, of course; but have you seen how much taking a case on the plane is now? Jean and me...well...we were looking at flights to Malta, and it was more for the bag than it was for a person. Can you get that? More for a bag, than it was for me?"

Tag thought he was going to have a heart attack.

"Bag," he said, almost to himself.

Scarlet was a tad incredulous. "Yeah, you know, luggage, for your clothes and stuff?"

"Luggage!" said Tag, just a little too loudly.

He pulled his mobile from his pocket and fumbled for his wallet at the same time. Both fell on the table.

"Shit!" he spat. "I need to make a call, I need to go...sorry, Scarlet... I really am...it's just this case...I need..."

Tag threw forty pounds on the table. "That will get you a cab and pay for the food...look...I'm sorry...I wouldn't do this if it wasn't really important."

Scarlet was shell-shocked.

"What? You're going? You're leaving me here?"

Tag grabbed at Scarlet, his hands gripped her gently either side of her face; he pulled her to him and kissed her firmly on the mouth.

"You're special, and beautiful," he said, and walked out of the door.

Scarlet was left alone. The diners all around were staring. She held the gaze of a woman at the nearest table.

"He's a doctor," she said, with more than a hint of the dramatic. "Urgent operation."

The diner's husband seated opposite looked impressed; the woman was open-mouthed, "Oh, I see. You must be very proud of him."

Scarlet collected the money from the table and stood.

"Actually," she preened, "I am."

Tag sprinted to the Audi. He dialled Striker as he hit the driver's seat and started the engine.

The phone rang once and a rabid dog answered.

"Where the fuck are you?"

"Never mind that, I'll be ten minutes, listen, I have a thing."

"Oh you have a 'thing' alright. I'll tell you what you have, Westland, you have my fucking cop car; a cop car that I signed for, and you..."

Tag rarely shouted, unless very stressed. He considered that this counted as very.

"Shut the fuck up about the car, Striker...I have a thing...a...lead...I mean.... yeah, a lead...that's right...the luggage...you know, the fuckin' pink and white suitcase that Ismi had? That and the brown wheelie case Zachari was dragging...where the fuck are they? Not in that flat!"

There was a short silence as Striker took in the babble of information.

"Not in the Merc either, son, they found it an hour ago, just around the corner from the safe house. Maybe Zachari took the cases with him and dumped them?"

Tag was racing toward the M6, foot hard to the floor. Rain poured into the car from the broken rear screen.

"He wouldn't take the kid's case though, would he?"

"Maybe."

"Yeah and maybe not; *maybe* he was coming back for the cases, saw the cops and dumped the Merc? *Maybe* those cases are somewhere we didn't look! Maybe there are clues in there!"

"Clues?"

"Yeah, you know? Clues?"

There was a silence again, before Striker growled. "How long you say before you're here?"

"Eight minutes."

"How's the car?"

Tag looked over at the rear. The leather Recaro interior was drenched; water poured down the back seats and pooled where a discerning bottom would travel.

"Okay, the car is ....okay."

Tag hit the off button and said a little prayer.

Abu Al Zachari sat on a hard chair, opposite the two Sudanese. He crossed his long legs and sat back.

He had eaten well enough. The curried goat, the rice and roti, finished with fruit, yogurt and honey, had filled his stomach, and revived him further. He thanked God for his food and his good fortune.

Across the table the two young Africans sipped tea.

Okot was tall and rangy, where his younger cousin Ismail was stocky, with powerful shoulders and arms.

Zachari sat further back and folded his arms. This was always the way with Al Qaeda. Different soldiers for different tasks; none could know or even see the others before the jihad. His role had always been to provide the weapons or explosives. He would finally meet with the shooter, just hours before the attack, just as he had before, back in Spain when he had handed the IEDs to his warriors. The shooters were always young, scared and rarely lived to tell the tale. This occasion was different, in that he too would be present at the moment of glory, and if God was willing, all his soldiers would survive.

"So you know this weapon well, my brothers?"

Okot put down his cup.

"The FIM 92 Stinger was first manufactured in the late 1960's. It was used by the Russians against our Afghan brothers and against our Serbian brothers in the war of Yugoslavia. It weighs 15.17 kilos and has an effective range of three miles.

Both Ismail and I have fired this weapon before. Now, with God's will, we will use it against the non-believers. All we need to know is where and when, my brother."

"In good time, Okot; first we shall pray, then I shall collect the weapons. Tonight we will prepare and rest, and in the morning we shall destroy our target. I will be with you every step of the way, my brothers. Unlike many of our soldiers, we shall all return from this holy crusade. That is my promise to you."

Ismail had been quiet for the duration of the meal. He seemed a deep soul with dark eyes, that gave him the appearance of a man with an old head on the youngest of shoulders.

"I am ready to die for Allah, my brother. To be martyred is a great honour. I came to this country to fight, to be part of the holy war against the infidel. This life is of no consequence. It is the next that is important."

Zachari nodded.

"Allah in his wisdom has brought us all together this night. It is his will and understanding that gives us the strength and resources to wage the holy war. It will be his spirit that decides all our fates tomorrow."

"Praise be to Allah," said Ismail.

"God is great," said Okot.

Tag pulled up outside Striker's house.

The rain and wind were whipping young saplings back and forth. They had been planted either side of the street, in an attempt to make the new village look more homely. It would be many years before they made a difference.

The young cop couldn't stop his left leg from shaking.

Striker was waiting in the doorway. He was not a happy bunny. He strode out into the foul weather, dipping his head against the sheets of rain.

Before he made the driver's door he walked around the back of the car and surveyed the damage.

He bellowed at Tag.

"Out! Get the fuck out now!"

Tag defiantly slid over to the passenger seat. He intended to stay dry, and temporarily out of the reach of the marauding sergeant.

The rain was so incessant Tag had to shout to be heard over it.

"Get in, Striker! Stop being a hard arse. It's a cop car, for Christ sake. "

Striker almost ripped the driver's door from its hinges.

"Yes! My fuckin' cop car!"

He dropped into the seat and looked back at the drenched upholstery; pebbles of shattered glass floated in pools of rainwater that had formed on the contoured seats.

"Fuckin' marvelous, Westland! I leave you alone for a couple of hours, and you wreck my car."

"It was the rioters," whined Tag.

Striker pulled the offending blue light's connector from the cigarette socket. Tag, in his excitement, had forgotten to remove it. He gave the rookie a 'disappointed dad' look and traced the cable back to the rear foot-well. The busted light was half submerged in water. His eyes burned into Tag.

"Let me guess; you've been to see a woman?"

"Erm..."

"Don't fuckin' answer yet, son, I'm not done...You've been to see some sweet little honey. I know this, because you think with the little head in your pants, rather than the bigger head on your shoulders. Correct so far? And, you're unable to keep the smaller appendage in your trousers for longer than twenty four hours...yes?"

"It wasn't quite like tha..."

"Shut up! So you thought you would impress said female by fixing the blue light to the roof and driving her around for a while?"

"Not exact..."

"You couldn't be bothered to read the fuckin' label on the light that expressly tells you not to go over seventy miles per hour."

"Just a minute..."

"The light flew off the roof, broke the screen and smashed the trunk to within an inch of its fuckin life. Am I warm so far, you fuckin' bollocks?"

"Well not..."

"Am I fuckin' warm?" bellowed Striker.

Tag hung his head. "Suppose," he mumbled.

Striker felt like he would explode. He pointed a finger at Tag, but words would not come out of his mouth. He took a breath, then another; then another.

When he felt calm enough, he started the engine.

"We'll change the car. Then we'll check on your lead."

"Okay," said Tag meekly.

They pulled away with a screech of tyres.

"When we get to headquarters," said Striker. "I'll do the talking."

"That would be good," said Tag.

It took the pair just under an hour to acquire a new car from the suspicious VMU officer. Much to Tag's amusement, Striker had stuck rigidly to his own version of the rioting hordes story. The uniformed constable, whose role it was to protect the fleet of police vehicles from misuse, hadn't believed the tale any more than Striker had, but nonetheless, they now had a shiny new Ford to play with.

They arrived at the flat in Burnley just before midnight. The forensic team had left, and a solitary officer sitting in his patrol car, sheltering from the foul weather, had replaced the two cops guarding the scene.

Striker's mood had lightened somewhat, buoyed by him finding some random jazz station on the Mondeo's radio.

Tag walked over to the marked patrol vehicle and flashed his ID at the cop inside. The guy seemed disinterested. If you had put Tag in this cop's shoes, a couple of days ago, he would probably have behaved in the same way.

Bored and pissed off.

Striker and Tag started their search in the room where they had found Tariq Hussain and poor Ismi. After that they checked a dirty bathroom that made Tag retch, and a box-room, which was totally empty.

It was obvious that the two cases they sought were not on display. There was a loft hatch in the box-room.

"Up you go, son," said Striker, with more than a hint of pleasure.

Tag gave a sarcastic smile and used the chair that Hussain had been tied to, to gain access to the hatch.

After ten minutes of thrashing around in the dark and using his full swearword vocabulary, Tag emerged empty-handed.

"He took them with him," said Striker, his tone matter-of-fact.

Tag brushed dust from his hair, and ignored his sergeant's comments. "This is a safe house for a terrorist. There has to be more hiding places."

Striker shrugged, impressed by the rookie's newfound positivity. "Go on, kid."

Tag shook his head and stepped out to the small square of carpet at the top of the stairs. The door that Striker had pushed off its hinges hours earlier was propped up against the wall.

Tag moved it; behind was a cupboard.

"Ha!" he declared triumphantly, pulling at the handle.

Inside was no more than an electricity and gas meter.

Tag pushed his hands into his pockets. He'd been sure the cases would be here. He stared at the grey boxes inside the cupboard, watching the disc on the electricity meter turn slowly.

Striker put his hand on Tag's shoulder. "It was a fair call, son, but it didn't come off."

Tag looked again. Something wasn't right.

"A gas meter," he mumbled. Then he turned to Striker. "A fuckin' gas meter! You see any appliances up here? There's no kitchen! Where is the kitchen?"

The two men strode downstairs and out onto the street. The rain that seemed intent on drowning them instantly drenched their clothes. Tag pulled up his hoodie and followed the wall to the left of the entrance door. It turned into a small yard. An out-building, that had once been a wash-house and toilet back when the property was built, sat in front of them.

Striker didn't mess about and leaned into the door. The lock gave way and the wood around it splintered.

They were inside in seconds.

Sat in the middle of the floor of the tiny kitchen were the two cases.

Tag thought he might burst. He reached for Ismi's luggage.

"Whoa!" shouted Striker, grabbing the young cop by the arm. "Not so fast, son."

Striker didn't need to explain his actions. Tag felt suddenly stupid. Opening a known terrorist's suitcase was not the best idea he'd had this week.

Striker pulled a Maglite from his pocket and carefully checked the seal around the child's case for any sign of a boobytrap. Then he removed a second device from his jacket. It looked like a miniature vacuum.

"Sniffer," he whispered. "Detects most common explosives. I brought it on the slim chance you were right."

Tag mouthed a couple of obscenities as the detective moved the device slowly across the case, back and forward.

"Clean," he said.

He pushed the case to Tag, who opened it and commenced a search.

Striker worked on Zachari's case. Again, the sniffer did its job. Striker sat the case on its back and carefully opened it.

Resting on top of neatly folded clothing was a computer. He gently lifted the notepad and held it up in his hand. "I reckon it's this baby we need to look at."

Tag hadn't quite mastered the term 'methodical' and had pulled all Ismi's belongings onto the floor in a pile.

Striker stood.

"I'd pop those back in the case, son."

Within minutes they were speeding back to Striker's house; the car was touching its limit of a hundred and fifty mph as the sergeant showed off his expert driving skills, despite the shocking visibility.
"Why your gaff then?" asked Tag.
"I have some kit there. We can examine the laptop at my house."
"I thought Forensics did that?"
Striker nodded.
"They do, but they take time. I have a feeling we don't have much of that."

Abu Al Zachari slipped out of the terraced house, leaving the two boys sleeping.
It was amazing to him that he had been able to remain the grey man for so many years. The same grey man the British SAS pride themselves on.
After all he was not a man that was easily concealed from view.
His great height had always set him apart from his peers.
The Sikh people were notoriously tall, they also had massive natural bull strength. Pakistani and Afghan men were coltish, but as an Arab, Zachari was muscled differently. Yes, he was of great height, but his ligaments matched his bone; he was lean, but his quads and glutes were tremendously strong. His long arms boasted long powerful muscles. Add to that his almost inhuman tolerance of pain, and he cut a formidable figure.
He stretched himself. The tracksuit and baseball cap, the street-clothes that were the norm for the area he was walking, meant he cut a younger shadow than his actual years. Take away the cap and add a suit jacket to the mix, dip his shoulders, put on a slight limp, and he was ten years older than his forty-two.
He had long since mastered the art of blending into the brickwork.
The two boys had prayed long and hard, cleansed themselves, in preparation for the rigors of battle. They thought they understood death. They thought they knew why they might die in conflict. It was because God willed it.
Zachari doubted that.
They would die if they messed up; if they didn't pull the trigger at exactly the right time, they would definitely die there and then.

Zachari would execute them where they stood. Failure was not an option.

The next stage of the operation was one of the most dangerous. Moving weapons from the safety of their hiding place to the safe house, and then to the firing point, was perilous in the extreme. The best laid plans had been foiled by a nosy policeman; look back at the most infamous arrests in history. Most of those poor bastards had been incarcerated completely by accident.
This job was best done alone. The boys could never know the location of the weapons. Should they be captured, they would talk. Maybe not when questioned by the police, but when faced with the rigors of the security services, well, that was another matter.
Zachari strode purposely toward the centre of the city; even at this late hour, and with the relentless wind and rain, people still went about their business. Meals were bought and sold, cigarettes were smoked, students drunkenly loved and lost.
He walked the Curry Mile, until it became Oxford Road. He passed the Palace Theater and headed right toward Piccadilly station.
He was soaked to the skin by the time he reached the car park at the rear of the station.
The black cab was parked exactly where it should be; the ignition keys were hidden on the front near-side wheel.
Zachari started the cab and switched off the fare light.
He pulled out into traffic, to the casual observer, just another Asian taxi driver.
In reality, he was the man who about to commit the biggest atrocity ever achieved by any terrorist organisation on British soil.
"Allah Wah kourodia," he said.
God is all-seeing.

CHAPTER NINETEEN

Tag sat in Striker's 'study'. He did a full circle in the swivel chair.

"Welcome aboard the Enterprise, Spock."

He ran his hand over a massive server.

"Fuck me, Striker. You have enough kit here to start a small cyber-war."

"It's a hobby."

"Yeah, right."

Striker plugged Zachari's net-book into his system and started to type.

Tag leaned over to see massive amounts of code being written at breakneck speed.

"Hey, this is like the Matrix, man!"

"Shut up."

Tag was still buzzing about the luggage, and the none-too-shabby fact that it was his idea, his *clue*, which had almost, definitely solved the case.

Not forgetting the stark reality that *he* was the one that found said cases. Vis a vis, he now had hero status.

Therefore, Tag reckoned that all car-related problems were now written off and the slate was clean.

He spun another three-sixty in the chair.

"I've been thinking, Striker."

"Uh uh?"

"Well, now that I am part of the team, you know, solving stuff and that."

"Yes."

"Well that, and the fact that you are only eight years older than me..."

"Yes."

"Well I think you should stop calling me...son."

"There!" said Striker ignoring the rookie.

"Where?" asked Tag peering at the screen.

Striker cracked his fingers and stretched himself in his chair.

"Terrorists don't send e-mail to each other anymore. It's too risky, the guys in the CIA don't give a monkeys about your privacy. They will intercept anything with a perceived risk to it. That includes every time you book a trip by air, mention a war or the government; talk to an Arab or an Afghan, whatever. So your modern day terrorist types write an email in the draft section of a provider and leave it there. The sender and recipient both know the address and password and simply open the account and read the draft section. It's like a dead letterbox on the net. The message never gets sent. It can't be intercepted."

"Right," said Tag tentatively. "So what have we got?"

Striker turned the screen. "This."

Tag peered. The message read: LS740 بلاكبول إلى يصل 1325 ساعات 241013.

"Oh fuck," said Tag under his breath.

"What?"

"You hacked Zachari's mail?"

"Exactly," boasted Striker.

Tag pulled the keyboard toward him, opened a new window and started a Google search.

"That," he pointed at the screen. "Is the Jet2 flight LS740 arriving from Malaga into Blackpool at thirteen twenty five hours tomorrow."

"You read Arabic script?"

"Erm...yeah, well a little..."

Striker patted Tag on the head.

"Well done, son."

To the west of Leyland lay Moss Side. It had been nothing more than green fields and older housing, back in the day. It was now a mix of modern urban dwellings and business premises. An industrial estate, nestled between the old town of Leyland and the relatively new sprawl of private, and not so, social housing.

The 'Moss' had a reputation for being what the better-heeled residents of Leyland called 'rough.'

It had joined Wade Hall estate on the list of areas to look down your nose at.

Danny liked it.

The place was white.

Slade sat in the driver's seat of his eight day old Range Rover Sport.

Things, and times, were very fuckin' good for Danny.

He'd spent his childhood in Harehills, the area of Leeds a stone's throw from where Peter Sutcliffe plied his trade in the late nineteen seventies. These days, it was what Danny called a 'spot the white man' place. Other than the odd Bulgarian, it was like fuckin' Bangladesh. From age eight, he'd cooked, cleaned and cared for his addict mother in that town. He grew up tough. Things had been shit.

The British army had both saved him and deserted him in equal amounts. He loved being a soldier. Everything was always organised, clean and tidy. It couldn't have been more different from Danny's life at home.

Rather than kick out against it, he loved the regimented life and discipline, the constant battle to push your body further and further.

Most of all, he loved that you got to kill people.

Danny had killed lots of people.

Four Irish, dozens of Serbs, and countless Arabs.

Whenever Private Danny Slade was sent into conflict, he ensured that he got himself bodies.

What was the fuckin' point otherwise?

Later in life, thanks to Grant Bliss, he'd managed to dodge a court martial that would have ended his military career.

Should the proceedings have materialised, they would have ensured he shared a cell with other sad bastards serving a life sentence. Slade was accused of disciplinary offences that involved torturing Iraqi prisoners of war. Bliss's influence had ensured his otherwise perfect army record remained unblemished.

On his very honorable discharge from the army, he walked straight into the job of his dreams.

He looked out toward his small industrial unit that nestled behind a newly built German-owned pizza factory. Slade would never eat a pizza from 'Dr Oetker'. His dislike of the Teutonic race was verging on the psychotic. The fact that they hated the Jews didn't mean shit.

The football thing was enough to ensure anyone who was even suspected of being German deserved to fuck off and die.

If you were white, English and Protestant, you had a chance with Danny. If not, it was best to jog on.

Danny Slade once killed an Iraqi man for wearing a Celtic shirt. He pushed both his eyes into his skull.

A security light flickered over the door of the building. It revealed a newly painted sign above a solitary roller shutter.
'3D Skip Hire'.
The previous company had ceased trading during the double dip recession the government said didn't happen.
The downturn may not have given the residents of greater London much cause for concern, but anyone north of the Watford Gap had been firmly in the shit. Danny had rented the building seven months earlier. Bliss had given him the money. It was a good location, nice and quiet.
Rain lashed against his windscreen, and what had become a gale rocked the car with each gust. On the Range Rover's six speaker sound system, the nice people at the Environment Agency were dishing out flood warnings for fun.
He pushed open the heavy door of the English flagship 4 x 4 and braced himself against a very nasty night.
By the time he'd managed to unlock the two deadbolts on the shuttered doors, he was piss-wet through.
Danny stamped his feet on the concrete floor and pulled off his coat. Inside the unit was warm, and dry, he'd fitted it out himself, it was a safe place to work, plan and store his kit.
Daniel Slade had provided the Heckler and Koch weapons for the hit on the two Paki kids. The impressive guns shown off in the Abdullah Hussain pictures; the weapon that shot Ayesha Chowdry. Slade didn't just find firepower. He sourced and supplied the anti-surveillance kit that kept the Right Honorable Alistair Sinclair clean in the eyes of the law.
Danny spent many hours ensuring Sinclair's safety, yet the man didn't like Slade, and the feeling was mutual. Danny knew what people like him were all about, all mouth and no bottle.
Sinclair had Danny's closest ally, Grant Bliss, in his pocket. The politician always got what he wanted. The two men may have grown a fledgling political party between them, but Sinclair was the alpha male. Whatever he said was gospel.

Despite all good sense, Sinclair had insisted on visiting Danny's unit. It was just hours before the job on the girl. He'd wanted to play with the guns, like some kid in a secret toyshop; he wanted to have his picture taken holding them. He'd been so desperate to fire the weapons, pleading with Bliss to take him somewhere, anywhere, so he could shoot them.

Danny had refused and, for once, Bliss had backed him up. It was a stupid risk, a small threat admittedly, but why take it?

He'd overheard Sinclair bad-mouthing him on his way out to the car; the spoilt brat not getting his own way for once.

Bliss continued to support his friend, he always had, but Danny remembered every word Sinclair had said about him.

Slade was like an elephant; unpredictable and lethal with it.

Danny stepped over to a metal table.

The best bomb maker he'd ever known had delivered the device, on time, and on budget, as arranged.

Inside a vacuum-packed plastic bag was a rucksack similar in appearance to the ones carried by the 7/7 London bombers. Danny didn't get the irony.

The colour and styling of the cheap bag may have been comparable to those carried by the Islamists, but there the similarity ended.

Inside this rucksack was enough plastic explosive to flatten the unit he stood in and kill everyone in a fifty yard radius outside.

The cool thing about the bomb was its stability; you could throw it on a fire and the only thing that would burn would be the rucksack itself.

However, once the mobile phone that sat in a separate pocket was attached to the main charge, it became a different animal. It could be detonated by a call to the phone. On the other hand, some poor bastard making or receiving a call, or even checking messages close to the device, could set it off.

In modern wars, you didn't check Facebook when searching for improvised explosive devices.

It could just blow your limbs off.

Danny checked his watch. 'Mad' Barry Williams would be arriving within minutes. He smiled to himself. All his life he'd been able to spot a complete loser, and Danny would quite enjoy dealing with the cocky little piss head.

Providing he survived the drop of course; either way, Barry would not see his fee.

The violence on the streets had come to a virtual halt.

Even rioters took a break when it was pissing down and blowing a gale. It had given the cops a few hours respite; enabled them to regroup.

The reprieve would be short-lived.

Williams would drop the device over the wall of the Al Jazeera Mosque, in Fulwood. It was the newest and largest place of worship for the Muslim community outside of Manchester. It had still to be completed and as yet had been unused. Barry Williams thought he was going to destroy bricks and mortar. But unbeknown to the fool, tomorrow dozens of dignitaries of the Muslim community would be kneeling in reverence to their God and blessing the new mosque. Within a split second they would be blown to pieces.

Rain or no fuckin' rain. That would wake 'em up.

Westland had never ventured to the second floor of Police Headquarters. It was a deified place of secret offices and the hushed corridors of power. The ACPO conference room was dimly lit and wood paneled. The muted lighting and dark mahogany only added to the feel of quiet authority.

Westland would normally have been nervous in such hallowed halls, reminding him of the bad old days at university.

However he was convinced he was on a course, an unstoppable journey toward something huge in his life.

He could only imagine what lay ahead. His worst nightmares hadn't come close to the real events that had brought him to this place. Right now, a few suits were small potatoes.

Striker fired up his iPad. Westland sat to his right. Directly opposite was an immaculately dressed man from the security services, to his left sat Errol Graham and next to him Geoff Green, some high flyer in the civil aviation authority. The Chief Constable managed to look like he was actually in charge by sitting at the head of the grand table.

Striker would have liked to have his boss present; but this was an invitation only party, and Slick Jemson wasn't on the guest list.

The Chief nodded toward Striker.

"Go on, Sergeant, it's late. Let's get this over with."

Striker stretched his neck. He didn't like the vibe in the room. This was a hanging jury.

He cleared his throat and went straight to the heart of the matter.

"We have information that a passenger aircraft is about to be the subject of a terrorist attack on the UK mainland. We believe the perpetrators have access to surface to air missiles and intend to use them against a Jet2 flight landing in Blackpool later this afternoon."

The secret service guy, who looked like a cross between James Bond and an accountant, held up a hand and offered an affected smile to the room.

"Blackpool?"

Striker's mood grew instantly dark.

"Okay, sir. As our friend in the security services can't comprehend that a northern bound airliner is not worth attacking, I'll get to the nitty-gritty.

Two days ago Ayesha Chowdry was about to deliver a package to the occupant of 307 Penrith House, Preston."

Striker tapped some keys and the body of the beautiful, posed and pale girl, filled a screen at the end of the table.

"She was professionally executed, but the perpetrators were disturbed by my colleague here and they left the package that you see in her left hand; a box containing an electrical component."

Striker hit another key; the image on the screen changed. In the new shot, the body of a young man dangled grotesquely over a garage pit.

"We believe she had been given that component by this man, her secret lover, Abdullah Hussain. We think that the package got them both killed."

"Tell us something we don't know," barked Errol Graham.

Striker gave the tired-looking senior detective a withering stare and his trademark sigh. He hit a key and another shot filled the screen.

Striker went for the big sell.

"This is Abu Al Zachari, an Al Qaeda quartermaster. The picture on the left was taken from his fake Iraqi passport, the one he used to obtain his UK residency, the one he used to enable him to live in the midst of the people of Preston. The picture on the right was released by officers investigating the Madrid train bombings. Zachari provided the explosives for that atrocity. He was identified from that single shot, by an American reporter he attacked in Iraq. Not content with being a murderer and terrorist, Zachari is a rapist. His victim produced DNA evidence to back up her claim, and this snapshot became the definitive image of one of the most wanted men in the world."

Striker turned to the spook.

"Isn't that right, sir?"

Even the most sceptical could see the similarities, but the MI5 agent showed no emotion at all.

"You have the floor, Striker," he said.

The detective knew he had to play the game. "The image on the left is definitely the occupant of 307. We have an ID from a taxi driver who worked with him. The same guy, Iftikar Din, picked him up outside the flats, and took him to Burnley. His statement is in the evidence pack.

That was around twelve hours *before* Ayesha was murdered. Zachari was forced to leave prior to the delivery because, once again, he'd given into his weakness, and raped a woman in his flat. He intended to kill her, but she escaped.

By the time Ayesha Chowdry got there, he was long gone; forced into the move as his would-be victim had survived. A clean up team was there within hours."

Striker hit another button and the documents from the taxi office filled the screen.

"He has been using the name Mustapha and traveling with a young girl.

We know virtually nothing about the child, but believe her to have used the name Ismi. We do know, however, that she is dead."

Striker pulled up a shot of the Burnley crime scene. It drew a gasp from the Air Safety guy.

Westland turned his head.

"She was strangled using a ligature and her body found in a safe house used by Zachari. The premises were a short walk from where Din had dropped him that same morning. This is the same flat that Tariq Hussain QC was taken to; the place where he was beaten within an inch of his life; beaten until he gave Zachari the combination to his safe."

Errol Graham leaned in.

"And what was in the safe?"

Striker flashed up a close-up of the circuit-board recovered from Ayesha Chowdry's hand.

"More of these; the components he needs so badly, the components that Abdullah had been hiding in Tariq Hussain's Nelson office."

The Chief Constable had taken on the look of a bamboozled quiz participant.

"And what is this...err...component, Sergeant?"

"A trigger mechanism, sir; and not just one, there were four in the safe. We believe they are essential to his plan to bring down the aircraft."

The security services guy coughed into his hand. He used the Chief Constable's first name to maximum effect.

"John, I am the first to agree that we have a problem here, but two photographs of a similar looking forty-something Arab, some dead kids and a couple of circuit boards do not make a terrorist plot."

Striker felt the muscles in his neck seize. He clenched his fists.

"You pompous asshole."

The Chief held up his hand. "Ewan! Settle down."

The MI5 man smiled and flipped through the report in front of him. "Yes, settle down, Sergeant. I don't see any forensic reports backing up this evidence of yours. Where are the fingerprints, the DNA? This guy could be Zachari, he has a passing resemblance, but can you be sure? I don't think so."

Striker was sure he had him.

"We have a partial fingerprint and DNA sample at the lab right now. It will be identified as Zachari, I'm confident..."

"Confident of what, Striker?"

The spook held his fake smile. He wafted his report in the face of the detective.

"And where did you get this partial print and DNA sample from? Where did you find this...evidence?

Striker wanted to punch his lights out, but he kept his voice level and measured.

"From a shoe; a shoe belonging to the rape victim."

"And does this victim have a name?" sneered the spy.

"Mackintosh, Sandra Mackintosh," spat Striker.

The man sat back in his chair and flicked through his papers. "So where is her statement, corroborating the evidence?" He lifted his arms. "More to the point, where is Sandra Mackintosh?"

Errol Graham had heard enough. He leaned his bulk into the table. He had little time for Striker, but he could see what was happening, and didn't like it one bit.

His face was haggard, he looked exhausted.

"She was beheaded by a mob. Last night, a few hundred yards from her flat. She...no they... Sandra and a guy called William Wilson, walked into a street barricade on Avenham.

They cut off her fuckin' head with a knife and hung Wilson from a lamp-post."

Graham slammed his fist into the table.

"So, right now, I think we should listen to the Sergeant."

The spook was not intimidated. He looked around the table and met everyone's eye, one by one.

"So we don't have a witness to tie the shoe to the suspect?"

There was more silence.

"And this circuit board, what is it exactly? Again, I don't see any expert testimony in this evidence pack. I didn't realise that Sergeant Striker and his trained poodle were electronics experts. A trigger mechanism, you say?"

Tag was incredulous, he hadn't a clue about the bloody circuit boards, but the poodle comment was well out of order.

His mouth got the better of him.

"Yeah, but there was this like spy type guy that…"

Striker stopped Tag in his tracks with a look he knew well, but it was too late.

The room waited.

"A spy, you say?" said the MI5 operative. A broad smile appeared on his face and he opened his arms to the table.

"You really expect the security services to start major incident procedures? Scramble the RAF? "

He gestured toward the man to his left. "You want the Civil Aviation Authority to change the flight paths of passenger jets? Declare a state of emergency for Blackpool funfair? All this, on the basis of the evidence sitting in front of us tonight?"

Striker could feel the job falling through his fingers. He dropped his head and voice.

"We will have further fingerprint and DNA evidence later today; taken from the Burnley flat and Hussain's Mercedes car. It will identify this man as Zachari, I'm sure of it. We have recovered a laptop belonging to the suspect. If you don't want to call him by his name, that's okay, but he is a kidnapper, a rapist and a murderer. On that laptop, we discovered an email targeting the Jet2 flight."

The MI5 man flicked at his pages.

"As I've already said, your fingerprint and DNA evidence is nonexistent. Tomorrow is another day, Sergeant. We don't identify terrorists by hunches. As for the forensic examination of the computer, again I don't see any expert testimony here, so I take it that it was you who 'found' this information?

You used your expertise as a hacker to obtain this so called evidence, didn't you?"

There was a sharp intake of breath from the Chief as the spook went for the jugular.

"You have illegally obtained this so-called evidence. We couldn't even use it in a court of law. You are a maverick, Sergeant, you may mean well, but your behaviour falls well short of what is expected. At best, hacking into a personal computer is a disciplinary offence, if not a criminal matter."

Striker exploded. "Well you'd better arrest me then!"

Westland grabbed Striker by the arm and pulled him back into his seat.

"Sergeant Striker didn't hack anything," said Tag calmly. "The laptop wasn't even password protected. I was a witness to that."
The MI5 man sneered at the young cop.
"Your loyalty is touching, Officer. Even so, all you have is a single draft document that lists the arrival time of one aircraft to a provincial airport in the middle of the afternoon. Correct?"
Striker remained silent.
"Any suggestion of a threat? A launch site? A method?"
The agent waited another beat.
Tag wanted to burst.
"I didn't think so."

Tag found half a bar of chocolate in the glove box of the Mondeo and offered Striker a square.
The detective shook his head.
Tag sniffed it himself and decided against it. After what seemed like an age, the young cop broke the silence.
"They aren't going to do anything, are they?"
"No."
Tag nodded slowly. He was exhausted. He was so tired he felt sick.
"So that's it then?"
Striker was looking in the rear view mirror.
"Not quite yet, son."
The rear door of the car opened and a very wet Errol Graham dropped heavily onto the back seat.
"Sir," acknowledged Striker.
The senior detective brushed rain from his hair. "Skip the formality, Striker. I'm not a fool. Why don't the security services want to catch this Zachari guy?"
Striker looked over his shoulder and gave Graham a cold stare.
"Oh, they want to catch him alright. They just don't want *us* to catch him."
Graham quizzically raised both eyebrows and waited.
"That would be a need to know situation, sir."
The superintendent's eyes flashed.
"Don't give me that, Sergeant! All this cloak and dagger shit doesn't wash with me. I've seen it all and bought the fucking T shirt."

Striker held up a hand. "All I'm saying, boss, is that some pretty heavy hitters will not rest easy now they know Zachari is in the country. Someone on the inside of MI5, or more likely MI6, chose to drop us some pretty serious information. They also chose to tell us what that circuit board was for. Now shit for brains in there, is doing his level best to stop us. You work it the fuck out."

Graham rubbed his chin. "I think the question is, which spook is toeing the company line?"

Striker shrugged. "I don't really care, boss."

The powerful detective dropped his tone and decided his brief of 'need to know' was a pile of shit.

"Look, boss, what I know is this.

Zachari is cutting all his ties to the UK. The girl may have been getting to an age where she understood too much about his extra-curricular activities; but I think he killed her because her usefulness had run its course.

She was not his preferred type of victim; he has always picked women in their mid thirties to late forties; big brash and brassy. Ismi's clothing was torn, but I'd lay a hundred bucks right now that there was no sexual contact. It was one for the cameras, like the knife he left after beheading a British agent. He's thinks he's a star. In his head he's tying up loose ends and doesn't give a shit if we know he's here; he's on the red carpet."

To Striker's shock, Tag was in there. The rookie sat back in his seat, didn't turn, just looked at the raindrops chasing each other down the screen.

He'd picked up some of the Lancashire accent the last months, but this was as measured a message as any statesman. "They aren't sure if the target, the Jet2 flight, is a definite. That message we found could be the arrival of another fighter, another poor fucker brainwashed enough to kill his own countrymen. Even so, it could be right on the money. Unfortunately, there are two very different power sources working against each other here. One is for us, one against. I think the question is, sir, are you going to help us catch this fucker or not?"

The senior detective pursed his lips for a second.

"I've got every last cop to the man working twelve hour shifts. We arrested seven suspects for the Mackintosh and Wilson murders two hours ago, and as a result, the town will go up like a tinderbox as soon as this fuckin' weather stops. I don't have a single lead on the Hussain and Chowdry killings. Every jack working on the initial murder is on their knees. I don't have anything to give you."

Striker eyed his senior.
"I want a helicopter and a pilot from first light, until that plane lands."
Graham met the stare, pushed open the car door and stepped into the rain. He shoved his head back inside.
"I'll make the call," he said. "You'll have the chopper. Don't let me down."

CHAPTER TWENTY

Barry Williams stared at his bottle of Stella. He'd tried to get his head down but after tossing and turning, head spinning, he'd left his wife Gina snoring quietly upstairs.

Barry decided on a couple of beers in the kitchen, just a couple, mind, just to calm the nerves.

The last days had been a whirlwind for him.

He'd missed most of the riots; he'd been too busy with his new job. Barry would dearly have loved to have been part of the tear-up with the Paki bastards. Smash a few heads.

But he had to look on the plus side. He now had the ideal job, looking after Mr. Sinclair; and what a role it was turning out to be. His new mate Danny had given him the opportunity he'd been waiting for to make a real difference, to really hurt the black twats. It was almost like an honour. Like God had looked down and said, 'Yeah, Barry, I always knew you were the man to sort this out'.

Barry knew that Pakis didn't believe in the real God. They didn't believe in Jesus or Christmas or anything like that. To them it was all Allah this and Allah that. They pretended to be religious, going to the mosque and all, but Barry knew the truth, he saw them out drinking and smoking pot, dealing it too.

All these years they'd made his life a misery, taking white men's jobs, riding around in their flashy Mercs and BMWs, turning local pubs into fuckin' curry houses; showing off to the young white girls on the estate; and Barry knew all too well what they got up to with them, he'd seen the programmes on telly, dirty black fuckers, giving drugs to little girls so they can fuck them and hand them round their Paki mates.

"Dirty black cunts," he said to himself. "Deserve all they get, they do."

The package that Danny Slade had given him sat on the chair next to him. Barry split his time between staring at the rucksack and studying his beer.

He felt a shiver, even though the kitchen was warm.

"Dirty fuckin' black cunts," he repeated.

Westland carried two coffee cups into Striker's lounge. He was desperately tired, so fatigued even, that his hands shook slightly as he lay down the brews next to an open laptop.

Striker seemed himself; Westland hadn't even seen him yawn. He may have detected a slight darkening under his eyes, a thickening of Striker's normally close cropped beard, but other than that, the machine kept on running.

"Found what you needed?" he said.

Striker tapped away at the keys.

"LS725 will approach from the east. The captain will only disengage the auto-pilot in the final couple of minutes of the flight, so unless the tower advises otherwise, due to weather or other traffic, we know the exact path of the aircraft to the meter."

Tag sipped his brew. "Trouble is, Zachari will have that same information."

"Maybe," nodded the detective. "But the weather will be shitty. We have heavy rain, high winds and low cloud forecast for lunchtime." Striker walked over to a printer and took four A4 sheets from it. He laid them on the table. They formed a map of Preston, Kirkham and Blackpool.

"This red line here," he pointed, "is the flight path of the Malaga plane. The numbers that run along its length is the height of the aircraft on final approach. Now, as the cloud cover tomorrow is forecast at around eight hundred feet, the plane won't be visible to a shooter until it reaches...here."

Tag leaned in to take a closer look.

"That's the M55 junction at Broughton. Jesus, Striker, the aircraft has more than fifteen miles left to run. Zachari could position himself anywhere along the rest of that route. It will be like looking for a needle in a haystack."

Striker nodded. "That's why we need the helicopter, so you can find the fucker before he pulls the trigger."

Tag straightened with a jolt.

"Me? In a helicopter?"

"Sure. I need to be on the ground to take him down. I can't leave that to a rookie, can I?"

Westland shook his head. "Oh no Striker. No...no...I don't do flying. I don't even do planes. I tried them twice, big ones with four engines. It was still shit. I'm a boat person; a nice comfortable ferry to St. Malo, a little shopping and a leisurely lunch in the flower market at Antibes, that kind of thing. I don't do planes, and I'm definitely not going to get into a helicopter."

Striker gave Tag a withering look and let out the trademark sigh. "All you have to do is sit there and look for the bad guys. It's perfectly safe."

Tag shook his head vigorously.

"Safe? Are you having an episode there, Striker? Flying at a hundred feet, in heavy rain, wind gusting to sixty miles an hour. Oh and some nutter on the ground with a bunch of surface to air missiles. Better still... you... fuckin' Yank, ginger twat...there will be a plane arriving blind above us, travelling on the same flight path, at what, two hundred and fifty miles per hour?"

Striker shrugged his shoulders, and brushed away the insult.

"No need for the hair comments, Westland. Anyway, helicopters can fly in bad weather these days. The pilots are experts, these guys have done it all before, and I don't think Zachari will risk firing at a police helicopter, not unless he has more than one MANPAD."

Tag was incredulous. "He's got more than one! He's got bloody five!"

Striker was losing that temper again.

"Don't be a big girl about this, Westland. This isn't a fucking democracy we have going on here. You are going in the chopper and I'm going to nail this guy, simple as."

Tag jutted out a petulant chin.

"And if I don't?"

"If you don't," spat the detective. "Then we will be picking up body parts from Blackpool promenade for the next month."

Zachari loaded two rockets and one launcher into the black cab. It was essential to the cause that the launchers were sparingly used. He had fitted one of the newly acquired components, to the grip of the precious device. The circuit boards were as prized as the launchers themselves. Many thousands of hard-fought dollars had been paid to the Chinese for those units. More rockets were already on their way from Bulgaria. From there they would find their way to the UK; ready for the next mission.

Rockets were easy to obtain, but the launchers were gold.

The British Secret Service had thought they were so clever. He had personally met with their spy and agreed to buy the MANPADS. The agent was a Muslim, an Arab by birth. Zachari knew he was a traitor the moment he had met him. Yet the brothers would not believe him, shouted him down; nonetheless he had been right.

He was always right.

Zachari had enjoyed punishing the British for their sniveling poor attempt to foil the cause.

He had personally beheaded the spy. He had screamed and screamed and screamed. Leaving the knife that had cut off his head, was the icing on the cake. It was his calling card. Catch me if you can.

Zachari covered the weapons with a blanket and pushed the door of the cab quietly closed.

Then he turned to the forty foot container. The nondescript metal unit held the biggest Al Qaeda weapons stash north of London. It was one of hundreds of international transport containers stacked in the Trafford distribution centre. He secured it with its padlock and seal.

The armourer sat heavily in the driver's seat and briefly closed his eyes. He let his head fall backward against the rest and exhaled slowly.

A broad smile drifted across his face.

Within hours a passenger jet carrying almost two hundred souls would be blown out of the sky.

Men, women and children, all nonbelievers, the infidels would pay for their lack of faith in Allah.

It would be a glorious victory.

The smile grew, then his chest heaved, his laugh exploded in the confines of the cab.

How he laughed.

At exactly 0700 hours Zachari pulled up outside the safe house. Okot and Ismail stepped from the door. It would be the last time they saw Manchester, their house or their jobs. They both had tickets to different European destinations. The cousins would remain separated for many months. They would form new identities, until the time came for them to strike again. The

Africans were the new breed of terrorist, almost impossible to track or trace.

They dropped their very different frames onto the small pull-down seats in the back of the cab.

Both were dressed in white dishdasha with waterproof coats to shield them from the foul weather. Zachari pulled off his street clothes where he sat, and dressed in identical clothing.

Rush hour was the very best time to travel. It was the least likely time to be stopped by a nosy cop. The sheer volume of traffic and number of commuters gave the men the perfect cover.

Just another taxi.

But with all three now in national dress, statistics told them that cops were less likely to stop them.

The two greeted their revered warrior and then fell silent, both eager to find out what their mission was to entail.

Zachari sensed their impatience.

"Keep calm, my brothers, all will be revealed in time. Just settle in and enjoy the ride. You will have your chance of glory."

He selected first gear and pushed down the accelerator.

"You will strike a blow to the infidel today. A blow like no other they have ever taken."

The car pulled away from the curb, carrying its own parcel of death.

CHAPTER TWENTY-ONE

Westland had fallen asleep in the chair. Striker shook him.

"Come on, big boy. It's eight. It'll be light in half an hour and you have a date with Captain Flash, and the chopper squad."

Tag had been dreaming of Scarlet one 't', and to be woken by Striker's less than pretty countenance was a shock to his system. His brain turned its ignition key and all the lights came on.

He rubbed his face awake. "You're not really going to make me get in a helicopter, are you?"

Striker slapped him heavily on the shoulder.

"You'll love it, son, and the weather is changing, the wind is dropping and the cloud cover is up to a thousand feet."

"That still doesn't make me feel any better, Striker."

Striker grabbed his wrist and pulled him from his seat. It felt like he'd been gripped in a vice.

"The search area is bigger now. We need to look as far east as Preston centre."

Tag was inspecting himself in a Jack Daniels mirror to his left. He definitely looked older...definitely older.

He stopped his preening at that snippet. He was wide-eyed.

"Jesus, if they bring it down there, it will kill thousands."

Striker nodded. "And as no fucker is listening to us, we'd better get on with the job, son."

The detective turned and pulled on a Berghaus jacket. "I'll drive you to BAC at Warton. They keep the aircraft there. The captain will fix us both up with personal radios so you can direct me where I need to go."

Tag nodded slowly. Striker could see the turmoil in the young cop's eyes. There was the merest tremor in Tag's voice.

"This guy Zachari, do you think he will be alone?"

""I doubt it," said Striker flatly." "These guys usually work in teams of three."

Tag swept his hair from his forehead, his mind working overtime. Reality had kicked in.

"Will they be armed? I mean other than a fuckin' rocket or two? Will they have guns?"

"I would think so."

Tag laughed; it had a touch of hysteria mixed with the usual sarcasm.

"My vest is back at the nick, I don't suppose you have a spare, just in case these chaps take exception to me flying over their heads as they are about to blow the tail off an Airbus 320?"

Striker turned. "I can do better than that, son, follow me."

Tag padded behind the bulky frame of the sergeant until they reached the door of his integral garage. It was no ordinary internal access. It had a standard facade, but the massive hinges gave away the sheer weight of the door itself.

Striker punched a code into a panel on the right of the opening, and there was a double click-clunk as the locking mechanism released and the door swung open.

As the fluorescents flickered on, Tag's eyes were immediately drawn to the vehicle sitting dead centre.

"Nice car," was all he could think of.

"I like Porsche 911's," said Striker with more than a hint of pride in his voice.

Tag was about to run his hand over the roof of the classic sports model, but caught Striker's gaze and thought better of it.

Tag once again thought about the expensive pictures in the hall and the coffee maker his mother had dreamed of. Now he was feasting his eyes on ninety grand's worth of German babe magnet.

Striker read his mind.

"You will have noticed I don't drink. I don't smoke. I don't have a girlfriend."

Tag walked around the car, admiring the immaculate condition; all thoughts of being shot at temporarily forgotten.

"Yeah, yeah, and that is how you afford the good things in life. I can get my head around the teetotal bit, and the no smoking, but why have a car like this and no woman to sit in it?"

Striker was working on opening a large grey safe. His voice was low. It had a tone to it that Tag had never heard before.

"There was one once."

Tag, always one for not noticing the need to shut the fuck up, perked up no end at this gem of information.

"Really? Go on, tell all."

Striker opened the heavy cabinet and passed Tag a ballistic vest.

"Here, put that on and stop asking questions."

Tag wasn't going to be so easily dissuaded. He pushed his arms into the vest and fumbled with the fastenings.

"Oh come on, Striker; at least tell me a little bit about her. What happened?"

Striker didn't answer his question. He just handed him a revolver. "You ever fired one?"

Tag looked at the Ruger .45 nestled in his palm.

"Err...yes...actually I have. My dad was a keen sports shooter. When we lived in Bahrain, he took me to the range."

"Good," said Striker, selecting an SLP for himself.

He pushed a magazine into the stock, slid the action forward, checked the safety and stowed the weapon behind his back into his belt. "Just make sure you only use it if you have to."

Tag shook his head and handed his gun back to the detective. "I have no wish to go to jail for carrying an illegal firearm. I'll take my chances without it."

Striker groaned. "It isn't illegal; it's my spare. I'm licensed to keep both here at home."

Tag wasn't impressed. "Maybe, but I'm not licensed, I'm not an authorised firearms officer and I would end up inside if I used it."

Striker pushed the gun back into the rookie's hand.

"Trust me on this one. Take the gun. It will make me feel better."

Tag opened the chamber and checked that all six rounds were present.

"I'm beginning to wish we hadn't met," he said.

Abu Al Zachari pulled the taxi into a back street, just one hundred yards from where the body of Mohammed Hussain had been found hanging from the meat hook.

On the left of the street was an industrial unit which displayed a sign announcing it was 'To Let'.

He stepped from the taxi, removed the padlock securing the gates and pushed them open wide enough for him to drive inside.

Once he had edged the cab up to the doors of the unit he alighted again, removed two dead bolt locks and raised the shutters by a chain.

With the taxi safely inside, tucked away from the prying eyes of the world, he sent Okot to secure the gates.

That done, the shutters were pulled down and the three men, together with their deadly cargo, were in position on time and as planned.

Without any order from Zachari, Ismail and Okot unloaded the MANPADS and began to check the weapons for faults.

Once they were happy with their test, they loaded their cargo back into the taxi and joined Zachari at a small wooden table in the corner of the unit.

The great warrior had made tea and had laid out flatbread, hummus and dates. The three ate in silence, until Zachari broke it. His deep commanding tone filled the space between the men. The younger two were spellbound by his magnificence as he laid out the great plan.

They would bring down a passenger plane over the city of Preston, killing two hundred in the air and hundreds more on the ground.

The launch site had been chosen well. All that was left to do was to wash, and pray together.

Allah would guide them to the most glorious of victories against the nonbelievers. If they lived, they would be heroes, if they died, they would be martyrs.

This was a good day to live and a good day to die.

No man cared which.

It was seven minutes past ten a.m. In just over three hours, death would rain from the sky, onto the filth that inhabited the streets of the city.

Should any of their own Muslim brothers be killed, then so be it. It was Allah's will.

'Mad' Barry Williams had fallen asleep at the kitchen table. His dreams caused him misery. When his wife Gina shook him awake, he jumped and cried out in shock.

Gina took a step back. "Oh dear, Barry, are you alright, love?"

Barry rubbed his eyes, his heart was pounding.

"Course I'm fuckin' alright, you silly cow. I was fast asleep there."

Gina was used to Barry's verbal abuse. It was just the way he was.

"Oh okay, love, sorry. I was wondering why you hadn't come up to bed, that's all. I've been awake for a couple of hours; it's gone ten, you know? Are you working for Mr. Sinclair today?"

Barry looked up at his wife.

What a mess you are, just look at the state of you; you've got old and fat before your time; no wonder I never want to fuck you, with your droopy tits and saggy belly. Fuck knows what you would have looked like if you'd ever carried the kid full term. Probably be the size of a fuckin' house.

He sneered at Gina; his heart had stopped pounding, now his belly rumbled.

"Workin'? Oh yeah, love, I will be later, I've got a big job on for the security lads. I was knackered, wasn't I? Workin all fuckin' hours and that? Fell asleep down here, didn't I? But now you've woke me up, I reckon some bacon and eggs wouldn't go amiss."

Gina nodded nervously. She could see Barry wasn't in one of his better moods. Time had taught her not to mess with her husband when he was cranky like this. Too many times she had felt the back of his hand or worse.

"Of course, love, I'll get the bacon on now. You want some fried bread or toast with it?"

Barry was busy rolling a cigarette. "Aye, some toast, and some mushrooms if you've managed to get the shopping done."

Gina busied herself in the fridge.

"I've got some, and they're fresh too, not tinned."

Barry didn't answer. His eyes had drifted back to the rucksack. It sat on the dining chair next to him. It goaded him. He felt briefly sick.

What a fucking idiot you are, Barry. Fell asleep, didn't you? Too many fuckin' Stellas as usual, could've easily hid the bag. The silly cow will be asking questions next.

As Barry recovered from his troubles, Gina was indeed looking directly at the very same item.

"That's new," she said breezily, doing her best not to irritate her tetchy husband, but curious as to the contents of the bulging bag.

Barry was never too good at thinking on his feet. The right answer never came easy, hence his various prison terms.

"It's nothing," was all he could manage. He could have said it was his new work bag, anything to keep Gina sweet; but he just couldn't think quickly enough.

If there was one thing that Gina had learned over the years, being married to 'Mad' Barry Williams, it was not to trust anything that came out of his mouth.

"It doesn't look like nothing, Barry," said Gina bravely. "It looks brand new and full to the brim."

Barry stood, his face contorted into a menacing grimace. He couldn't take his eyes from his wife. He stood, pale and shaking.

Stupid bitch! I'm never going to let you interfere with my new job. Just keep on, bitch, and I'll fuck you up.
How many times have I had to tell you not to interfere with my work? Not to be a fuckin' nosey fat bitch? What happens when you stick your beak in, eh?

Gina saw the venom in his eyes and took a step away from her husband. She grabbed the handle of the nearest saucepan. She knew how violent Barry could be, she had the hospital visits to prove it; but Gina was not one for lying down and taking a beating anymore. She was quite prepared to clock him with whatever came to hand.

Barry saw that she was ready for him, saw the heavy pan on the stove, and like most bullies, backed down.

He sat heavily and his stare couldn't hide his hatred for her.

"Just get me my fuckin' breakfast and shut your mouth," he spat.

Gina took one last glance at the rucksack sitting in her dining-kitchen. The kitchen she had almost paid for from her own salary; the kitchen she would have finished paying for if Barry hadn't forced her out of the job she loved.

Gina didn't like the look of that bag.

More importantly, she didn't like the way her Barry was sweating.

Westland was indeed a rookie, but he wasn't a fool. Even he knew that cops didn't keep guns at home. They certainly didn't have a 'spare' to hand out to their mate in a crisis.

Only certain cops carried guns. On occasions, Striker would indeed be one of them, but he would need to be issued with it, and be given the authority to carry by a senior officer; it was the British way.

Despite all that, Tag felt some comfort from the heavy weapon tucked into his belt.

He had been dropped at the BAC Warton, a major player in the manufacture of defence weapons and aircraft. It boasted its own runway, as the fighters that it sold to over seventeen countries took off and landed there.

In addition to the jets, the arms manufacturer was home to Lancashire Constabulary Air Support Unit.

Now under normal circumstances, Tag would have been interested in the technical specification of the police helicopter and all its ancillary kit. He would have loved to have known how fast it flew, how many candle-powers the lights were, all of the above.

He would've asked all those questions; but as the rotors turned lazily on the bright yellow machine, he was being blown off his feet by the wind. Tag didn't give a shit what the thing could do. He was terrified.

Earlier, Striker had briefed the pilot. He'd left nothing out. All the dangers had been explained. They had pored over the map Striker had printed out earlier.

The plan was to make two or three sweeps of the possible launch area. The first was to try and identify possible launch sites, the second and third, to find the shooters. Striker was insistent that they fly a minimum of fifty meters north or south of the flight-path of the Airbus, so the shooter may consider the helicopter to be on a routine flight, and that if anyone was sighted, they fuck off as quick as.

No U-turns, no second looks.

The pilot simply took in the information, made some notes and nodded.

When it had been Tag's turn to have his safety brief, he discovered that the man was called Captain David Tennant. Tag considered he looked nothing like the actor, or Doctor Who for that matter.

He did have that 'pilot' voice. So much so, that Tag considered the guy might shout 'Tally ho' as the swung into action. One thing was for certain, the guy had just been told he was looking for some nutters armed with stuff that would blow them out of the sky, and he hadn't so much as flinched.

Then it came time to visit the helicopter itself.

Tennant was in his late forties, a rather handsome chap, with salt and pepper hair. He was calm, courteous and walked Tag through all he needed to know about how to behave when they crashed. Tag wasn't impressed.

Neither was he overwhelmed by the fact that Tennant had been a Royal Navy helicopter pilot, and then worked for ten years in the treacherous conditions of the North Sea oil installations.

As far as Westland was concerned, Tennant could have been James Bond, Bruce Lee and John Wayne, all rolled into one. He was still shitting himself.

It had been fully light for almost an hour, but the day remained grey and unsettled. As Tag strapped himself into the observer's seat of the aircraft, rain droplets poured down the screen and the wipers worked overtime.

Tennant increased the power of the engines and indicated for Tag to put on his headset.

"Ready for take-off," he said. It wasn't a question, just a statement. If it had been the former, Tag would have answered with a resounding, "NO!"

The aircraft seemed to lurch upward and forward at the same time, leaving Tag's stomach somewhere on the helipad. He grabbed the side of his seat as Tennant gunned the engines and banked hard left heading for the A583 which they would follow until they reached the start of Blackpool airport's easterly runway.

"Sit back and relax, old chap," said Tennant with a knowing smile. Tag didn't answer, but if a look could say 'fuck off', his was damn close.

Gina Williams was in turmoil. She had never seen her Barry so nervous. She'd made his breakfast, yet despite his hunger, and temper, he'd pushed it around his plate, eating under half. Barry never left food on the plate. Never.

He had moved the rucksack from the kitchen. She didn't know where exactly, and she wasn't about to start a search, as being discovered would surely mean a violent start to the day.

Barry had taken a shower and changed into his favorite clothes, black tracksuit, black trainers and a black baseball cap.

He was too old to carry off the look, but the last youth to tell him so had ended up with a broken jaw, so it was best to let him look like mutton dressed as lamb.

Just after eleven fifteen, he found his keys, recovered the rucksack from its hiding place and slammed the door behind him.

Gina watched him down the path; watched him turn right towards Plungington. Then, in a moment when her heart seemed to stop, he was gone.

She hesitated for a moment, unsure of what to do. She had the strongest feeling of foreboding she had ever known. Stronger even than the day she had started to bleed and lose their baby.

She had no way of knowing what was in that bag, but she knew one thing, whatever it was, it was scaring her Barry, and that was bad.

Gina picked up her sensible coat, pushed on her sensible shoes, flung open her front door and started the dangerous task of following her husband.

Zachari checked his watch for the fourth time. It was exactly two hours before the Jet2 flight LS740 arrived from Malaga. He logged on to the live stream for Blackpool airport and checked the flight for any delays. He smiled as an icon flashed next to the flight number announcing 'on time'.

. Choosing a target bound for a provincial airport and striking at a minor northern city, had been frowned upon by the council of brothers.

It wasn't until he pointed out the possibility of the major prize of a nuclear disaster, they agreed to it.

His calculations could not have been more precise. The launch site he had chosen many months earlier was eighteen miles from the runway. The aircraft would pass directly overhead at fourteen hundred feet between 1310 hours and 1312 hours.

He stretched his long limbs and opened a live weather forecast site. It showed winds gusting to forty-five miles an hour, persistent heavy rain, but the worrying cloud cover was now up to two thousand feet.

As soon as Okot could see the plane, all he had to do was point and shoot. Now the launcher had the necessary component, the secondary phase of the rocket would guide it directly to the aircraft. He couldn't miss. The missile would explode on impact and burning debris and bodies would fall from the sky onto the city of Preston.

Travelling at a hundred and seventy-five mph, the bulk of the plane would strike the ground just before Kirkham and if Allah was looking down on them and bestowing his most gracious of gifts, it would hit the British Nuclear Fuels facility at Salwick.

Zachari anticipated casualties in their hundreds; but if the plane hit BNFL, it would be thousands. Not only that, Lancashire would become desolate and uninhabitable for centuries.

He glanced over at his two brothers in arms. They knelt on brightly coloured prayer mats and muttered quietly.

They were good Muslims; they observed the teachings of Allah and the Quran. They understood the true meaning of Jihad; they knew that the true believer could not water down the true teachings to suit the soft western settlers.

Glory will come. God is great.

Striker was finding it difficult to keep pace with the helicopter, and Westland's directions were not the best. He had bellowed into his radio on more than one occasion, when Tag had sent him down a dead end, or to the wrong building entrance.

Tag was far too scared of crashing to be worried about Striker's temper.

They now had less than an hour before LS740 was due to land and they had identified sixteen different possible launch sites stretching a mile from the runway to fourteen miles away.

That said, although it was preferable for a shooter to be up on firm, high ground and away from prying eyes, the MANPAD was easily deployed anywhere, even from the back of a pick-up. So when Westland had described the search as a needle in a haystack, he had been underestimating the task at hand.

Captain Tennant had done his best to keep Westland comfortable, but wind sheer is unpredictable, and at such low altitude, dangerous in the extreme.

Tag had managed not to scream like a girl on the fairground, but he couldn't prevent the occasional profanity.

That meant that his directions had a surreal feel to them; a strange mix of 'left...no...right...fuck...oh God...straight on...Jesus Christ...'

Striker was throwing the car around in the wet like Mika Hakkinen showing off to his new girl. The flying Finn would have been proud of him, especially as his co-driver was two hundred feet above him and didn't know left from right.

So far, every building was secure, with no sign of tampering. More importantly, there was no sign of Abu Al Zachari and his rockets.

Beneath the banter, fear of failure was edging ever closer.

Gina Williams was soaked. She'd followed Barry to his favorite watering hole, the Princess Alice, just off Plungington Road. Barry would be in the tap room and on his third or fourth pint by now. Gina had tried to huddle in a shop doorway to avoid the worst of the rain, but after fifteen minutes or so, the owner had asked her to move, so she had been standing in the wind and rain for over an hour.

The daughter of a Preston dock worker was made of stern stuff. Whatever Barry was up to, she intended to find out; rain or no rain.

Barry himself was in far more comfortable surroundings. He was holding court with two of his regular drinking cronies, Jimmy and Matty Smith. The rucksack was tucked behind a chair in the corner of the snug. He had yet to connect the mobile phone to the main charge as Danny Slade had instructed him, so he knew the package was safe. After all he didn't want to blow up his favorite boozer and his mates, did he?

He guzzled his beer, feeling the alcohol take effect. His bravado was returning. The fear he had felt sitting at the kitchen table had evaporated into a beer glass. He was warming to his task.

Jimmy and his brother looked up to Barry, and he considered them part of his crew.

Barry drained his Stella and waved the empty glass at the barmaid. "And one each for the lads here, love," he said winking at Jimmy.

"Cheers, Baz," said Jimmy

"Yeah, cheers," mirrored Matty who was ten years younger than his brother and equally stupid.

Barry puffed out his chest, "No worries, lads, I'm feeling flush, aren't I? With this new security job I've got, I'm proper on it."

"You always were lucky when it came to work though, Baz, eh?" said Matty, unaware of how long Barry had been unemployed.

Williams took his pint from the bar and made a show of paying for all three drinks with a twenty.

"Can't keep 'Mad' Barry down, lads."

All three clinked glasses and toasted their luck. There was a brief silence, until Jimmy motioned toward the rucksack.

"What yer got there, Baz?"

Now even someone as dim as Barry Williams knew he should keep his mouth shut on this little matter. Trouble was, Barry didn't like to work alone, and once he had a pint or two inside him, he just couldn't help but brag.

He tapped the side of his nose and leaned forward conspiratorially. "It's a big job I've got on, but it's like real hush-hush."

No-one could be quite sure which of the Smith brothers had use of their solitary brain cell on any particular day. That said, Barry knew he had their attention as they nodded simultaneously, slack-jawed.

"You know we all hate the Pakis, eh?" he began.

More nodding.

"Well, you know the black cunts are building that new mosque on Watling Street Road; fuckin' millions it's costing us taxpayers, that cunt."

"I've never paid tax, Baz," said Matty.

Barry grabbed him by the arm. "Course you have, Matty, we all pay don't we, even when you get the dole, mate, they take tax out of it. When you buy a beer, there's tax on it. I bet you didn't know that the fuckin' council have given 'em thousands towards it n'all."

Matty scratched his head. "I never knew that, Baz."

Barry dropped his voice so the barmaid couldn't hear.

"Anyway, never mind that. I'm gonna blow the fucker up."

Jimmy may have been short on brains, but even he knew this was bigger than anything he'd ever considered.

"Fuck me, Barry; I'm not up for killin' any fucker, Paki or no Paki."

Williams shook his head.

"We ain't killin' any fucker, Jimmy. The place isn't finished, is it? It's a fuckin' building site. All I'm gonna do is fuck the building up. I just need a couple of good lads to keep watch for me while I throw the fuckin' bag over the fence."

Jimmy scratched his head, glanced at his younger sibling and then rubbed his thumb and forefinger together.

"How much?" he said.

"Fifty each," said Barry. "That and all the ale you can drink back here after the job's done."

Jimmy turned down the corners of his mouth, seemingly unimpressed with the fee. "Not much for helping blow somethin' up, Baz. I reckon a hundred would be nearer the mark."

Barry was getting narked. "Listen, you ungrateful fuckers, how long has it been since you earned fifty quid for half an hour's work?"

Matty nodded at his older brother. "He's right, Jim, that's nearly a hundred quid an hour, that is."

Barry pointed at the younger Smith. "Exactly right, Matty; and I'll get you both in at this new firm I'm working for. I'll introduce you to Danny Slade, the guy who organises everything. You'll be quids in when he finds out you've helped me out on this one."

Jimmy still wasn't sure. He nodded toward the rucksack. "So how'd you set it off then?"

Barry got even closer. "That's the sweetest bit, lads, we don't. It's got a mobile phone attached to it, so once we drop it in the gaff, I let Danny know; he dials the number when there's no folk about to get hurt, and boom! Fuckin' simple, innit?"

Jimmy was warming to the task. "So all we do is keep nicks for you, till you drop the bag over the fence, then come back here for free ale all night and fifty quid each in our back bin?"

"In one," said Barry smugly.

"You're on," said Jimmy.

"Yeah, Baz, you're on, mate," said Matty.

Zachari slid forward the action on his AK47 assault rifle and clicked on the safety. He had cleaned the weapon carefully and loaded two spare magazines with the 7.62 high velocity ammunition that the gun required. He wasn't expecting problems, but it was always better to be safe. He draped the rifle over the front seat of the cab and covered it with his coat.

It was time.

The short drive to the launch site would take less than ten minutes. They would then have to climb the fire escape, fourteen floors high, whilst carrying the rockets, and launcher. No easy task, but Ismail and Okot were strong and Zachari was the strongest of them all.

Once the rocket was deployed and they were happy the aircraft was destroyed, they would climb back down the same stairs and slip into a flat on the third floor. There they would change clothes, hide the remainder of the weapons for collection by the council of brothers, and disappear on their own separate journeys. As the carnage unfolded around them, it could be months before anyone found the launch site, if ever.

Zachari knew the place well. He had lived in the flat under the pseudonym Mustapha for several years.

He had spent many hours looking from his window in 307 Penrith House as the jets turned lazily in the sky above the block.

He would sit on the ledge with Ismi, reading the names of the airlines, they were so low.

Sometimes the greatest plans are the simplest.

The cousins were watching him closely.

"Come, my brothers," he commanded. "It is time for glory."

"God is great!" they cried together.

Westland was losing the will to live and Striker was so angry at the lack of success, he was ready to kill something.

It was 1249 hours and the plane was due to enter Lancashire airspace in four minutes. The pair had taken to bickering, as each building, each possible launch site refused to bear fruit. Even Tennant had felt the need to intervene as the arguing had become so unconstructive.

He'd calmed them slightly by informing the pair that LS740 had been struggling with a headwind since the channel and was eight minutes late.

Tag held the flight-path map on his knee as the helicopter bounced around and lurched in the crosswinds. He studied their route again, for the umpteenth time, tracing the line of flight back from the runway to the edge of the printed map.

As his finger reached the very periphery, he felt his stomach lurch. This time it was not the fault of the captain or the weather.

"Striker! Come in, Striker!" he bawled into his headset.

"Go," shouted Striker, gunning the car at its limit.

"I know the launch site! I'm bloody sure of it!"

Striker didn't reply for a moment. He was the one who had the strange moments of clarity, the bizarre feelings that led him to people and places essential to his investigations. Tag was just a rookie.

"Inspire me," he shouted into the radio.

"Penrith House! Zachari's old flat! The place he attacked Sandra. LS 740 flies directly over the junction of Oxford Street and Avenham Lane!"

"Height?"

Tag checked the map again. "Fourteen hundred feet!"

There was another silence before Striker addressed Tennant.

"What's the cloud cover right now, Captain?"

The pilot was as cool as a cucumber. "Cover here is at one one zero zero, clearing easterly. The site is a possible, Sergeant. Roger that?"

Tag didn't wait for Striker. "See! Roger that! I'm damned right on this one, I'd bet my life on it."

Striker was calculating time and space in his head.

"Even with the delay, the plane will pass over the flats at 1320 hours. In this traffic and weather, that doesn't work for me on the ground. I won't make it."

Tennant hit his radio. "Do you see the farmland off to your left, quarter of a mile, maybe a touch more?"

"Roger."

"I'll set her down there, pick you up; then drop you as close to the site as I dare."

Tag turned to the captain, all thoughts of crashing forgotten. "You are a fucking beauty, Tennant."

Abu Al Zachari didn't believe in coincidence. He didn't believe in fate, he didn't believe in luck.

So after his team had completed their climb up the fire escape stairs, past the various stinking objects discarded by the residents of Penrith House, they set up their kit and took stock. They sat with their backs against the lift housing doors fourteen floors up, listening. Even against the blistering wind and lashing rain, one sound he hadn't counted on was the thud of rotor blades.

"Keep tucked in here! Don't move, my brothers!" he barked as he crawled along the concrete floor on his belly, soaking his chest and legs in the process.

He pushed himself over the lip of the low wall that surrounded the roof of the flats.

The chopper was further away than he had first thought, but as soon as he saw the yellow design on the fuselage of the aircraft; he knew where it had come from.

It hovered precariously in the strong winds directly above the multi-storey car-park on Avenham Lane.

There was always the possibility that it was there to chase a car thief. But when he saw two figures jump from the aircraft onto the roof of a parked car, he knew his disaffection with luck and coincidence was well-founded.

He checked his watch.

13:00.

The Air Support Unit helicopter banked hard right and quickly became little more than a dot over the city centre.

The two figures had also disappeared from view, but Zachari had the feeling that he would be seeing those two very shortly.

He stood from his hiding place. Now was the time for his glorious victory.

"Okot, prepare the missile! Ismail, assist your cousin! The plane will come from the east!"

He looked at his wristwatch again. He was forced to shout against the swirling wind and incessant rain.

"Twelve minutes, my brothers! Twelve minutes and glory will be ours! Allah Akbar!"

Striker pumped his arms to keep pace with Westland as they sprinted across the top floor of the car-park.

The young cop was taller, but lighter than the sergeant, and despite Striker's excellent fitness levels, physics could not be beaten. The first hundred meters, he was with the younger man, but Striker's sheer muscular bulk ensured that his distance running was done at a sedate pace. Westland, however, was used to training as a boxer. Endurance was his thing, and he made the stairwell a good twenty meters ahead of the sergeant.

They had five floors and twenty concrete flights to negotiate. By the time they were halfway down Striker was catching Tag using sheer willpower.

Westland slipped at floor two and landed with a crack, smashing his elbow into the wall and sending a river of pain up his arm. As he dragged himself to his feet, Striker jumped over him and hit the front.

"Come on, Westland, no time for a breather!"

Westland pulled himself to his feet, but by the time he had Striker in his sights again, the big man was half way across Avenham Lane.

Tag's chest was burning as he hit the front door of Penrith House. Nothing had changed since his regular visits, and the electronic door was wedged open with a beer can. Sweat poured down his back as he found himself just four steps behind Striker on the fire escape. By floor five, Tag was once again in front, as he took the stairs two at a time. His legs were on fire, his thighs and glutes worked so hard that they were starting to cramp.

Tag knew the flats; he knew where the stairs led. He knew the door at the top opened inward. With one flight to go he stopped and waited for his sergeant.

He rested his hands on his knees. He was blowing hard. Striker appeared seconds later, equally exhausted. They took silent seconds to recover.

Striker stood straight first and pulled his gun from his belt, Tag mirrored him and they walked to the top landing.

Tag's heart was beating faster than he thought possible. He had never experienced such fear. He had never experienced such exhilaration.

Striker nodded toward the handle on the door that would lead to the roof and the unknown.

"Let's go, son."

CHAPTER TWENTY-TWO

The two men burst onto the roof, hands outstretched, weapons pointed forward; ready to strike.

The second they stepped from the door, Striker knew they were in trouble. Before they had moved six feet, he felt the cold barrel of a gun against his temple. The voice attached to the gun was calm.

"Drop your weapons, infidel. It is not your turn to die just yet."

Striker knew it was Zachari. The man the western world had sought for years, the most wanted of wanted. He could not turn his head to see the man's face, but he knew it was he.

Both cops did as they were told and their guns rattled on the concrete floor.

"Well done," said the voice. "Now kick them to my brothers. Don't be brave and dead. Think of your families, think of your wives and children."

Striker watched as two men, one lithe, the other stocky, picked up the guns and stowed them behind their backs. Both were dressed in dishdasha and were soaked to the skin. The wind and rain were indiscriminate. The elements soaked every soul, despite their quest, race or religion. The two young men appeared of African origin; maybe Somalian or Sudanese. Neither showed any fear and simply watched their superior for any command.

For a brief moment Striker felt genuine fear. All three were prepared to die.

Why did I bring the boy here?

Once Zachari was happy he had control, he bellowed over the wind. "Now, my brothers! Now! Prepare!"

Both men immediately went about their business, robotic, unquestioned.

The stocky male uncovered a FM92 Stinger missile launcher, whilst the taller one picked up a spare rocket.

The taller of the two men handed his partner a BCU. In order to fire the missile, a battery coolant unit is inserted into the hand guard of the launcher. This shoots a stream of argon gas into the system, as well as a chemical energy charge, that enables the acquisition indicators and missile to get power.

The unit made a high pitched whirring sound, which told everyone being drenched by the rain that the unit was ready.

Tag had stopped being frightened, another emotion had taken over; an emotion he had been brought up with all his life.

Reason.

He couldn't help himself, and turned to face Zachari.

"You are crazy, man! There are hundreds of innocent people on that plane. What is in your head? Children, man! Women! What the fuck do you think you will achieve by this shit? I mean, come on! How is this going to change a thing?"

Zachari clicked off the safety of the automatic weapon and brought it to his shoulder.

His voice was barely audible above the weather, but his eyes burned with hatred.

"Shut your mouth, infidel scum!"

Tag was convinced Zachari would shoot; he steeled himself for high velocity bullets to tear into his body, to end his life.

It didn't come. The Arab was suddenly distracted by a noise that was now audible above the howling wind.

It was the engines of flight LS720.

Zachari stepped away, but kept his weapon trained on the two cops. A broad smile drifted across his drenched face.

"Now you will see, British man! Now you will witness the supremacy of Al Qaeda. Now you will believe in the power of Allah."

Striker could make out the landing lights of the Airbus. The aircraft was in plain sight. The stocky African started the firing process on the MANPAD and the lights on the display turned green as it acquired its target. The plane was a sitting duck. The rocket would deploy and within seconds would reach sixteen hundred mph, the Argon cooled seeker head would point its way through the weather and the annular blast fragmentation warhead would tear the Airbus apart.

Okot wrapped his hand around the grip of the launcher; he felt the cold metal of the trigger against the skin of his finger. "Target acquired!" he shouted.

They were his last words before all his bodily functions stopped in the blink of an eye.

The African's head exploded. His skull was ripped apart in a split second and his brain was sprayed on the roof of the flats. The sound of the high velocity sniper round followed a split second later. The man fell backward, his legs twitched for a second before he was still. The Stinger dropped to the floor.

Zachari turned in shock and lifted his AK47 toward the two policemen, but before he could fire, his jaw exploded, taking the top of his throat with it. A fountain of blood spurted from his neck as he dropped to his knees. The rifle fell as he clutched at his throat making a horrible gurgling sound, eyes bulging. Seconds later, he fell face down and was silent.

Ismail, the slender one, was in shock. He wasn't sure if he should go for the Stinger or shoot the policemen. He decided on neither and ran to cradle his cousin.

As he lifted Okot into his arms and started to pray, another expertly aimed bullet took out the back of his head.

Flight LS740 to Blackpool, carrying a hundred and ninety-four passengers and crew, banked right and lined itself up for final approach. Striker watched it for a moment. He wiped the rain from his face; the pilot deployed the aircraft's landing gear.

You'll never know how lucky.

He turned his attention to the roof of the next block of high rise flats, Richmond House.

There was nothing to see of course. The shooter was gone, as would be all trace of him.

He shook his head ruefully and then went about the task of recovering his two handguns from the dead Africans.

He stowed them both in his coat.

Least said, soonest mended, is what his mother used to say.

Tag had slid down the wall of the lift housing until his backside hit the wet floor; he'd turned his head from the carnage in front of him and retched. Nothing came out, but tears did flow. He wasn't sure if they were tears of relief, or joy. Either way, he knew he'd cheated death.

Striker left him to it. He pulled out his mobile and called the office. There would be no bells and whistles to this job.

This will be an interesting report.

Striker pulled Westland to his feet. The tears had stopped and mild embarrassment had taken over.

"Fuck," said Tag. "Did you order that?"

Striker shook his head.

"No, but I have a feeling I know who did."

CHAPTER TWENTY-THREE

Barry carried the rucksack into the Gents at the back of the
Princess Alice. He'd had seven pints and was feeling pretty pissed.
Danny Slade had showed him how to arm the bomb. It was as
simple as putting your own mobile on charge. Barry attempted to
push the micro USB connector into the phone three times before he
achieved it. He swore under his breath.
"Fuckin' Pakis, you'll fuckin' get it now, eh?"
He exited the toilet and gave the nod to his two would-be lookouts.
Jimmy Smith was close to legless, Matty never looked any
different no matter how much alcohol he consumed, he just wore a
daft grin.
Barry threw the bag over his shoulder and the three stepped out
into what had become a fine drizzle.

Gina saw the three men stagger into the street and gave an inner
groan. She watched her husband closely from her vantage point.
He carried the rucksack that worried Gina so much.
*Look at the state of him, pissed again, what was it my mum said?
'You make your own luck, girl'.*
A plane flew low over her head, its landing lights flashing as it
flew into Blackpool airport. It was so low she could read 'Jet2' on
the fuselage.
*I always wanted a holiday abroad; wanted to go to Greece, like
that Shirley Valentine in that film. Instead I got him.*
She was soaked, she was cold, but this was important, she just
knew it.
Now she had seen that the Smith brothers were part of Barry's
plan, well, it could only mean one thing; trouble.

Westland had been whisked away from the scene by a very
important looking suit, with a black car and no sense of humor.
The guy had remained silent all the way to Fulwood police station.
Tag was so delighted at being alive, that all common sense had
deserted him, and he nicknamed him 'Buddy'. He didn't seem to
appreciate it.

A second suit, with a body odour problem, was waiting for him in an upstairs office. He was not so silent, and was firing questions at Tag left, right, and centre.

Striker had been put in a different car and was now in a different office, being quizzed by different suits.

Body odour boy reminded Tag four times that he had signed the Official Secrets Act. Then the general line of questioning seemed to revolve around the misuse of a police helicopter, damaging a car roof by jumping on it in order to get out of said helicopter, and two illegal firearms. The matter of three dead terrorists with their heads shot off was either not important, or it was as if they had never existed.

Tag got the impression that if he agreed that the three dead guys were indeed a figment of his active imagination, all the other stuff would go away.

He played dumb. It wasn't hard.

He spent much of the time shrugging and asking for food as he was starving.

Gina kept a safe distance as her husband crossed Blackpool Road and headed north toward Fulwood. It took him and the Smith brothers a good fifteen minutes to make it to the junction of Watling Street Road. When they got there, Gina couldn't quite work out what was going on. Jimmy Smith wandered up Watling Street itself until he got as far as the gates to the old Sharoe Green hospital. There he sat on the wall, seemingly oblivious to the rain, and lit a cigarette.

Matty, the younger of the two, not known for his astuteness, stayed at the bottom of the road, hands in pockets, looking just about as suspicious as was possible.

It was only as Barry started his trademark strut up the road that the penny dropped. Gina felt physically sick.

Oh Jesus, the new mosque.

After much whining, Tag finally got a pie, chips and gravy sent in from the local chip shop. 'Mr. Smelly', the noisy suit, had got so fed up with Tag's incessant references to food, subliminal or otherwise, that he allowed him to eat. As Westland stuffed his face noisily, he reminded the suit about his constitutional rights, and how his uncle was a very swanky barrister, who was a personal friend of Boris Johnson, and that his mother played bridge with the Deputy Chief of MI5.

He was also very vocal about how 'Buddy', who had kindly driven him to the station, could benefit from anger management classes.

"You're not taking this seriously are you, Westland?" said Mr. Smelly.

"No," said Tag.

"Well, don't you think it would be better if you did?"

Tag pushed the last of the chips into his mouth and stood.

"I think it would have been better if you guys, from whatever part of Canary Wharf you are from, had listened to us in the first place."

He dropped his fork onto his plate and grabbed his wet jacket.

"I'm tired, I'm wet and I'm fuckin' traumatised. Strangely enough, I'm not used to regular near death experiences, I *really* don't like to fly, and I *really* don't like seeing people get their head shot off. I'm perfectly aware of my constitutional responsibilities, my loyalty to Queen and Country and my signature sitting at the bottom of the Official Secrets Act. So, unless you are going to arrest me, this debrief is over."

The suit was about to open his mouth when Striker opened the office door, just on cue.

"Westland! We're out of here."

Tag gave Mr. Smelly a narrow smile. "We were just saying goodbye, weren't we?"

Gina walked across to the service station on the opposite side of the junction and stepped inside the shop. It was the only place she could think to hide as Barry strolled back down Watling Street Road, minus the rucksack. He stopped on Blackpool Road and waited for the Smith brothers to catch him up.

Gina watched as they drunkenly slapped each other on the back and made their way back toward Plungington and the Princess Alice.

The Asian guy behind the counter was eyeing Gina suspiciously. "You here to buy, love?" he said.

Gina jumped as he shocked her from her thoughts.

"Oh...err...sorry...no...I'll leave now," she said absently.

"Well you need to," said the man, straightening his skull cap. "I'm closing up. They are blessing the new mosque soon. I want to be there. It is a very important day for us."

Gina shot the man a look of horror. "A blessing? For the mosque?"

The man walked around the counter, a look of genuine concern on his face.

Gina was drenched and shaking from a mixture of cold and fear.

"You okay, love? You look like you've seen a ghost and you're soaked."

She looked the man in the eye.

"I'd stay open if I were you," she said, and bolted from the shop.

Barry, Jimmy and Matty had made it back to the warm tap room of the Princess Alice and were in ecstatic mood.

Barry was playing king of the castle and had dished out the wages and bought the first round. He took a large gulp of beer and laid his pint on the bar.

He rummaged in his pocket and found the business card he was looking for. It had Danny Slade's number on it. Danny had told him to destroy it, but Barry wasn't that good with numbers.

He did his best to focus on the small font and dialled the number into his mobile.

"Mr. Slade?" he slurred.

"Yes," said the voice.

"It's done," said Barry.

Williams was hoping for a 'well done' or a pat on the back, but the phone simply went dead. Worse still, there was no mention of payment, or when to collect it.

Barry looked at the phone, his face like a puzzled pug. He'd blown all the wages he'd earned for the security work at the festival, on paying the Smiths and a few beers. "Everything alright, Baz?" chirped Jimmy.

Barry straightened. "Err...yeah course it is, Jim. I'll give Mr. Slade a bell tomorrow, nip to the unit, pick my cash up then."

Gina barreled up to the front door of Fulwood police station and found it firmly locked. It had long since stopped being a public access station. A sign on the door proclaimed, 'In case of emergency please use the phone to the right of the door and dial 999'.

"Oh no!"

Gina was almost at the point of breakdown. She didn't know how she would cope without her Barry. But she had been brought up as a good girl, a good person, and she could not stand by and watch this terrible thing happen. Maybe if she stopped it, maybe, just maybe, they would go easy on Barry.

She grabbed the phone and punched in the three nines. The operator answered at the first ring. "Police emergency."

Out of the corner of her eye, Gina saw two men stroll from the back of the police station. One was heavy set, scary looking with ginger hair and dark stubble, the other taller, leaner and very handsome.

Gina dropped the phone into the cradle and ran over to Striker and Westland.

Tears fell down her face, she shook uncontrollably.

"Please...please," she stammered. "Please help me."

Striker was about to call a uniformed officer when Gina blurted, "There's a rucksack...I mean a bomb, well I think it's a bomb...in the mosque... down the road..."

The detective took hold of Gina by the shoulders. His voice was steady and level. He looked her in the eye.

"Now just stay calm, madam; just run that by us again."

Gina pulled herself from Striker's grasp. She was close to hysterical. "How can I stay calm? I followed them...my husband...my husband...Barry Williams...and his mates... they had a rucksack...they've thrown it over the fence...and there's a...a...blessing today."

The sergeant focused on Gina.

"Listen, madam, pick up that phone again, tell the operator what you told us, and tell them two detectives are on their way to the scene, okay?"

Gina steeled herself and nodded, "Okay...I can do that."

Westland looked Striker in the eye as they set off at a slow jog toward the mosque. "You got anything left in those legs of yours, Striker?"

"More than you have, rookie."

Tag started to stride out. "Two detectives, eh? Have I been promoted?"

"Slip of the tongue, son."

As the pair approached the near-completed mosque, they could see cars starting to pull up on the pavement across the road. Men in national dress were walking along the street, and a small gathering was standing outside the gates of the building site. They were shaking hands, greeting each other. An important looking man with a henna beard seemed to have the attention of the small crowd.

"How we going to play this?" asked Tag as he jogged alongside the sergeant.

"The guy with the red beard is the Imam," said Striker. "We speak to him first. Then get everyone across the road."

As the pair closed the last twenty yards, the gates to the site were opened by an excited man in his thirties, who seemed delighted that the Imam was being ushered inside.

Striker pulled out his warrant card and held it aloft. "Gentleman, please, gentlemen! Police officers! Please step across the road."

Thirties man stepped toward them.

"What is this? What do the police want here? This is a private ceremony. Have the police not done enough these last days to disgrace themselves; to drive a wedge between our communities?"

Tag tried his best. "Sir, we need to complete a search of the site before you enter...we..."

Thirties was instantly incensed, and stood defiantly in their path. "Nonsense! Go away and leave us in peace. Do you have a warrant? What on earth could the police look for in this holiest of places, on this, of all days?"

Striker stepped in. "We believe there is an explosive device inside the site, sir. Now get your people across the road now!"

The Imam had been listening intently. He placed his hand on the shoulder of Thirties.

He spoke in Urdu, gained his immediate attention, and addressed the group.

Moments later, the men shuffled across the road toward the corner of Highgate.

"Thank you," said Striker.

The holy man nodded his acceptance. "So, what are we looking for exactly?"

Striker held up a hand. "*We* aren't looking for anything, sir. A witness has reported a suspicious package. The bomb squad will complete a search and..."

"Nonsense," said the man. "Surely you can have a cursory look around? If this so-called package is there, then we will await the specialist officers; but should a search prove fruitless, then our community can get on with this very important religious event. That is not unreasonable, detective."

"We could have a look," said Tag.

Striker eyed the young cop for a moment and made a snap decision.

He turned to the Imam and pointed down the road, "Okay, you get your guys at least two hundred yards along the road, and leave this to us."

The man nodded and moved off, encouraging his followers further away from the mosque.

Tag turned and walked to the gate of the site.

Striker shouted after him. "And where are you going?"

"Searching," said Tag.

Then the bomb went off.

CHAPTER TWENTY-FOUR

Striker found himself in the middle of Watling Street Road. He was deaf, a high pitched whine blocked out all sound. Debris dropped all around him; everything from insulation boards, to shards of bricks and lengths of scaffold.

He couldn't see from his right eye. Blood poured into the socket from a deep head wound. He attempted to stand, and pain shot through his right knee.

He wiped his face with his sleeve and inspected his leg. A shard of glass was buried into his kneecap.

His left ear popped and the whine disappeared, only to be replaced by sirens, shouts and cries.

Despite the horrendous pain, he forced himself upright and staggered toward where he had last seen Westland.

All he found was a mountain of rubble.

He focused on the mound of bricks and concrete and staggered toward it.

The fragments of brick under his feet caused him to stumble and fall. Each time his legs gave way he fell and his hurt was tripled.

He reached the place where he knew that Tag had stood moments before, and fell to his knees.

Striker started to pull rubble away with his bare hands. The bricks were hot and burnt him. No matter how hard he tried it was just layer after layer of solid metal, brick and concrete.

He filled his lungs and they burnt as much as his fingers.

"Westland!" he screamed.

He held his ear to the rubble, praying for a reply, but none came.

He dragged at the debris, and tore the skin from his hands. He screamed at the gathering of men who stood shocked, but unhurt on the footpath opposite what had been their flagship mosque.

"Help me!" he screamed. "For God's sake, help me!"

The men stood still rooted to the spot their white national dress covered in brick dust.

Striker bawled at them. "There is a police officer under here! He saved your lives! For heaven's sake, help me!"

The Imam was first to step forward.

When the first ambulance arrived, the crew attempted to treat Striker. He was having none of it.

He was straining to move a concrete lintel from the pile, but even if he had been fit, even if he'd had all his bull strength at his disposal, it would have been impossible.

Striker was not a man to give in and he shouted encouragement to the other men as they moved brick after brick.

Then he heard a cry.

It came from the Imam.

"Here! Medic! Here!"

Striker sat on the curb and watched four paramedics work on Westland's battered body.

Another green-suited girl was fussing around the detective, attempting to treat his wounds, but he felt nothing. All he saw down the narrow tunnel of his vision was Tag. They pumped at his chest, pushed a tube down his throat, wrapped a support around his neck. It took them an age to move him.

As they wheeled him to the ambulance, Striker pushed himself to his feet to get a better look. He couldn't tell if Tag was alive or dead.

From the look on the faces of the ambulance crew, it wasn't good news.

He felt suddenly sick and vomited. He rested his hands on one good knee. His head spun. He grabbed at the medic for support. Striker was unconscious before he hit the floor.

CHAPTER TWENTY-FIVE

Ewan Striker opened his eyes to find Detective Superintendent Errol Graham sitting at the side of his hospital bed.

"How long have I been out?" he said, looking at his wrist where his Omega would usually sit.

Graham's deep baritone filled the small room. "Long enough for them to stitch you up."

Striker pushed himself to a sitting position. He swallowed hard. "Westland?"

Graham rubbed his chin.

"Early days, Striker, he's in surgery, and likely to be there some time. He has some internal issues. He wasn't breathing on his own. He's alive, that's all we can say for now."

The sergeant nodded, winced and touched his head.

"What about the bombers?"

"We arrested them in the Princess Alice pub about an hour ago."

Striker swung his legs from the bed.

"Whoa!" exclaimed Graham. "Where do you think you are going?"

"I want the interview," growled Striker. "I need this one, Graham. Me and Westland have the right...You can't..."

Graham held up both hands.

"Stop right there, Sergeant! Williams and his two cronies are as drunk as skunks! They won't be fit for interview for at least eight hours. So you can't speak to them, as you well know. Not unless you want to fuck up the whole investigation before it starts?"

Striker steadied himself. He took some deep breaths, raised a hand and pointed at the senior detective.

"Okay, but I still want the..."

"The interview, yes, I know, and you'll get it. But right now, you need to get some rest."

Striker, grabbed at his trousers that lay on the chair next to him. He inspected them. "Any chance of some clothes that aren't covered in blood and shit?"

Graham gestured toward a holdall on the floor.

"In there."

Striker met Graham's eyes and nodded.

"Thanks, boss," he said.

Just after ten p.m. Striker pulled into the car-park of the Princess Alice pub on Plungington.

Striker's usually thick mop of dark red hair had been shaved by the hospital staff, prior to seventeen stitches being inserted into his wound. His right knee was heavily bandaged and as he limped into the tap room of the pub, people would have been forgiven for thinking he was an extra from 'One Flew Over the Cookoo's Nest'.

The landlord was straight over.

"Now we don't want any more trouble in here tonight, pal, so if you're lookin' for 'Mad' Barry, he's not here, he's been locked up."

Striker pulled his ID.

"Oh, err...sorry, pal, just that you look a bit...err...y'know...a bit rough like."

Striker gave the man a weak smile, which quickly disappeared into a scowl.

"So you know Barry Williams then?"

The landlord nodded. "Oh aye, everyone knows 'Mad' Barry round here; and the two numpty brothers he was with today, you know, the Smiths, like."

Striker sat painfully on a barstool.

"Go on, tell me more, I'm all ears today."

The landlord seemed to relish in his gossip. "Oh, they've been drinking' in here for years. Barry has always been trouble, especially after a few pints, but today they were steaming; all three of 'em. God knows what they've been up to; but when your lot came in to lock 'em up, well, it proper kicked off. Barry knocked one copper clean out, they reckon."

The landlord pointed to a pile of wood in one corner.

"Damaged my table n'all; and broke six glasses."

The man suddenly seemed to remember his job in life.

"Would you like a pint, mate?"

Striker's throat was dry and his stomach was empty.

"Do you do food?"

Mr. Hospitality pointed at a blackboard and chirped. "Only until eight o clock, sorry."

Striker leaned forward onto the bar and flexed his considerable biceps. He glowered at the landlord.

"I've had a really bad day, and I kinda lost track of the time."

The landlord took a step back.

"I...err...can fix you a sandwich, sir, bit of chicken maybe?"
Striker nodded. "What's your name, matey?"
"Colin," stammered the man. "Colin Sanderson. I'm err...the landlord like."
"Well, Colin," said Striker, with more than a dollop of sarcasm. "That would be decent of you. I'll have a pint of diet Coke to go with it too."

Colin selected a glass and started to pour the drink.
"Were you serving Williams and his crew today?" asked Striker.
Colin shook his head. "No, they'd been in all afternoon. It would have been Gemma that was serving them."
"Is she working now?" asked the detective.
"No," said the landlord. "But she is in."
The man pointed over his shoulder toward the lounge area of the bar. "That's her, talking to the blonde girl."
Striker took his drink and drained half of it. "Thanks," he said, moving slowly off his stool and heading toward the lounge. "Be a good lad and bring the sandwich through."

Scarlet had the news on with the sound down. She chatted on Facebook, looking up occasionally to see what death and destruction was happening this week. Her father was sleeping at last. It had been a very difficult day, but thankfully the home help would be back in the morning, and Scarlet could return to her job. The awful weather seemed to have calmed things down. And now, even though the rain had stopped, the streets were quiet.
As she inputted text into her phone with her thumb, her attention was drawn to the television. She saw a reporter standing outside her workplace, the Royal Preston Hospital.
She put down her phone and turned up the volume.
...the explosion destroyed the newly constructed mosque and has left several people injured...the most serious of those is believed to be a police officer, who has been named as Thomas Westland, twenty-four. Westland is a probationary constable with less than two years' service...
A picture of Tag flashed up in one corner of the screen. It looked like his warrant card picture.

Scarlet put her hand to her mouth, she thought she might cry, but tears didn't come. She picked up her phone and dialled the hospital.

Striker found a stool next to Gemma and her friend. Both eyed him suspiciously. Under normal circumstances, Striker looked scary, but with the Frankenstein haircut and scar, he was even more frightening. His sheer bulk meant Gemma had to ease herself closer to her female companion.

Striker quickly realised that the two girls were a little more than drinking buddies and that squeezing closer together was not a big issue.

"You'll be Gemma then?" he said as casually as he could manage.

"And who are you, big man?" she answered in a thick Lancashire lilt.

Striker held out a ham-like hand. "Ewan Striker, Detective Sergeant, Anti Terrorist branch."

Gemma took his hand and shook firmly. "We could have done with you a few hours back when it all kicked off. I reckon you could have sorted it all out on yer own, pal."

Striker actually smiled. He took an instant likening to the red-headed girl. She wasn't intimidated by him. He got the impression she could look after herself just fine.

"That's what I wanted to chat to you about, Gemma. It was you that was serving the three of them this afternoon, right?"

"Oh yeah, that was my penance for the week, love. Dealing with Mad Barry and the Smith brothers is an occupational hazard in here."

"Did you notice anything unusual about Barry? Anything out of the ordinary?"

Gemma turned down the corners of her mouth and tapped her lips with a blood red fingernail.

"He had a big bag with him, a blue and yellow rucksack. It looked new to me. I've never seen Barry with a bag of any kind before." She nodded swiftly to herself, as if confirming her own information was accurate.

"Yeah, deffo a blue and yellow bag. He came in early doors. Matty and his kid brother tipped up soon after, couple of minutes maybe? They were putting it away like prohibition was about to start. Then they fucked off for a bit, about three-ish, I reckon. Weren't gone long though; they were back on the booze about four; all happy-slappy matey they were. Like they'd had a win on the horses or somethin'."

Striker's sandwich arrived, and he nodded his thanks at Colin, before turning back to Gemma.

"Did you see the bag when they came back?"

Gemma shook her head. "Funnily enough, no; I don't think he had it later on; but to be honest, I was more concerned with keeping them sweet. They can be a set of twats when they've had a few."

Striker nodded and started to pull the chicken from his sandwich, leaving the bread. He dropped a piece into his mouth. It was dry, and despite his hunger he pushed the plate away and gave up. Gemma watched him.

"Are you on the Atkins?" she asked quizzically.

Striker screwed up his face and then realised what the girl was talking about.

"Wha...? Uuh...no I'm not. I just don't eat bread. Anyway...did you hear any of their conversation; anything they might have been up to?"

Gemma shook her head and grabbed her blonde friend's hand for support. The helpful and friendly barmaid was turning bandit on him. Her voice became flat, monotone.

"I don't hear anything in this pub, Sergeant."

She sat forward and wagged a finger.

"Hearing things can get you in the kind of trouble you've been in, by the look of that very nasty cut on your head."

Striker touched his wound absently. "I don't want a statement, Gemma; this is off the record, just between us; nothing written down, no names."

The barmaid's blonde girlfriend leaned in to get a better look at Striker.

"No one gives evidence against the likes of 'Mad' Barry, mate. We all know what he's like. As soon as he gets bail, he'll be all over this pub like a rash, wanting to know who said what. It just ain't worth it."

Striker's mood turned black. His lack of patience was starting to get the better of him.

"Williams won't be getting bail, love, in fact he won't be drinking in here again. Not tomorrow, not next week; not ever. That bag he

was carrying was an IED. Do you know what that is? A fuckin'
bomb; and it has put a young cop in the hospital fighting for his
life."

Gemma's mouth dropped open.

"The bomb at the mosque up Fulwood...that was in that bag....
Barry did that?"

Striker just stared into her eyes. Gemma saw something in there.
Deep behind the hard man stare. He didn't need to add anything.

"You have to be fuckin' joking," she said, then glanced at the
blonde, hoping to get some moral support. It wasn't forthcoming,
but she went with it anyway.

"Look, I never take much notice of what them three morons are
talking about; but it don't surprise me, them doin' somethin' like
that. They're always slagging the Asians off."

She took a drink.

"It's always Paki bastard this and, black bastard that, with them
three. They go to them EDL meetings every week; they're all the
same, fuckin' racists the three of them."

Striker drained the last of his Coke and stood gingerly. The
painkillers he'd been given in Casualty were wearing off and his
knee was giving him hell. He pulled a card from his pocket.

"Take this, Gemma. If you think of anything, anything at all, just
give me a call, okay?"

She nodded and pocketed the card, despite the withering looks
from her blonde friend.

Striker limped from the bar and made his way back to the hospital.

The relative's room attached to the ICU suite was the only place
that Striker could stretch out and get his head down. He was
thankful to have the place to himself. Westland's parents were
holidaying in the Bahamas, and as yet were unaware of his
situation. The boy was still in theater. The detective checked his
Omega, 0410 hours. Tag had been in there almost eleven hours.
Striker's stomach rumbled. He wandered a corridor and found a
vending machine. He bought himself a plastic sandwich that he
pulled the ham from, a truly awful coffee, dropped a couple of co-
codamol with the first mouthful, and sat. He found himself on a

plastic chair, specifically designed by the NHS to give you back problems for the rest of your life.

At 0511 hours the door to the room opened and a tired looking doctor dressed in blue scrubs wandered in.

He was a slender man with sharp Arabic features. He sat next to Striker without being asked. "Mr. Westland?" he asked.

"No, I'm a colleague, a police officer working with him. His parents are on holiday abroad. We are trying to contact them." The doctor pulled his mask over his head and threw it in the wastebin.

"I see." He rubbed his face and yawned. "Well, your colleague is a very poorly man Mr.?"

"Striker."

"Ah, yes, yes, Mr. Striker. Well, as I said, very poorly. Thomas has suffered severe shrapnel wounds from the explosion. I have seen these many times from the conflict in Iraq."

"You served in Iraq?" asked Striker.

The doctor shook his head.

"No, Striker, I didn't serve. Well not in the sense you say. I am Lebanese, and I am a Christian. But I trained in Baghdad because it was a good place to learn, to be educated. Of course, later came many injuries, many lost causes."

The doctor trailed off.

"What about Westland?" asked Striker. "Is he a lost cause?"

He cocked his head to one side. "Do you smoke, detective?"

"I don't."

The doctor stood. "Well I do, and as I have been fixing up your colleague for the last twelve hours, I need one. Why not walk with me?"

Striker hobbled behind the doctor until they reached the front entrance of the hospital.

The man lit a cigarette and inhaled deeply.

"I thought they were bad for you," said Striker, more a matter of fact than question.

"They are; but not as bad as an IED."

Striker nodded resignedly.

The doc blew out a long plume.

"Your friend has some very serious internal issues. The device at the mosque was designed to kill and mutilate. It had nothing to do with destroying a building. In some ways he is fortunate to have all his limbs intact. It would seem that he has taken most of the blast to his torso. But he suffered secondary damage, due to falling masonry. That caused the compression injuries to his chest and stopped his breathing for several minutes until he was pulled from the rubble."

"You must have seen worse injuries in Baghdad," said Striker.

"Not many," said the surgeon. "But some. The city was a good place to learn, even if I say so myself. Your friend has had the benefit of my experience, and the benefit of many of Baghdad's ...lost causes."

The doctor flicked ash into a sand bin and added, "You are American, are you not?"

Striker was starting to feel irritated, his gut churned.

"Don't preach to me right now, doc. I know all about the war, all about the reasons why, all about hate.

Striker also knew about death, and he wanted information.

His father had been taken young by illness, then his mother by joy-riders. The only woman he had ever loved, gone at thirty years old from liver cancer. She had never even taken a drink. Everyone he ever got close to ended up dead.

He swallowed hard.

"My ancestry has nothing to do with that young boy in there. So how about we stick to the script, doctor. Just tell me, will he live?"

The man extracted the last nicotine from his cigarette and dropped it into a large ashtray.

"I'm a surgeon, detective. I'm not God. If I were you, I would rely on your Gaelic roots and religion."

"I'm not religious," spat Striker.

"Neither am I anymore, detective. After the Americans' shock and awe tactics; after all the death and destruction, I decided God did not exist."

The doctor turned to go inside. "All the same, I'd say a prayer for your friend if I were you."

Striker drove back to his house on Buckshaw, showered, changed and drank good coffee. He didn't want to think about how little sleep he'd had since this thing started.

By 0800 hours he was sitting in Errol Graham's office, watching the senior detective eat a McDonald's muffin.

Graham wiped his mouth and pushed the wrappers into his wastebasket. He felt instantly guilty. His wife would kill him if she knew.

"How's the kid?"

Striker shrugged his massive shoulders. "Not good. I spoke with his surgeon earlier. He said to say a prayer." The sergeant turned down the sides of his mouth. "Are you a religious man, boss?"

The senior detective shook his head. "My wife is, she goes to the chapel two or three times a week, reads the bible; she's a good person that way. Me? Well I lost my way a little."

"Me too," said Striker. He instantly changed tack. "Is our boy 'Mad Barry' fit to talk to?"

Graham stretched. "Doc says so. We have the wife in protective custody until we know who was really behind this shit. It isn't down to the three clowns we have downstairs, that is for sure."

"Lawyers?"

"The Smith brothers have opted for the duty brief, he's with Jimmy, the older one now. Williams has requested his usual face, some guy from Randle and Villiers in town. We called him up about two hours ago. He arrived just before you; he's a pompous prick called Evans."

Errol dropped his voice. It was his turn to change the subject. "Listen, Striker, I know we got off on the wrong foot, but you did a great job out there yesterday."

"Thanks."

"I mean it; you should both have a commendation." The senior detective blew out his considerable cheeks, "The kid especially." Graham sipped his coffee. "I suppose the boys from the ministry have given you the hard word and waved the Official Secrets Act under your nose."

Striker nodded.

"I've never known such pressure from upstairs," continued the senior detective.

"The dead men on the roof will go down as three dealers fighting a turf war. You know that, don't you? They've already put out a press release saying we are not looking for any other suspects."

"Figured as much."

"There'll be no mention of plots or rockets or planes, it's a disgrace if you ask me."

Graham leaned forward and eyed Striker intently. He was impressed with the guy who he had once thought a rude nuisance. His strength and his integrity were beyond doubt, but there was something more, something Graham could not quite put his finger on.

"Are you still certain that all this business ties in with Abu Al Zachari? The murders? Hussain? Chowdry? The bomb at the mosque?"

"I reckon so."

"Shit, I hope you're right, Striker. We need a break on this one. The streets have been quiet since the bomb. The whole town feels strange. People are just eyeing each other in disbelief. It's as if the whole population has taken a valium."

Errol stood and pulled on his jacket.

"You are too young to remember, but during the miners' strike in the eighties, some pickets targeted a taxi taking a strike-breaker to work. They threw a rock off a motorway bridge at the car. It killed the driver instantly.

Almost from that moment, the violence stopped. It was if the whole community said, 'enough is enough'.

I think that's where we are right now, but unless we show some progress, it will start again. I just know it. You can feel it when you walk the street. And this time, if it gets out the bag, nothing and no-one is going to put it back in again."

Striker pushed back his chair and winced. He didn't want to take any painkillers. He needed to be fully functional for the interview.

"Has the Williams woman got an armed guard?" he said flatly.

"No," said Graham.

"Get her one," he said, standing gingerly. "I want the prick ready to interview by nine, and I don't care what his lawyer says. I'd prefer it if you interview the Smith brothers, and that you do that alone."

He checked his Omega.

"Let's say we meet back here at ten."

Scarlet stood outside the thick glass that protected the patients in ICU. She touched it, somehow hoping it would transfer something to the broken human being on the other side.

All she felt was the chill of the plate against her fingers and she shivered.

Tag lay in the semi darkness, a respirator breathed for him, drugs induced a coma in the hope the swelling on his brain would subside. Tubes and wires surrounded him; monitors flashed and beeped.

A duty nurse walked by; Scarlet knew her by name, she had sat with her in the canteen a few times.

The woman was surprised to see the auxiliary nurse. "Hello, honey," she said in a hushed tone. "What brings you up here?"

She followed Scarlet's eyes to the young man behind the glass. The look on the beautiful girl's face said it all.

"Oh my," she said.

Scarlet dropped her eyes. "Is it that bad, Sarah?"

The nurse didn't answer, but gently placed her arm around Scarlet's shoulders. "I didn't realise you had a boyfriend, hun. How long have you been together?"

She shook her head. "We aren't really together, it was just one date, we just met, he's..."

Her voice faltered, but she swallowed hard and regained her composure, "...he's just a nice guy, you know...one of the good ones."

Sarah squeezed Scarlet. "Come on, love, there's nothing you can do here, let's get a coffee before your shift starts, eh?"

The willowy girl forced a smile, touched the glass once more and nodded. "Okay, that would be good, I start at nine."

Sarah checked her watch, "We've got twenty minutes, love, come on."

The two women walked the corridor. As they reached the heavy doors, an alarm sounded behind them.

Sarah turned on her heels and ran back toward ICU.

Striker stepped into the interview room. He had just spent fifteen minutes talking to Gina Williams on the phone. She was distraught and asked about Barry over and over. But she was still a coherent witness who could clearly identify all three suspects.

Inside the cool dimly lit room, Williams sat back in his seat. He wasn't restrained, and his hands were clasped in front of him on the table. His fingernails were bitten to the quick. He looked hungover, needed a shave, and from the smell in the room, a shower. His right leg bounced up and down nervously, but as the detective strode into the room, the bouncing stopped and Williams sat up. He sneered at Striker, revealing his awful teeth.

Barry nudged his brief. "Hey look, Nigel, they've sent fuckin' Frankenstein to interview us."

Striker kept his counsel, but his hair stood up on his neck and arms.

I know you. You were at the rally with Sinclair's lot. Well, well, well.

Sitting next to him was a smartly dressed if overweight man, who wore thick glasses and a haughty expression.

Striker was accompanied by a uniformed constable who was laughingly present to ensure Williams didn't attack the detective sergeant.

The detective sergeant prepared the recorder and signed the tapes. "We all ready?" he said.

Nigel Evans wagged an expensive-looking pen in the detective's direction. "I have advised my client that, due to the lack of any solid evidence against him, he should make a 'no comment' interview."

The sergeant shrugged. "Up to you," he eyed Barry with some disgust. "I'm still going to ask you the questions though, son."

Barry put on his best 'fuck you' smile.

"Ask away, ginger-nut."

Striker hit 'record' and the machine buzzed as the leader tape passed over the recording heads. When the sound stopped, he began.

"The time is 0911 hours on Saturday the ...."

There was a sharp knock on the interview room door. Errol Graham stuck his head inside.

"Sorry, Striker, I need a minute."

The sergeant stood. "For the purpose of the tape I am leaving the room to speak to a colleague."

Evans gave a plastic smile. Barry slumped in his chair and the uniform paused the tape.

Once Striker was in the corridor, Graham filled the space in front of him, ensuring they were not interrupted. The chief detective looked pale and drawn. He studied his feet for what seemed like an age and then looked Striker in the eye.

"He's gone," he said.

Striker felt sick.

He knew he was responsible. He should have left Tag where he was, sitting in a shitty cop car, bouncing drunks and reporting motorists, should have let him walk into his inspector's office and tell him to stick his crappy job, let him go back to his comfy life down south. It was Striker who'd seen the potential in Tag Westland. He was always one to spot talent, it was so obvious to him. It was he who pushed the boy, dragged him through the investigation. Now he was dead, a kid who had it all, snuffed out like a birthday candle.

Pure hate tore through his body, his anger and guilt taking over; common sense, normal behaviour, logic, all gone.

That was the word wasn't it...gone?

"I'm going back inside," he said, clenching his fists to stop his hands from shaking.

Graham wagged a finger. "Don't do anything crazy now, Striker. The suspect in that room is just that, A SUSPECT! UNDERSTAND?"

The senior detective couldn't think of anything else that might stop his sergeant from tearing Williams limb from limb. So he added, "And he has his fat stupid lawyer sitting next to him!"

Striker's mouth was dry. He licked his lips before he spoke. His heart was in his throat. He fought with his body, so he could speak.

"I'm going back inside this room, and I'm going to finish this interview. Then I'm going to find the fucker who really delivered that bomb."

Graham nodded, sweat beaded on his forehead.

"Okay, Sergeant. Just stay cool, okay?"

Striker pushed the door open.

Williams had sat so deep in his chair that his shoulders were level with the seat back. His arms were crossed over his chest, his eyes closed.

As Striker got to the table, he opened them.

"What did the nigger want?" he said.

Striker ignored the comment and hit the record button. He turned and dropped forward so his hands sat in the centre of the table. His massive arms propped him up. His triceps twitched as his body continued its fight with the masses of adrenalin pouring into his bloodstream. His face was inches from Barry's.

He used all his self control to keep his voice level and stop himself from smashing his fist over and over into the racist thug's face.

"I am resuming the interview with Barry Williams. Present is his lawyer, Nigel Evans and Police Constable John Barry. Before we go any further, I must tell you that I am arresting you for the murder of Police Constable Thomas Arthur Gordon Westland. You do not have to say anything, but it may harm your defence if you do not mention now, something which you later rely on in court. Anything you do say may be given in evidence. Do you understand?"

Barry's mouth dropped open. He looked at his lawyer for help. The portly man remained stoic.

Williams was in a blind panic. "What's all this about? They can't do this, can they? I mean, I never set the thing off, did I?"

Nigel Evans held up a small podgy hand.

"That's enough for now, Barry, remember what we discussed."

Williams was having none of it.

"That was before. I never wanted to kill anyone...it was just supposed to be the Pakis' place, weren't it? Just the mosque. I'm not going down for setting the thing off, that weren't us."

Striker pushed a plastic evidence bag containing Danny Slade's business card across the table. Then he added a second bag that held Barry's mobile phone.

"You called this guy at 1608 hours yesterday. The call lasted eleven seconds. Two minutes later, the bomb went off."

Barry was pale, he shook with fear. He eyed his phone like it was some kind of alien object. His mind worked overtime, clinging to any excuse, no matter how flimsy.

"I...I...never rang anyone...I... must have given my phone to..."

"To who, Barry?" snapped Striker. "To one of those dimwits sitting in the next interview room? Do you really think they are going to back you up, now they are in the same boat? They are looking at the same life sentence as you, pal; killing a copper. A life sentence, Barry, a full life term with no hope of release. That's what you and your chums are looking at, just ask your fat lawyer here. Ask him what a judge will dish out."

Striker stood straight, his voice boomed.

"Conspiracy to cause explosions, and a cop killer to boot; it's goodbye to 'Mad' Barry Williams, do not pass go, do not collect two hundred pounds, go directly to jail for ever and ever, son."

Evans placed his hand on his client's shaking shoulder and looked at Striker.

"Let me speak to Mr. Williams. Maybe we can come to some kind of arrangement."

Striker almost exploded. "You think I'm going to plea bargain this piece of shit?"

He stabbed his finger onto Slade's business card.

"As God is my witness, Williams, if you don't answer my next question, I will make it my lifelong quest to ensure you do every minute of your time inside with a Muslim cellmate.
Now...where can I find this guy?"

CHAPTER TWENTY-SIX

Striker sat heavily in his La-Z-Boy armchair and raised his injured leg onto a cushion. Miles Davies was playing, 'So What?'
He tried to read, but his mind wouldn't allow him the level of concentration required for the task.
Not on this day.

The investigation was effectively over.
Danny Slade had put up a considerable fight when the support unit and ARV crews went into his unit to arrest him. It took three blasts with a taser, before they could get the cuffs on him.
Once the specialist search teams went into the Moss Side building, it became apparent that the cops had struck gold.
Two Heckler and Koch MP7 automatic weapons were found, together with hundreds of rounds of ammunition.
Within days, one of the guns was identified as being the weapon used to kill Ayesha Chowdry.
The forensic lab painstakingly checked every unused round in the gun's magazines and found an unidentified partial thumbprint on one shell.
The party really started when the guys checked a memory stick stuffed in the bottom of Slade's briefcase.
On it were eleven pictures of Grant Bliss and Alistair Sinclair posing with the machine guns.
Bliss was arrested the same day attempting to board a flight to Vietnam. He had the best lawyers money could buy, but once his prints were taken and were matched as the ones found on the solitary bullet, he was in trouble. The final nail in his coffin was a further set of pictures found on his personal laptop. They were encrypted, but once the boffins had finished with them; they revealed six images of Ayesha Chowdry being posed limb by limb. In one image, the picture taker had placed the 'terrorist' sign around the girl's neck and his gloved hand was clearly visible. So was Bliss's one-of-a-kind wristwatch.

Throughout Danny Slade's interrogation, he remained totally loyal to Bliss, and refused to offer any information that might harm his closest ally and dearest friend. The same level of loyalty did not carry through to the Right Honorable Alistair Sinclair MP.

Danny knew he was fucked. They had enough on him to put him away for four lifetimes. He couldn't do anything for Bliss, but he could help himself.

He made a deal and told the spooks everything he knew about Alistair Sinclair.

The leader of the Justice for Great Britain Party was arrested by Errol Graham himself. The irony of a black man leading the MP away in handcuffs was not lost on the newspapers.

Along with Bliss, Slade, Williams and the Smith brothers, he was charged with conspiracy to murder and conspiracy to cause explosions.

All except Sinclair were remanded in custody awaiting trial. The party leader's legal team argued that he wasn't a threat to society and was unlikely to abscond; therefore he remained with his family. His wife was reported to be 'standing by him'.

The detectives had concluded the investigation into the murders of Sandra Mackintosh and William Wilson.

Five adults, Fahad Hussain, Jalal Chauhan, Naheem Ibrahim, Sadiq Naheem and Wajid Farooki, together with a juvenile, who could not be named for legal reasons, were charged. They all denied murder at their initial court appearance.

Striker had attended the funerals of Abdulla Hussain and Ayesha Chowdry as part of his duties. He'd joined Errol Graham at the cemetery. Both cops kept a respectful distance.

Next were the funerals of Sandra Mackintosh and William Wilson. Sandra's was a small quiet affair, just her sons and a few faces from the estate. The detective had expected fireworks or demonstrations from the locals, but there were none. It was as if the town was in mourning for itself.

Wilson's send off was a different matter entirely. Striker had predicted a pauper's funeral, with a witness provided by the state. The old scrapper had no living relatives and his ex wife would not be in attendance.

But somehow the bush telegraph had worked its magic and more than a hundred gypsy travelers from England and Ireland gave 'Fighting Billy' a memorable send-off, which included an arm wrestling contest and a bare knuckle brawl.

Now he had one more funeral to attend.

He sipped the last of his coffee, found his suit jacket, checked his tie in the mirror and left the house.

The city of Preston came to a halt.
Tag Westland was to be buried in his home town, some two hundred miles away. This ceremony was about remembrance. His coffin was draped in the Union Jack, his helmet placed carefully on top. Two black stallions with blinkers and black plume feathers drew the carriage to the parish church.
On foot behind were his mother and father; pale but somehow proud. The woman held on tightly to her husband, each step, each movement a memory of her child, alive and well.
His father had his walk, but Tag had been handsome because his mother was classically beautiful. She dabbed her eyes, head held high.
Behind them were other relatives; uncles, aunts, nephews, nieces, all touched, all torn between anger, hate and hurt.
Behind them came the suits, the higher ranking officers who had never even heard of Tag Westland.
All except one.
Errol Graham walked with his wife, head bowed.
Striker looked along the street. Hundreds of people were standing in the steady drizzle. Muslim, Christian, black, white.

The Imam who had been the first to help clear the rubble at the bomb site, and the one to find him, followed the coffin into the church. As the bearers trod steadily to the altar, and rested the casket, the holy man turned and seated himself alongside a Methodist minister.
Striker sat at the back of the church, he didn't hear the service. He didn't hear the choir. But he saw something special.

As Tag's father started his reading, a sparrow of a girl stood from the congregation. She was one of the most beautiful women Striker had ever seen; strawberry red hair; pale skin. She wore a blue uniform, half hidden by a damp brown coat.

She shook as she walked, but everyone could see that nothing was going to stop her.

She walked the narrow corridor toward the altar.

Tag's father fell silent.

He dropped his notes on the podium, his face a mixture of surprise and intrigue. There was a murmur from the congregation, but as the girl drew ever closer to Tag's coffin, they fell silent.

Scarlet kissed her forefinger and rested it against the Union Jack.

She had always thought that she had no tears left.

She was wrong.

CHAPTER TWENTY-SEVEN

Striker stood outside the church, hands in pockets.

The press was mingling with mourners. It was time for him to make his exit and he limped toward Cheapside. As he reached the old market square, he became aware he wasn't alone.

"Good boy, that one," said the voice.

Striker turned. It was Des, the guy who'd been standing outside the flat where he and Tag had found Ismi and Hussain.

"You again," said Striker.

"I'm a bad penny, pal, keep turning up."

"I noticed; you turned up in time to blow the heads off three terrorists."

"It wasn't me."

"No?"

"No, pal... I never was a sniper...but I know a man who is, like."

"Well tell him from me...he did a good job."

"I might do that."

Striker turned to Des and managed a thin smile.

"You fancy a Guinness? I think Tag would have invited you...he thought you were a spy, you know?"

"I am...with my little eye, like."

The two found O'Neil's Irish pub on Friargate. Striker pulled off his black tie as he walked to the bar.

The Scot followed him inside.

"I mean it, pal," said Des. "He was a good boy, that one, you could see it. It's not a fair one."

Striker passed Des his pint.

"Spare me the bleeding heart."

Des shrugged, he was a man used to death. It was an integral part of his working life.

"Listen, pal, as I said, he was a good boy; that's all...nothing more. Back in the day, when we lost a bloke, we would have a piss up, and fight over his boots."

"I don't think Tag Westland would've owned a pair. Not his kinda thing."

Des nodded and changed the subject.

"Weird how William's wife used to work for Hussain, eh?"

Striker eyed Des, his mouth turned downward.

"The whole thing was tied together; it was like some kinda film script...Zachari...Hussain...Sinclair...Mackintosh...like you say...weird."

Des found his pipe and started the process of filling it.

"My brief was all about Zachari. Once you identified him, my team came into play, simple as."

Striker straightened. "Of course you did. It was never going to look good if an airliner was blown out of the sky by a rocket sold to Al Qaeda by the British Secret Service, was it?"

Des prodded the tobacco in his small metal pipe. He was so matter of fact.

"That kind of thing doesn't go well in high places."

Striker found his blood pressure rising.

"And you made sure that Zachari and his little disciples were wiped off the face of the earth without a trace. No chance of spilling the beans, eh?"

Des attacked his pint. "Someone has to do the real dirty work, Striker."

The detective made for the door.

"And some have to pay, eh, son? Enjoy your beer."

The CPS reviewed the evidence in the Sandra Mackintosh and William Wilson murder case; they came to the conclusion that it would be impossible for a jury to agree which of the six individuals struck the fatal blows. Therefore all were given the opportunity to plead to an alternative charge of affray and malicious wounding. The adults received prison sentences ranging from four to six years. The juvenile was released.

Barry Williams, together with James and Mathew Smith, were all found guilty of the murder of Tag Westland.

Both Smith brothers received a nineteen year penalty. Williams was sentenced to a full life term.

Barry committed suicide the day after he received notification that Gina had started divorce proceedings.

Bliss was found guilty of the murder of Ayesha Chowdry. He received a twenty-five year term.

Danny Slade made full use of his deal with the authorities; he received a nine year sentence for conspiracy to murder Abdullah Hussain.

Alistair Sinclair was the last to stand trial at Preston Crown Court Before the jury was sworn in, his legal team challenged the Crown's evidence, the majority of which was testimony from Danny Slade. They claimed that Slade had been kept in custody seven minutes longer than was legally allowed during his questioning, and therefore all testimony was inadmissible.
Judge Fotheringham upheld the claim and praised Sinclair's legal team for their attention to detail.
The leader of the Justice for Great Britain Party was found not guilty of all charges and released.
He stood on the steps of the court, flanked by his wife and family, and vowed to continue his political career.
His defence lawyer slipped quietly away. He still needed another operation on his eye in an attempt to restore his sight.
Tariq Hussain QC had maintained his reputation of defending the un-defendable.
His family would never forgive him.

Ewan Striker resigned the same day.

END

Printed in Great Britain
by Amazon